PRAISE FOR LINCOLN CHILD AND

THE FORGOTTEN ROOM

"Chilling. . . . Child makes the most of the creepy setting, his unusual lead character, and an intricate plot." —*Publishers Weekly*

"Child's characters are first-rate, as is his writing." —*The Washington Post Book World*

"[A] very imaginative story for those who prefer a soft blending of mystery and paranormal." —*Booklist*

"Lincoln Child's novels are thrilling and tantalizing." —Vince Flynn, #1 *New York Times* bestselling author of *The Last Man*

"The genius-touched Child writes paragraphs of polymathic detail. . . . Terrific." —*Kirkus Reviews*

LINCOLN CHILD
THE FORGOTTEN ROOM

Lincoln Child is the *New York Times* bestsell-ing author of *The Third Gate*, *Terminal Freeze*, *Deep Storm*, *Death Match*, and *Lethal Veloc-ity* (formerly titled *Utopia*), as well as coau-thor, with Douglas Preston, of numerous *New York Times* bestsellers, most recently *Crimson Shore*. He lives with his wife and daughter in Morristown, New Jersey.

www.lincolnchild.com

THE FORGOTTEN ROOM

THE FORGOTTEN ROOM

· A NOVEL ·

LINCOLN CHILD

ANCHOR BOOKS

A Division of Penguin Random House LLC

New York

FIRST ANCHOR BOOKS OPEN-MARKET EDITION, MAY 2016

The Library of Congress has cataloged the Doubleday edition
as follows:
Child, Lincoln.
The forgotten room : a novel / Lincoln Child.—First Edition.
pages ; cm
I. Title.
PS3553.H4839 F67 2015
813'.54—dc23
2014044677

Anchor Books Open-Market Edition ISBN: 978-1-101-97229-8
eBook ISBN: 978-0-385-53141-2

Book design by Maria Carella

www.anchorbooks.com

Printed in the United States of America
10 9 8 7 6 5 4 3 2 1

For Veronica

THE FORGOTTEN ROOM

1

It was perhaps the most unusual sight ever beheld on the august and stately grounds of the Glasgow Institute of Science, founded in 1761 by grant of charter from George III. A large podium, studded with microphones, had been erected on the Great Lawn, directly in front of the administration building. Before it had been set some three dozen folding chairs, on which sat reporters from local newspapers, the *Times* of London, *Nature*, *Oceanography*, *Time* magazine, and a host of others. To the right of the podium were two television cameras, one from the BBC and the other from CNN. To the podium's left was a large wooden scaffold, upon which sat a large, strange-looking machine of dark metal: a cross between a cigar tube and a pincushion, about thirty feet long, with a bulky attachment protruding from its upper edge.

The restless chatter among the reporters grew muted as the main doors to the administration building opened and two men stepped out into the September afternoon sunlight. One was plump and short, with a shock of white hair and wearing a thick tweed coat. The other was tall and quite thin, with rather severe features, light brown hair, and alert gray eyes. Unlike the first man, he was dressed in a conservative dark suit.

The two approached the podium and the older man cleared his throat. "Ladies and gentlemen of the press," he began, "thank you for coming. I am Colin Reed, provost of the Glasgow Institute of Science, and to my right is Jeremy Logan."

Reed took a sip from a glass of water on one side of the podium, cleared his throat again. "You may well know of Dr. Logan's work. He is perhaps the only, and certainly the preeminent, enigmalogist operating in the world today. His job is to investigate, interpret, and explain the—for lack of a better word—unexplainable. He throws light upon riddles of history; he separates myth from truth and the natural from the supernatural."

At Reed's side, Jeremy Logan frowned slightly, as if uncomfortable at this bit of panegyric.

"About two months ago, we contacted Dr. Logan on his home ground of Yale University and asked him to undertake an assignment for us. That assignment can be briefly explained: to definitively prove, or disprove, the existence of the creature popularly referred to as the Loch Ness monster. Dr. Logan has spent the last six weeks in Inverness, doing precisely that. I will now ask him to share his findings with you."

Reed stepped back from the microphones and Logan approached. He surveyed the crowd of reporters for a moment, then began to speak. His voice was relatively low and mild, the mid-Atlantic accent contrasting with Reed's Scottish burr.

"The Loch Ness monster," he began, "is the most famous of all the supposed Scottish lake monsters, perhaps the most famous of all cryptids. The institute's aim in hiring me for this particular task was not to stunt the local tourism industry or to put peddlers of Loch Ness iconography out of business. Rather, it was to put a stop to the amateur and misguided attempts at searching for the creature—attempts that have been on the increase recently and, at least twice in the last year, have resulted in deaths by drowning."

He took a sip from his own water glass. "I quickly realized that proving the existence of the creature required only one thing—observing it in its element. Proving that the creature does *not* exist, however, would require a great deal more work. Technology would be my greatest ally. Hence I persuaded the United States Navy, of which I was once a part, to lend me this one-man research submersible." And Logan waved at the strange-looking machine sitting on the wooden scaffold to his right.

"The submersible is equipped with continuous-wave radar, synthetic aperture sonar, pulse-compression echolocating devices, and numerous other technologies for both underwater mapping and target acquisition.

"There were two important factors to take into account. First, the loch is quite long and unusually deep—seven hundred and fifty feet in places. Second, so-called sightings of the creature suggested a morphology similar to a plesiosaur, which would put it at something between twenty and forty feet in length. There were several unknown variables to contend with, of course, such as the creature's range of movement and environmental preferences, but these could not be determined until such time as it was located.

"I began by familiarizing myself with the features of the submersible and the layout of the loch—both above and below the surface. My service in the navy made the former relatively straightforward. I spent one week in this shakedown period, during which time I uncovered no sign of the creature.

"Next, I had the institute procure for me some netting—rather a lot of netting, in fact. Using spools of military-grade nylon mesh, we put together a net ten thousand feet by eight hundred feet."

This brought murmurs of surprise.

"What came next was rather tedious but—after the first few run-throughs—quite straightforward. I was lucky in the fact that the loch, although some twenty miles long, is not particularly wide: just under two miles at its widest point. We started at the northernmost point of the loch and worked south. My work was aided by two research assistants from the institute and two motor launches out of Inverness. Each day, using the submersible, I would comb an area of the loch consisting of a single mile in a southerly direction. A mile-long slice of the loch, as it were, along the x, y, *and* z axes. For each of these discrete slices, I would make three separate passes at different depths, using the submersible's movement and targeting technologies to search for any objects the size of the creature. This equipment has significant range and precision; had any object of the requisite size been in the slice, I would have located it. At the end of each day, with the help of the research assistants—one on each shore of the loch—and the two boats on the loch itself, I moved the netting one mile forward, to the terminal point of my search for that day. This vast mesh covered the entire loch laterally, like an antisubmarine net. The mesh was broad enough for any normal fish to swim through without difficulty, but narrow enough to prevent anything larger than forty centimeters wide from passing. Watercraft were dealt with on a one-by-one basis.

"Each day I explored an additional one-mile slice of the loch, searching for the creature. At the end of each day, as mentioned, we pulled the net forward another mile. After twenty days we reached the southern end of the loch—without result. And so, ladies and gentlemen, you can take as fact the four words I'm about to speak—though I speak them with some regret, since I enjoy cryptozoological legends as much as the next man: *There ain't no Nessie.*"

This was greeted with applause, a scattering of laughter.

A low sound became audible in the distance: a droning, repetitive thudding. As the sound drew closer, it became identifiable as helicopter blades cutting through the air. Then a fat chopper with military markings appeared over a nearby hilltop lined with redbrick row houses. It approached quickly now—an American navy aircraft—then descended, hovering directly over the Great Lawn and the dark gray submersible. Grass flattened out in a circular direction, and the reporters were forced to grab hats and papers to prevent them from flying. A technician in a jumpsuit trotted out a side door of the administration building, climbed up the wooden scaffolding, and attached two huge hooks that had been reeled out of the helicopter's belly onto fastenings on the upper surface of the submersible. He crawled back down, gave a thumbs-up, and the helicopter began to rise gingerly, the craft swaying beneath it. Higher and higher it climbed, and then it turned slowly and began heading eastward, its peculiar cargo trailing behind it by the two lifelines. Within sixty seconds it was gone. The entire operation had taken less than five minutes.

Logan watched the distant horizon for a moment, then turned back to the press. "And now," he said, "I would be happy to answer your questions as fully as I can."

———

Three hours later, in the snug of the Edwardian-era bar within Glasgow's most opulent hotel, the same two persons—Colin Reed and Jeremy Logan—toasted each other over glasses of a peaty single-malt scotch, served neat.

"An excellent performance," Reed was saying. "And I don't just mean at the press conference today—an excellent performance from beginning to end."

"Acting is new to me," Logan replied. "But it's nice to know that, if the ghost-hunting business ever dries up, I can always supplement my Yale salary by treading the boards."

" 'I would be happy to answer your questions *as fully as I can*,' " Reed said, chuckling at the memory. "Nice bit of prevarication, that." He took a sip of his scotch. "Well, I think we can safely say that with today's announcement—in addition to the new rules that have been instituted regarding use of watercraft in the loch—all this hunting for the monster will die off."

"That's the plan."

Reed started, as if forgetting something. "Oh, yes." He reached into his pocket, pulled out a slender envelope. "Here's your stipend."

"I still feel bad taking money from the institute," Logan said as he pocketed the envelope. "But I console myself with the thought that it's recompense for the damage my reputation would suffer should the truth ever become known."

"We thank you—and, more important, I'm sure Nessie thanks you." The provost paused. "You have the, ah, *data* with you?"

Logan nodded.

"And you still believe the best thing is to destroy it?"

"It's the only option. What if those images got into the open—or, God forbid, went viral on the Internet? It would undo everything we've accomplished. I'll burn them as soon as I get up to my room."

"You're right, of course." Reed hesitated. "May I . . . may I have one last look?"

"Of course." Logan glanced around the bar, then unlocked the Zero Halliburton attaché case that sat on the banquette beside him, extracted a folder, and passed it to Reed. The man took it, opened it, and leafed through the pages within, his eyes glittering with hungry fascination.

The pages contained images produced from a variety of technologies: acoustic backscatter, synthetic aperture pulse, active beam-forming sonar. The images all showed the same thing, in different positions and from different angles: a creature with a bulky, ovoid body; lateral fins; and a long, slender neck. Reed lingered over the images for a moment. Then, with a rueful sigh, he closed the folder and passed it back to Logan.

Just as Logan was returning it to his attaché case, a man in the hotel's uniform walked up to their table. "Dr. Logan?" he asked.

Logan nodded.

"There's a call for you. It's waiting at the front desk."

Logan frowned. "I'm in the middle of a meeting. Can't it wait?"

The man shook his head. "No, sir. I'm afraid the party on the line said that the matter was urgent. Most urgent."

2

Approached from the west along Rhode Island's Route 138, the Jamestown Verrazzano Bridge was a four-lane, concrete box girder affair of a pleasing— if rather alarmingly pitched—design. It was mid-day, out of season; traffic was fairly light; and Dr. Jeremy Logan prodded the accelerator of his '68 Lotus Elan just a little. The coupe obliged, rising effortlessly up and over the span. A narrow nub-bin of land shot by beneath, and then a second bridge appeared ahead: the Claiborne Pell. This bridge was both much longer and much taller. Logan knew just enough about structural engineer-ing to find suspension bridges faintly disquieting, and he pushed a little harder on the gas pedal. The car climbed; he topped the apex of the span—and then the view ahead and below drove all thoughts of resonant frequencies from his mind.

Newport, Rhode Island, lay before him, jewel-like and sparkling in the early autumn sun, like Oz at the end of the yellow brick road. Coves, marinas, harbors, wharves, and gleaming buildings dressed in stone or white-painted clapboard—barely discernible at this distance—stretched out to the left and right. In the middle distance, a handful of sloops and catboats coursed through the water, heeled over by the wind, their white sails taut and full. It was a sight that never grew old, and Logan drank it in.

It was almost enough to make him forget the nagging mystery of why, exactly, he was here.

At the end of the bridge he turned right onto Farewell Street, then cut through the narrow, traffic-heavy lanes of the old downtown until he reached Memorial Boulevard. Like all tourists, he turned first left, then right onto Bellevue. But then, instead of veering off to the east—toward the Cliff Walk and the impeccably manicured facades of such "cottages" as Marble House or the Breakers— Logan made his way south and west until he reached Ocean Avenue. He passed a series of small beaches, a country club, the inevitable summer mansions. And then, some two miles on, he slowed before a narrow road of paved stone that led south from the main thoroughfare, with no other name than PRIVATE fixed to its road sign. He turned onto the lane. A hundred yards on he reached a tall wall of weathered brick, leading off to each side as far as the eye could see. Directly ahead was a gate in the wall, and a quaint slate-roofed structure that served as a security station. Logan stopped to show some papers; the guard within the station glanced at them, nodded, and passed them back; the gate across the road lifted and, with a wave, Logan drove on.

The narrow, winding road passed through a tiny wood, over one low rise of land, and then another. And then, rounding a corner, Logan stopped as he caught his first glimpse of Lux in almost ten years.

It was even larger than he remembered. Modeled after England's Knebworth House, but on an even grander scale, the sand-colored structure stretched away on both sides for what seemed leagues before terminating in East and West Wings. An odd mélange of Jacobean, Palladian, and high Gothic, leaded-glass windows winking in the sun, the mansion seemed even more Oz-like than Logan's initial impression of Newport—save for the fact that the dark veins of ivy covering the facade; the oddly hooded, watchful appearance of the gables and turrets; and the low crenelations that ran along its roof as if in readiness for battle gave the building an appearance that was faintly sinister. No—that was too strong a word. "Disquieting," Logan had termed it upon first sight, and he settled on that term again now. The high brick wall he had passed through could be seen far away on both sides, running up and down with the vagaries of the grassy terrain, and terminating on both sides at the steep, rocky cliffs above the Atlantic. Scattered around the flanks of the main structure were at least a dozen outbuildings of various shapes and sizes: a power plant, greenhouse, storage facilities, and a series of windowless structures that Logan knew to be laboratories, together forming a campus comprising almost a hundred acres.

Easing the car ahead now, he drove up the lane to a parking area on the near side of the East Wing—the front entrance, with its four massive Solomonic columns supporting a marble pediment, was much too grand to actually be used for anything save decoration—got out of his car, and walked down a short tree-lined sidewalk to a set of double doors. Only here, screwed into the facade on a weather-darkened panel of bronze, did the place allow itself to be named: LUX.

To one side of the doors were several devices: a numeric keypad, an intercom with a buzzer, and another technologic gadget Logan couldn't identify. A printed sign above all three announced RESIDENTS AND GUESTS: USE KEYPAD AFTER HOURS. Logan was neither, and since it was noon, he pressed the buzzer.

After a moment, a woman's voice rasped through the speaker. "Yes?"

"Dr. Jeremy Logan," Logan said, leaning in toward the microphone.

A brief delay. "Please come in."

There was a buzz; the doors sprang open; and Logan entered. Ahead lay the long, broad corridor he remembered. It quite clearly conveyed the double uses of the vast mansion. While the walls and ceilings were trimmed with elegant, almost rococo molding—implying the palatial abode of some robber baron of a previous century—the book-covered tables, heavily used wall-to-wall carpeting, door signs, and conspicuous red exit signs bespoke its second and quite different purpose.

Logan walked about ten yards down the hall, then turned in at the door marked RECEPTION. Telephones rang, and fingers tapped busily on keyboards. And yet there was a strange, subdued feeling in the air that Logan was immediately aware of: something that, for him, cut like a knife through the normal, professional tone of a busy office at work.

A woman was seated behind a long desk, and she watched him enter. "Dr. Logan?" she asked.

"That's right."

"I've notified the director. He'll be down in just a moment."

Logan nodded. "Thank you."

He looked around at the leather-upholstered wing chairs and sofas that made up the waiting room, decided on one, and was about to take a seat when the familiar form of Gregory Olafson appeared in the reception doorway. He was older, of course—his thick black hair had turned pure white, and there were wrinkles around his eyes that had once been merely laugh lines—but something other than years had aged his face. He smiled at the sight of Logan, but it was a brief smile, quickly gone.

"Jeremy," he said, walking forward and taking Logan's hand. "Good to see you again."

"Gregory," Logan replied.

"I know you must be wondering what this is all about. Come with me, please—I'll explain everything in my office." And he led the way out of the room and into the main hallway, Logan following.

3

Olafson's office was much as Logan remembered it. Dark, Edwardian-era wood panels, polished brass fixtures, and the anachronistic scribbly paintings hanging on the walls—Olafson favored abstract expressionism. Along one wall, tall, thickly framed windows afforded a view of the well-tended landscape: greenery that swept down southward toward the rocky cliffs overlooking an angry ocean. The lower sashes of the leaded windows were slightly raised, and Logan was aware of both the distant crash of waves and the briny odor of the sea.

The director motioned Logan toward a chair,

then took a seat beside him. "I appreciate your coming so quickly."

"You said the matter was urgent."

"And so I think it is. But I'd be hard-pressed to tell you precisely why. That's . . ." Olafson hesitated a moment. "That's where you come in. I wanted to secure your services before another assignment came up."

The room fell silent for a long moment as the two men looked at each other. "Before I say anything more," Olafson continued at last, "I need to know that you can put aside any prejudice, any ill will, that might have been caused by—ah—past differences."

This prompted another silence. From his armchair, Logan regarded the director of Lux. He'd been sitting in this same seat the last time he spoke to Olafson, a decade earlier. It had been about this time of year, as well. And the director had worn the same expression on his face: at once both anxious and eager. Fragments of Olafson's short speech came back to Logan now, filtered through a veil of time and memory: *Certain members are rather concerned . . . perceived lack of academic rigor . . . the good of the nation's oldest and most prestigious policy institute must come first. . . .*

Logan shifted in his chair. "It won't be a problem."

The director nodded. "And I can be assured of your complete discretion? Much of what I'm going to tell you is secret, even from the faculty, Fellows, and staff."

"That's part of my job. You shouldn't even have to ask."

"Ah, but I had to, you see. Thank you." Olafson glanced briefly out at the sea before returning his attention to Logan. "Do you remember Dr. Strachey?"

Logan thought a moment. "Willard Strachey?"

Olafson nodded.

"He's a computer scientist, right?"

"That's right. Strachey was recently at the center of a . . . very tragic event that took place here at Lux."

Logan recalled the atmosphere he'd sensed during his brief wait in the reception area. "Tell me about it."

The director glanced seaward again before answering. "Strachey hadn't been himself for the last week or two."

"Can you be more specific?" Logan asked.

"Restless. Apparently not sleeping, or sleeping very little. Irritable—which if you have any recollection of him, you'll know was completely out of character. And he . . ." Olafson hesitated again. "He'd begun talking to himself."

"Indeed?"

"So I've been told. Under his breath but extensively, sometimes even animatedly. Then, just three days ago, he experienced a sudden breakdown."

"Go on," Logan said.

"He became violent, began assaulting his assistant." Olafson swallowed. "As you know, we have only a skeletal security force here—we really aren't equipped to handle any . . . well, scenes of that sort. We restrained him as best we could, locked him in the visitors' library on the first floor. And then we called nine one one."

Logan waited for the director to continue. But instead, Olafson stood up, walked to one wall, and pulled away a decorative curtain, revealing a projection screen. Then he opened a drawer in the same wall, took out a digital projector, and plugged it in, aiming it at the screen.

"It would be easier—for you, and certainly for me—if you just saw for yourself," he said. Then he moved toward the door, flicked off the lights, and turned the projector on.

At first, the screen was black. Then a series of numbers scrolled quickly up its face. And then an image appeared, black-and-white, slightly grainy at this level of magnification: the video feed from a security camera. A date and time stamp ran continuously along the lower edge of the frame. Logan recognized the room. It was, as Olafson had said, the Lux visitors' library: an ornate space with elaborate sconces and a coffered ceiling. Three of the walls were lined floor to ceiling with books; the fourth wall contained several very tall windows of the same heavy sash construction as those in Olafson's office. Armchairs, ottomans, and banquettes were arranged around the gracious space. It was not a working library—that was elsewhere in the mansion, and much more fully stocked—but was instead meant to impress guests and potential clients.

From the bird's-eye perspective of the security camera, Logan could make out a man pacing back and forth over the expensive carpeting, clearly afflicted by extreme agitation. He plucked at his clothes, pulled his hair. Logan recognized him as a decade-older version of Dr. Strachey, perhaps sixty or sixty-five years of age. Now and then the scientist stopped and bent forward, clapping his hands over his ears as if to block out some unbearable sound.

"We put him in there," Olafson said, "so that he wouldn't harm himself or anyone else until help could arrive."

As Logan watched, Strachey went up to the door and yanked at it violently, crying out as he did so.

"What's he saying?" Logan asked.

"I don't know," Olafson replied. "Raving, I'm afraid. The audio quality is poor—only a few of our security cameras even have integrated microphones."

Now Strachey's agitation increased. He pounded the walls, yanked books from their shelves and threw them across the room. Again and again he stopped and covered his ears, shaking his head like a dog shaking a rat. He approached the windows and beat them with his fists, but the leaded glass was too thick to be easily broken. He began to stagger, flailing, almost as if blind, running into walls, turning over tables. He stumbled in the direction of the camera and, for a brief moment, his voice became clearer. Then he turned away again, panting raggedly, looking around. And then, suddenly, he grew calm.

From the corner of his eye, Logan saw Olafson turn away. "I must warn you, Jeremy—I'm afraid this part is terribly disturbing."

Under the gaze of the camera, Logan watched Strachey move toward the wall of windows. He walked slowly at first, then more quickly and confidently. Coming up to the closest window, he tried to raise it. The heavy, old-fashioned sash rose only a few inches.

Strachey went to the next window, tugged at it with sharp, violent motions. It, too, went up just an inch or two. The old-fashioned, metal-trimmed window sashes were very heavy to begin with, Logan knew, and they probably hadn't been cleaned and oiled in decades.

Now Strachey approached a third window; tugged again. This one rose more easily than the others had. Logan watched as Strachey pushed the sash up farther, first using both hands, then applying a shoulder. Logan could hear the grunts of effort. Finally, Strachey managed to raise the window sash to its maximum height: almost five feet above the lower sill.

There was no screen; the library was on the first floor of the building; the yawning window frame gave Strachey easy access to liberty. In another minute, he'd be through the open window and gone. What, Logan wondered, was the tragedy in one scientist gone rogue?

Except that Strachey did not go out of the window. Instead, he bent low before it, reaching in toward the right edge, fiddling with something in the groove of the frame. It was, Logan realized, the window's sash chain. He peered in at the screen, mystified. With one hand, Strachey now held the sash chain; with the other hand, he was performing some kind of twisting motion on an object that his body blocked from view.

Then the hand pulled away. In it was an iron sash weight, about ten inches long and obviously heavy. Strachey had detached the sash weight from the window chain. He let the weight drop to the floor. His other hand still held tight to the sash chain. Only Strachey's grasp on the chain now kept the window from crashing downward.

Suddenly, a terrible dread flooded through Logan.

Still holding tight to the chain, Strachey knelt in front of the window and rested his neck on the sill. There was a moment of stasis in which Logan, frozen in his seat, heard the man draw in several ragged breaths.

And then Strachey let go of the chain.

With a sharp screech like the whistle of a train, the heavy metal sash came hurtling down in its casing. There was a terrible crack of bone, audible even over the rattling of the window; Strachey's body jerked as if touched by a live wire. Logan looked quickly away, but not before seeing the head go tumbling down into the flower beds outside the library, and the heavy flood of blood running dead black in the pitiless eye of the security camera.

4

For at least a minute, neither man moved. And then, silently, the director turned on the lights, stowed away the projector, slid the curtain back over the screen, and returned to his chair.

"My God," Logan murmured.

"We couldn't conceal the fact that Strachey killed himself," Olafson said. "But for obvious reasons, we've tried to keep the details to a minimum. Nevertheless, rumors have been circulating." He looked up at Logan. "I have to ask—do you have any initial thoughts?"

"My God," Logan said again. He was in shock.

He tried summoning up a mental picture of Willard Strachey from his own time at Lux, but all he could recollect was a quiet, rather shy man with thin, mouse-colored hair. They had traded smiles and nods but never a conversation.

He tried to push the shock away and address Olafson's question. "I think," he began slowly, "that to kill oneself in such a way . . . can only mean this was a man who absolutely could not bear to live another minute. He couldn't wait until he had access to pills, a gun, a car, the roof of a building—he had to die. *Immediately.*"

The director nodded, leaned forward. "I don't concern myself with the day-to-day operations of Lux; I leave that to Perry Maynard. But I knew Will Strachey for thirty years. He was the most stable, the most gentle, the most rational of men. He was also one of my best friends. He was a groomsman at my wedding. There is no way he would ever attack somebody. And he would never, *ever,* commit suicide—especially in such a way. Will abhorred ugliness or scenes. An act like this would be completely outside his nature."

Olafson leaned a little closer. "The authorities, of course, just listed it as a suicide and had done. It seems they have a dim view of policy institutes and their residents to begin with. And the police psychiatrist dismissed it as, to the best of my recollection, a 'brief reactive psychosis brought on by a fugue state.'" The director scoffed. "But I know that isn't the case. And I know something else: *that man in the video is not the man I knew.* It's as simple—and as mystifying—as that. And that is why we've asked you here."

"It's not exactly my line of work," Logan said. "I'm no private detective; I'm an enigmalogist."

"And isn't *this* an enigma?" Olafson asked, passion adding a faint tremor to his voice. "I just told you—that man on the video can't be Strachey. He would never have done such a thing. And yet there's no denying that he killed himself. You saw him do it. *I* saw the body." He paused to pass a hand across his forehead. "We need to learn what happened to him. Not for myself—but for the good of Lux."

"You say you were one of his best friends," Logan said. "Was there anything troubling him—anything in either his personal or professional life?"

"I didn't see as much of him over the last year or two as I'd have liked." Olafson waved a hand toward his desk as if pleading a heavy workload. "But I'm sure there was nothing. He never married, never minded being single. He was independently wealthy. There were no health issues—annual physicals are one of the perks here, and nothing came up at his examination two months ago; I checked. I believe he was in the process of wrapping up his work; his assistant, Kim, or Dr. Maynard, could tell you more about that than I. But I can assure you the prospect of retirement didn't concern him. Will Strachey was a full Fellow here at Lux; he'd already made a lasting contribution to his chosen area of research. He had a lot to be proud of—and he had a lot to live for. The last time we had lunch together, he spoke of all the things he was looking forward to when he retired. Touring the cathedrals of Europe—he was a huge fan of architecture and architectural design, knew a great deal about it. Picking up the piano again; did you know that he was a talented pianist, classically trained? He'd had to put his more serious instrumental studies aside years ago when his database work became all-consuming. Sailing the Mediterranean—he was quite the sailor. This was a man with everything to live for. *Everything.*"

For almost a minute, silence descended on the office. And then, at last, Logan nodded. "One condition. I'll need unrestricted access to Lux's offices, labs, and records."

The director hesitated for just a second. "Very well."

"Am I going to need a brief? A reason to be here, poking around, asking questions? After all, there's my, shall we say, past history with Lux to consider."

A pained look crossed Olafson's face. "I've thought about that. Many of the people you knew ten years ago are still here. And, of course, you've become rather well known since then. But if you're to operate with a free hand, I don't see how there can be any coyness or dissembling. You're here, at the request of the board, to look into the circumstances surrounding Dr. Strachey's death. It's as simple as that—and I wouldn't be any more specific."

"Very well. Anything else I should know before I start?"

"Yes." The director paused a moment. "It's only fair to warn you that not everyone is going to be happy to see you. I'm not just referring to the 'past history' you mentioned. A lot of new blood has joined Lux since you were here, but at heart it is still a very conservative place. There are people who are going to question your motives; people who won't trust you. You might as well know that the board was deadlocked, three to three, on bringing you in. I myself cast the tiebreaking vote."

Logan smiled a little wearily. "I'm used to that. Unfortunately, it seems to come with the territory."

"You're still part of the Yale faculty, correct?"

"Correct."

"Well, that can only help." Olafson stood up. "Come on—let's get you processed."

5

At half past four that afternoon, Logan stood in his private office on the third floor of the vast mansion, looking thoughtfully out the window. It was of the same heavy, leaded, metal-lined variety that Strachey had employed; Logan knew he would never look at such a window in quite the same way again. It was closed, but nevertheless he could hear the faint roar of breakers as the Atlantic crashed and worried against the boulders below.

He raised one hand and lightly traced his fingers along the window sash. Lux had its roots in a private club, founded in the early 1800s by six Harvard professors to debate issues of art and philosophy. Over the years it expanded in both ambition and scope, its mission broadening, until finally, in 1892, it was organized into Lux, with a formal charter and an impressive endowment. This made it the country's oldest policy institute—"think tank" to the unwashed—antedating the Brookings Institution by more than two decades. It enjoyed unprecedented success in its early years, quickly outgrowing its Cambridge quarters and relocating first to Boston and then—in the early 1920s—making its final move here to Newport, where it purchased the mansion known as Dark Gables from the heirs of an eccentric millionaire. Over the years, Lux had continued to thrive in its areas of expertise: economics; politics; applied mathematics; physics; and more recently, computer science. The only subject expressly forbidden by its charter was any form of military application—which set it apart from other think tanks, many of which enthusiastically pursued such lucrative research.

Logan stepped away from the window and glanced around the room. Like the rest of the mansion, it was ornate, opulent, and expansive. In addition to the office, there was a small sitting room, a bedroom, and a bath. Logan's eye stopped when it reached his desk. He had already laid out some of his work materials: a laptop; a camcorder; a digital voice recorder; an EM detector; an infrared thermometer; and a dozen or so books, many of them bound in leather, most hundreds of years old.

A low knock on his door interrupted this survey. Logan walked over and opened the door to see a young man in a muted business suit hovering outside. "Excuse me," the man said, handing Logan a sealed folder marked PRIVATE AND CONFIDENTIAL. "Dr. Olafson asked me to deliver this to you personally."

"Thanks," Logan replied with a nod. The young man went off down the richly carpeted corridor and Logan closed the door with one shoulder, unsealing the folder as he did so. Inside was a single, unlabeled DVD.

Walking over to the desk and taking a seat, he powered up the laptop, waited for it to boot up, and then inserted the DVD. Moments later, a media player window opened on the screen and a video began to play. Logan immediately recognized it as the security feed he'd watched in Olafson's office: the grainy, black-and-white image of a man in an elegantly appointed library, pacing and pulling at his hair.

Logan clicked the pause button. He did not want to watch that again. He stared thoughtfully at the now-frozen image of Strachey. Olafson's words came back to him: *I knew Will Strachey for thirty years. He was the most stable, the most gentle, the most rational of men. This was a man with everything to live for. That man in the video is not the man I knew.*

He closed the view window, then fired up a utility to extract the audio portion of the DVD. Next, he opened the resulting file in a forensic audio-editing program and played it in its entirety. It was just four minutes and twenty seconds long. After listening to it once, Logan deleted the last thirty seconds: the screech of the descending window sash, the sickening crack, and the two thuds that followed were almost as horrifying to listen to as they'd been to witness.

Now Logan listened to the audio file again. The first forty-five seconds consisted only of heavy footsteps and stertorous breathing, and he deleted that as well. He was left with an audio file approximately three minutes long, of poor quality, full of hum and hiss and digital artifacts.

In the editor's main window, the audio was displayed as a waveform: a fat, ragged line that ran from left to right, studded throughout with needle-like spikes. Logan opened a smaller window and instructed the program to run a spectral analysis of the audio file. He peered at the resulting display, examining and adjusting the amplitude and frequency values. Next, he ran a glitch-detection macro over the audio, adjusting its threshold slider to an aggressive setting. He corrected the file for DC offset, increased the gain, then ran it through a parametric equalizer chained to a high-pass filter.

Now the file was louder and clearer, and the majority of the hum was gone. Strachey's voice was more audible, but it was still difficult to interpret—partly because of the poor audio, and partly because Strachey was alternately gasping and mumbling. Nevertheless, Logan made the best transcript he could, playing the difficult passages again and again and listening very closely. As much as possible, he tried to put himself in Strachey's shoes, imagining what the man might be feeling, then interpolating the results.

"No . . . No. I can't, I can't."

This was followed by a passage of rapid breathing, almost hyperventilation.

"Help me, please. It follows me everywhere. Everywhere. I can't, I can't escape!"

Logan heard the doorknob being rattled, books flung from their shelves.

"It comes from the [undecipherable]. I know it does."

Various crashing noises; the sound of a table being overturned. For a brief moment, the voice became clearer:

"The voices—getting too close. They taste like poison. Have to get away."

Then the voice grew more distant as Strachey staggered away from the recording camera.

"It is with me. They are with me. In the dark. No, God, no . . ."

That was it. Suddenly, the tremulous agitation in the voice eased. The breathing slowed, became almost calm. Logan stopped the playback; he knew what was going to happen next.

Saving the transcript to a text file, he closed the laptop and stood up, returning to the window and the view of the gray Atlantic. He had, for the purposes of deciphering the audio, tried to put him-

self in Strachey's shoes. Now he wished he hadn't.
There was nothing there but inexplicable, sudden
madness—madness and death.

They are with me. In the dark.

The sun beat down over the greensward that
ran away from the mansion toward the sea. In the
oak-paneled office, it was warm. Yet despite the
warmth, Logan felt a shiver run through him.

6

It was half past seven when Logan left his rooms, descended the sweeping central staircase, and entered the main dining room. Dark Gables, Lux's home, had been the product of the febrile imagination of Edward Delaveaux. During its construction, the reclusive, bizarre millionaire had purchased an ancient French monastery, disassembled it stone by stone, and brought sections wholesale back to Rhode Island to incorporate into his mansion. The dining room had once been the monastery's refectory. It was a large gothic space, with huge wooden beams forming a vaulted ceiling and decorative arches lining the tapestried walls. The only things breaking the illusion were the two opposing Solomonic, or barley-sugar, columns that—with their inlaid bands spiraling from bottom to top—matched those at the mansion's main entrance. Such columns were the primary load-bearing supports of the building, and could be found, in varying sizes, throughout Lux.

Logan paused just within the doorway a moment, looking around at the tables, the people dining at them, and the tuxedoed waiters hovering attentively here and there. There were several vaguely familiar faces, still more that he didn't recognize. The tables were all identical: round, seating six, covered with crisp white linen tablecloths.

One of the closest tables was almost empty. There were just two people seated at it, a man and a woman, and another place setting indicating that a third person had temporarily left the table. Logan recognized the seated man. He was Jonathan King, a specialist in game theory. While Logan hadn't been close to King during his time at Lux, the man had always been friendly. He began walking toward the table. As he did so, he was aware of people doing double takes as he passed. He'd had his image on the cover of enough magazines that he was used to this.

King looked up as Logan approached. He looked blank for a moment; then his face broke into a smile. "Jeremy!" he said, standing up and shaking Logan's hand. "What a surprise. And a pleasure."

"Hi, Jonathan," Logan replied. "May I join you?"

"Of course." King turned toward the woman who was seated beside him. She was perhaps thirty years of age, with black hair and bright, inquisitive eyes. "This is Zoe Dempster," King said. "Joined Lux six months ago as a junior Fellow. She's a specialist in limits and multivariable calculus."

Hearing this, Logan remembered how, at the think tank, people were automatically introduced not only with their name but their specialty. "Hello," he said with a smile.

"Hello." Dempster frowned. "Have we met before?"

"This is Jeremy Logan," King said.

The frown remained for a moment. Then a lightbulb went on over her head. "Oh. You're the—" and she stopped suddenly.

"That's right," Logan said. "The ghost detective."

Dempster laughed with something like relief. "You said it, not me."

Logan caught a glimpse of Olafson. He was seated at a table in the rear of the dining room, along with vice director Perry Maynard and several others. Looking up, the director noticed Logan's glance and nodded.

"Jeremy was in residence here for a time," King said tactfully. "That was— How long ago was it, Jeremy?"

"Almost ten years."

"Ten years. Hard to believe." King shook his head. "Are you back here for more research?"

Logan noticed the way the two were looking at him. He knew they were curious about his presence here, and he was considering the best way to answer, when somebody sat down at the third table setting: a man in his late fifties, with close-cropped black-and-silver hair and a beautifully trimmed beard that would have done Sigmund Freud proud. He set down a cup full of black coffee beside his plate, then looked over at Logan with an expression of theatrical surprise.

"Well, well," he said. "I was wondering if you might be showing up about now."

"Hello, Roger," said Logan.

"Hullo, yourself." Roger Carbon had a honey-eyed English accent that somehow made everything he said sound slightly disdainful. He turned to the others. "Jonathan, you remember Jeremy Logan, no doubt. Zoe, you wouldn't. Although you might have seen him on television. I happened to catch you on CNN just the other night. 'There ain't no Nessie.' How droll."

Logan merely nodded. Roger Carbon, specialist in evolutionary psychology, had been Logan's nemesis during his time at Lux, considering his work on enigmas and the qualification of supernatural phenomena to be sensationalist, beneath the institution. Carbon had been one of a small group that had been instrumental in seeing that Logan was asked to leave.

A waiter appeared at Logan's side with a small printed menu; Logan glanced at it, checked off his choices, and passed it back to the waiter, who quickly vanished.

"I must say, the modus operandi you described sounded remarkably scientific," Carbon went on airily. "And you have a name for your, ah, discipline now—don't you?"

"Enigmalogy," Logan said.

"That's it. Enigmalogy. As I recall, you had not yet gotten as far as a name during your time here at Lux."

"Remarkable what can happen in a decade," Logan replied, tolerating the man's snide tone.

"It is indeed. Can I assume, then, that you've codified this new field of yours? Systematized it, established its principles? Can we expect a textbook anytime soon? *Ghostbreaking 101,* perhaps? Or, no—*Spooks for Dummies?*"

"Roger," Jonathan King warned.

"I've gotten very good at ancient curses, too," Logan said, careful to keep his tone light. "In fact, I'm offering a special today: I'll hex two people of your choice for the price of one."

Zoe Dempster chortled, covered her mouth with one hand. King smiled. Carbon took a sip of coffee, ignoring the remark.

"But you are here about Strachey, right?" he asked, changing the subject.

"More or less," Logan said.

"Well, let's have some details, then!"

"Another time. Suffice to say the board has asked me to make some inquiries into the nature of his death."

"The nature of his death. Nobody's talking much about that, but the word is it was pretty ghastly." Carbon gave him a penetrating gaze. "Is it true Strachey's head was found in a rosebush?"

"I couldn't say," Logan replied, with a double meaning.

"Well, at least tell us how you're going to get started."

"I've started already."

Carbon digested this for a moment. Clearly, he did not like the insinuation.

Logan's first course appeared: frisée salad with lardons and a poached egg. "Actually, I thought I'd drop in on Perry Maynard."

"Ah. Well, when you do, be sure to ask him about the others."

Logan stopped in the act of raising his fork. "Others?"

"Others." And Carbon finished his coffee, dabbed primly at his mouth with a linen napkin, smiled at King, winked at Zoe Dempster, then rose and left the table without another word.

7

The office of vice director, Perry Maynard, was twice as large as the director's was. And although it naturally had the same Edwardian feel, it nevertheless managed to look quite different from Olafson's office, as well. It was located on the fourth floor of the mansion, in one of the gables beneath the massive, beetling roof; and it faced north, looking over the expansive grounds rather than toward the rocky, angry coastline. The power desk almost devoid of paper, the set of Ping clubs placed with deliberate casualness in one corner, and the sporting prints on the walls all gave the space the appearance of a CEO's lair. This was not really a surprise: Maynard's specialty had been macroeconomics before he was promoted to vice director. There were, Logan had noticed, two basic types at Lux. On one hand there was the academic type, who tended to wear white coats or slightly rumpled blazers and always seemed to be absorbed in whatever research they were conducting at present. The other was the corporate type, usually specializing in industrial psychology or business administration. They wore dark, well-tailored suits and habitually assumed confident, übercompetent airs.

It was just ten o'clock the next morning when Logan was ushered through the outer office and admitted to Maynard's sanctum sanctorum. "Ah, Jeremy," said Maynard, coming around his desk and shaking Logan's hand with a bone-crushing grip. "I've been expecting you. Have a seat."

Indicating a brace of leather chairs with a wave, Maynard retreated behind his desk. He did not, Logan noticed, take a seat beside him, as Olafson had done.

"Congratulations on your promotion to the vice directorship," Logan said.

Maynard gave another wave, dismissive this time. He had dark blond hair and a lithe, athletic body that made him seem younger than his fifty years. "I prefer to think of myself as head of operations," he said. "You know, most of the Fellows here are their own bosses. They know their areas of research, their own little fiefdoms, better than anyone else. I'm just the administrator."

This bit of self-deprecation didn't fool Logan. Maynard might be an administrator, but one possessed of great power should he need, or decide, to wield it. While it was true Lux was a think tank, it was also a privately held corporation that cared about profits. Naturally, it gave generous grants, awarded a number of annual scholarships, and funded chairs in various areas of academic pursuit—but such things were made possible by a steady stream of revenue. Though it wasn't often articulated, every Fellow at Lux knew that the most effective kind of research was the kind that could, ultimately, be put to practical use. Logan wondered whether Maynard was one of the three on the board of directors who had voted for his presence here, or one of the three who'd done the opposite.

Maynard settled himself in his chair. "No doubt you'd like to discuss Willard Strachey."

Logan nodded.

"What an awful business. Awful." Maynard shook his head.

"Gregory told me that you'd be in a better position to fill me in on just what Strachey had been working on recently."

"Mmm. Yes." Maynard leaned back and crossed his arms. "Well, you may recall that Willard's specialty was DBMS."

"DBMS?"

"Database management systems. He made some revolutionary progress in the relational database model first pioneered by Codd and others. Strachey's database, Parallax, was one of the breakthrough applications of the early eighties."

"Go on, please," Logan said.

"It was a database manager with a built-in programming language of Strachey's own design. It was legendary for its speed, scalability, and small footprint: not a behemoth like, say, DB2. It was popular with the VAX minicomputers used on many college campuses of the time. The time, of course, was thirty years ago." Maynard shrugged. "Programming languages have changed a lot since then."

"Are you saying Strachey had come to believe his best years were behind him?"

"I don't think he viewed it that way at all. He was exceptionally proud of the work he'd done. And he was a true academic: for him, the research itself was its own end." Maynard hesitated. "It was Lux, if you really want to know, that had issues with it."

Logan frowned. "I don't understand."

"It's like I said: programming has changed a lot. These days it's all about objects, class inheritance, scripting languages. The very things that made Parallax so revolutionary when it was first released also made it difficult to reengineer. And, let's face it, Willard was happy with Parallax as it was. He continued to refine it. But many larger clients were moving on."

"And taking their money elsewhere."

A pained look crossed Maynard's face, but he nodded, conceding the point. "In any case, Strachey was fully vested at Lux. He was a senior Fellow. He'd had his successes, done us all proud. Even though he could have retired with a full pension, we were delighted to see him continue his relational database work. But a decision was made that such work should be more of a . . . sideline."

"A hobby, in other words—rather than something he'd be paid for."

"Oh, he'd still be paid for it. But several months ago, we did with Willard what we do with many of our Fellows who are transitioning away from their primary research. We gave him *administrative* duties, as well—duties that could directly benefit Lux."

"Like a tenured professor transitioning to an associate dean. Making sure he was still of commercial use to Lux."

"Something like that."

"Could you tell me about these administrative duties?" Logan asked.

"It was Roger Carbon's idea, actually. Willard was given overall responsibility for the restoration of the West Wing, which as you probably know hasn't been updated in ages. In fact, it's been off-limits for the last several years. It's not unsafe, of course, but it's old and needs a complete retrofit to bring it into the twenty-first century. I don't have to tell you that the loss of all that square footage has put a crimp in our operations, even with the expansion of our outbuildings. So its restoration was viewed by Lux as a very important task."

"Did Willard Strachey view it as important, as well?"

At this, Maynard looked searchingly at Logan. "If you're harboring any thoughts that Will might have been unhappy with the assignment, or felt it demeaning, you're completely off base. He knew the way Lux works. And he was passionate about architecture. Here was a chance to take a beautiful example of late-nineteenth-century design and repurpose it into a modern, utilitarian space. He wasn't getting his hands dirty, wasn't wielding a nail gun: he was designing the functionality, balancing the practical with the aesthetic. It's like a homeowner telling his general contractor just what he wants done—only on a different order of magnitude. We had an architect working with him, of course, to vet the designs and verify the underlying engineering, but the ideas began with him. And by all accounts he was delighted with the task. Of course, I didn't see much of him on a day-to-day basis. You'd need to talk to Ms. Mykolos about that."

"Who?"

"Kim Mykolos. His research assistant."

"The one he assaulted?"

A brief pause. "Yes."

"Did you know much about Strachey's behavior over the last few weeks?"

"I'd heard reports from various people, yes. In

fact, I'd been intending to have a talk with him." Maynard's shoulders drooped, and he looked down at his desk. "Now it's too late. I'll never know if there's something I could have done, some way I could have helped."

"You mentioned he was working with an architect," Logan said.

"As it turns out, the great-granddaughter of the architect who originally built Dark Gables. Pamela Flood. She's carried on the family's architectural firm. We were lucky to get her."

Logan made a note of this as Maynard glanced at his watch. "I'm very sorry, Jeremy. There's a meeting I need to attend. I'll be happy to answer any other questions you have at some later point." And he rose from his desk.

"Just one more, if you don't mind."

Maynard stopped. "Of course."

"Last night at dinner, Dr. Carbon suggested I ask about 'the others.'"

Maynard frowned. "He did?"

"Yes. He mentioned you specifically as the one I should speak to."

Maynard shook his head slowly. "I've never understood Roger's sense of humor. He may have been pulling your leg—you know he never took your line of study seriously."

"I know. But what did he mean—'the others'?"

Maynard glanced at his watch again. "I'm sorry, Jeremy, I really can't be late for this meeting. Please keep me and Gregory apprised of your progress. And whatever you do, be discreet in your inquiries. An old, upstanding institution like Lux blemishes awfully easily." And with a smile, he waved for Logan to precede him out of the office.

8

An hour later, Logan made his way down the central corridor of Lux's third floor, canvas satchel slung over one shoulder. This hallway, familiarly known as the Lady's Walk, retained almost entirely the look it had sported when the mansion was a private residence. It was fantastically ornate, with wide, polished oaken floorboards; elaborate wainscoting; coffered ceiling; gilded sconces; and huge oil portraits in golden frames. It was also the longest unbroken hall in the mansion: running the entire length of the main building, it stretched nearly three city blocks' worth from the East Wing to the West Wing. And yet despite its magnificence, it was almost never seen by visitors. This was, in part, because the third floor was given over to the private offices and apartments of the think tank's Fellows. Another reason, Logan thought, could be the hallway's nickname itself. Awkward questions might arise.

The lady in question was Ernestine Delaveaux, wife of the original owner of Dark Gables. By all accounts, she had been a beautiful and accomplished woman, the product of one of Boston's finest families and Europe's best finishing schools. But she was also possessed of a nervous temperament and weak constitution. When the couple's only son died of smallpox, the shock proved too much for Mrs. Delaveaux. Uncontrolled weeping, lack of appetite, and insomnia followed. The doctors brought in by her husband, Edward—himself of an eccentric cast—could do nothing, save prescribe nostrums for what they pronounced to be neurasthenia. Then, one night in 1898, Ernestine Delaveaux saw, or thought she saw, her dead son, standing in this same hallway, hands outstretched toward her. After that, she wandered the hallway every night, tirelessly calling her son's name. She never saw him again. Finally, on a stormy December evening two years later, Mrs. Delaveaux left the mansion, walked down to the sea, and threw herself into the Atlantic.

Edward Delaveaux never recovered from the double loss of his son and his wife. He spent the rest of his life and fortune in seclusion, trying one scheme after the other to contact his family on the other side. He finally died himself, nearly destitute, in 1912. Dark Gables remained shuttered and unoccupied until Lux relocated from Boston to Newport and purchased it. Ever since Lux took possession of the mansion, however, rumors had circulated that, on certain stormy nights, the ghost of Ernestine Delaveaux could be seen roaming this long, extravagantly appointed corridor, holding a linen handkerchief and calling her son's name.

Logan had never seen her. Nor had he spoken to anyone who had. But the legend persisted nevertheless.

Now he stopped before a large wooden door, windowless and gleaming, set into the wall to his left. It bore a brief legend:

382

W. STRACHEY

K. MYKOLOS

Logan paused a moment, then knocked. A female voice from beyond immediately called out, "Come in."

Logan entered. The room he found himself in was fairly small, evidently an outer office, judging by the open door in the far wall leading to a much larger room. Nevertheless, the bookshelves here were stuffed full of technical journals, textbooks, boxed and labeled manuscripts; the lone desk was covered with notated papers and monographs. And yet the crowded space managed to look orderly rather than messy. The room had no windows, and there were no pictures or photos on the walls, but there were half a dozen glass frames full of butter-flies: large and small, some monochromatic, others as iridescent as a peacock.

A woman in her midtwenties sat at the desk, fingers resting on a workstation keyboard. She had short jet-black hair, an upturned nose, and—although she was slender—was possessed of a rounded, dimpled chin that reminded Logan of Betty Boop. He recalled seeing her in passing at dinner the night before, talking animatedly at a table with other young people. She was looking up at him now with an expression of expectation.

"You're Kimberly Mykolos?" he asked.

"Yes," she replied. "But that's quite a mouthful, isn't it? Please call me Kim."

"Kim it shall be."

She smiled. "And I'm terribly afraid I know who you are."

Logan gave a melodramatic sigh. "In that case, would you mind if I sat down?"

"I would insist."

Logan began to sit down when he caught sight of a brief Latin quotation, framed simply in black and set upon the wall beside the desk: *Forsan et haec olim meminisse iuvabit.* He froze.

"What's wrong?" the woman asked. "You look as though you've seen a ghost."

"An occupational hazard in my line of work," Logan replied. "But it isn't that." He sat down and pointed at the framed quotation. "Virgil, *Aeneid.* Book One, line 203."

"That's a remarkable bit of erudition to have at one's fingertips."

"I'm no savant. It's just that I have the same quotation hanging over my desk." And he quoted: " 'Perhaps some day it will be pleasant to remember even this.' "

Mykolos raised her eyebrows. "I guess that means we're going to be the best of friends."

"Maybe so. I like butterflies, too."

"I don't just like them. I'm passionate about them. Have been ever since I was a kid. When I'm not working, I'm out collecting. Look at this one." She pointed to a relatively small butterfly in the nearest frame: brown with black eyelets and orange-colored terminal bands on its wings. "A Mitchell's satyr. Very rare. I caught this at age thirteen, before it was considered endangered."

"Beautiful." Logan looked from the butterfly back to Mykolos. "You say you know who I am?"

"I remember seeing you on a PBS documentary. It was about an excavation of the tomb of a very ancient pharaoh—the first pharaoh, if I remember right. You stood out because of your occupation." She frowned. "They had an unusual word for it. An . . . an . . ."

"Enigmalogist," Logan completed the sentence for her. He decided that Betty Boop was an unfair comparison. This woman's chin more closely resembled Claudette Colbert's.

"Yes, enigmalogist."

"Well, I'm glad you saw the documentary. It saves me a lot of time in introductions."

She glanced at him curiously. "Are you here to investigate the Lady's Walk?"

"Unfortunately not. I've been asked by the board of directors to look into the death of Willard Strachey."

Mykolos's eyes slowly drifted down toward her desk. "I was afraid of that," she said in a very different tone.

"Ms. Mykolos, I know this must be difficult for you. I'll try to keep my questions as brief as possible. But you were as close to Dr. Strachey as anybody. I hope you'll understand why it's necessary I speak with you."

She nodded wordlessly.

"First, tell me a little about yourself. How you came to Lux, how you came to work for Strachey."

Mykolos paused to take a sip from a cup of tea that sat on the desk. "I don't know how much you know of the way Lux goes about hiring its staff. They're quite selective."

"That's probably an understatement."

"It's not unlike the way the Brits recruit potential spies to MI6. Lux has talent spotters at several of the best universities. If they see somebody who shows a certain kind of promise, along with the right temperament and intellectual curiosity—Lux has entire profiles for the spotters to use—then the foundation is contacted. An inquiry is convened and, if the results are positive and there's a suitable opening, an offer is made. In my case, about four years ago I received my MSE in computer science from MIT. It was my plan to go on directly for my doctorate. Instead, I won the Advanced Computing Society's Obfuscated Software Award. And then I got a visit from a Lux recruitment officer." She shrugged. "And here I am."

"What was your specialty at MIT?" Logan asked.

"Strategic software design."

"Never heard of it."

"It's a rather new field. It deals with how to protect programs from today's threat-filled digital environment: worms, tunneling programs, reverse engineering, intrusions by hostile corporations or governments. Of course, one learns how to write one's *own* reverse engineering algorithms, as well." And she smiled almost slyly.

"And were you hired specifically to be Dr. Strachey's assistant?"

Mykolos nodded. "His previous assistant had to leave to become a full-time mother." She paused. "Funny how married women tend to get pregnant from time to time, isn't it?"

"I've often wondered about that." Logan sat back in the chair. "But were you a good fit for the job? With Strachey, I mean. His specialty was relational databases, after all."

Mykolos hesitated. "I'm not sure how familiar you are with them. They're much more powerful and versatile than flat file or hierarchical databases. And Strachey's database management system, Parallax, was a revelation when it appeared. He was a phenomenal coder. Really phenomenal. The language he wrote it in, C, is tight to begin with, but he was able to make each line do triple duty. Still, Parallax was . . . well, a product of its time. Lux was looking for a way to market it to a larger, less demanding market."

"And that meant bringing in fresh blood."

"These days, programs that large corporations once paid hundreds of thousands of dollars for in site licenses don't necessarily need to be shelved as they age. They can be repurposed for the use of smaller companies that will pay a lot less per seat, but whose needs are more limited. But that also means, in effect, releasing the program into the wild—and so it needs to be protected by anti-tampering technology. That's where I came in."

"And the result?"

She glanced at him. "Sorry?"

"Well, a person like Strachey, nearing the end of his career, might become resentful . . . if he felt his life's work was being 'repurposed' by someone young, lean, and hungry."

There was a pause during which a change slowly came over Mykolos. From a friendly, open, even playful young woman, she became visibly distraught. She pushed herself back from the desk. Logan felt her pushing back from him, as well.

"May I take hold of your hand for a moment?" he asked.

She frowned in surprise.

"If you don't mind. It helps me get a better sense of the person I'm talking with. Sometimes I can understand things on a deeper level than with language alone."

After a moment, she extended her hand. He took it gently in his.

"I know," he said after a moment. "I know you're trying to deal with a terrible thing in the best way you can. One way to do that is to pretend: act and speak lightly, avoid the issue. It's a valid defense mechanism—for a time, anyway."

Mykolos's eyes filled with tears. Logan withdrew his hand. She turned away, reached into a tissue box, dabbed at her eyes. Perhaps a minute passed. Then she took a deep, shuddering breath and turned around to face him again.

"I'm all right," she said. "Sorry."

"Don't be. You've been through something awful."

"It's just that . . ." She paused again, and for a moment Logan thought she might begin to weep. But she pulled herself together. "It's just that Willard was such a kind man, such a *gentle* man. He loved his work. He loved Lux. And he loved me, too, I think—in a way."

"So he wasn't resentful—didn't see you as someone who wanted his job."

"No, no, nothing like that. I was a little afraid he might be, at first—it would be a natural enough reaction." Mykolos sniffed, dabbed at her nose with a fresh tissue. "But he was genuinely interested in retasking Parallax for a broader market. And I think he felt that . . . well, that he'd done enough. He'd made several breakthroughs in relational database theory, created a very successful RDBMS of his own—that's more than enough for any career. So while he remained interested in the work, remained dedicated to keeping Parallax the best it could be, he became less actively involved."

"And what did the work consist of, exactly?"

Mykolos paused again. "It gets technical. Obfuscation, for example."

"You mentioned that term before. What is it?"

"It's a subset of reverse engineering. Making software difficult for competitors to decompile and figure out. Lux likes to get paid for Parallax—they don't want to give it away. But really, much of what I ended up doing was code review. That, and helping him document his theories as they had developed and matured."

"In other words, playing Boswell to his Johnson."

Mykolos laughed softly despite the red eyes. "We were both playing his Boswell. Willard was proud of the work he'd done—really proud. So he wanted to chronicle it, not only for himself but for posterity. Or at least what passes for posterity here at Lux."

"I see." Logan thought for a moment. "So what about this other work he began a few months back? Overseeing the reconstruction and redesign of the West Wing?"

For a moment, a cloud passed over Mykolos's face. "He didn't say anything about it at first. Nothing negative, anyway. But then, that's not his way—he'd never bad-mouth anyone or anything. But I could tell he wasn't especially pleased. By that point, all he wanted was to complete his work, maybe reduce the number of weekly hours a bit so he could get in some sailing. But as time went by, he grew more and more interested. It involved a lot of architectural planning and design—he really enjoyed that."

"I understand he was working closely with the firm that originally built this structure."

"Yes. Flood Associates."

Logan took a deep breath. Now came the hard part. "Just one more question. Can you please tell me about the events leading up to Dr. Strachey's attack on you?"

Mykolos remained silent.

"Take your time. Tell me in your own words."

She plucked a fresh tissue from the box. "It came on so gradually I didn't notice it right away. I guess it was the irritation first—he'd never acted irritated, ever; he was always the kindest person you can imagine. He'd never once raised his voice in the more than two years I worked for him. But he started to snap at people—secretaries, attendants—even me, once. And he began developing odd mannerisms."

"Odd in what way?"

"Waving his hands before his face, as if to push something away. Humming, the way you might if you were a kid, and someone you didn't like refused to stop talking. And then . . . then there was the muttering."

"I heard he was talking to himself. Did you hear any of what he said?"

"Until the last day or two it was pretty much

under his breath. I don't think he was aware of it himself. And what I did catch was nonsense, mostly."

"Try me."

Mykolos thought for a moment. "Things like: 'Stop it. Stop it, I don't want it. Go away. I won't, you can't make me.'"

"And then?" Logan prodded gently.

Mykolos licked her lips. "The last couple of days, things got abruptly worse. He closed the door to his office, began yelling, throwing things around. He wouldn't speak to me. I'd see him walk by, abruptly clapping his hands over his ears. And then, last Thursday . . . he looked so agitated, so troubled, I came up, put a hand on his shoulder, asked if I could be of help in some way. He turned on me suddenly. . . ." She paused. "Oh, my God, his face—it was so unlike him, purple, enraged, eyes wide and staring . . . but it wasn't only rage, it was also despair, maybe helplessness. . . . He knocked my hand away, grabbed my shoulders, pushed me onto the desk . . . grabbed my neck, began choking me. . . . I picked up my keyboard, flung it in his face. . . ."

She stood up. "He let go then. I ran behind my desk, picked up the phone, dialed the front desk, then Dr. Olafson's office. A minute later, three lab assistants burst in and hauled Willard away. He was yelling and screaming at the top of his voice, kicking violently . . . and that was the last I ever saw of him."

She turned back now and sat down again at her desk, breathing heavily.

"Thank you," Logan said.

She nodded. A brief silence descended over the room.

"Please tell me something," Mykolos said at last. "They say he committed suicide. But I don't believe it."

Logan said nothing.

"Please tell me. How did he die?"

Logan hesitated. The information, he knew, was being kept as quiet as possible. But this woman had helped him, to her own discomfort. "It isn't supposed to be known."

"I'm not going to tell anyone."

Logan looked at her appraisingly. Then he said, "He used the heavy windows of the visitor's library to decapitate himself."

"He—" Mykolos's hand flew to her mouth. "How awful." Then she balled the hand into a fist. "No," she said. "No, that couldn't have been Willard."

"What do you mean?"

"Something was obviously not right with him. He might have been sick—I don't know. But he would never, *ever* have killed himself. He had too much to live for. He was the least rash person I've ever known. And . . . dignity was important to him. He would never have killed himself—especially not in that way."

This brief speech was remarkably similar to

what Olafson had said—and it was delivered with the same passion. "That's why I'm back here," Logan told her. "To try to understand what happened."

Mykolos nodded a little absently. Then she glanced at him. "What do you mean: *back* here?"

"About ten years ago, I spent six months at Lux, doing research of my own."

"Really? Six months is an odd length of time. Usually, research terms are measured in years."

Logan regarded her again. Something about this young woman convinced him he could trust her—and that, in fact, she might be able to help him in ways he could not yet know. "I was asked to leave," he said.

"Why?"

"You know Lux's record as the nation's oldest think tank. The respected position it holds among its peers."

"You mean, we're all a bunch of tight asses."

"Something like that. My work was adjudged to be inadequate. Not true science. Not intellectually rigorous enough. It was seen by some as hocus-pocus, smoke and mirrors. A cadre of Fellows, headed by Dr. Carbon, had me forced out."

Mykolos made a face. "Carbon. That prick."

"Well, I'm back here now. This time, as an investigator instead of a Fellow."

"Dr. Logan, I want—I *need*—to know what happened. If I can help in any way, let me know."

"Thanks. You can start by letting me putter around in Dr. Strachey's office, if you don't mind." And Logan indicated the far office.

"Of course. It's a bit of a mess, though. Let me go in ahead of you and clear things up a bit. I wouldn't want you to do an Alkan on me."

"A what?"

"Charles-Valentin Alkan. French composer. Wrote some of the strangest music you'll ever want to hear. Supposedly died when a bookcase fell on top of him."

"Never heard of him. You're quite the Renaissance woman."

"I guess the Lux talent spotter thought the same way." And Mykolos rose from her desk with a wan smile. "Come on—follow me."

9

Willard Strachey's private apartment—his "rooms,"
in Lux parlance—was on the third floor of the
mansion, just a dozen or so doors down the Lady's
Walk from where his office was located. Logan
let himself in with a key provided by Dr. Olafson,
closed the door behind him, let his bag drop to the
floor, and stood still a moment, taking in the feel of
the space beyond. It was just past nine p.m., and
the chamber was dark, its furnishings mere dull
shapes. After about a minute, Logan turned on the
lights.

He hadn't known what to expect, and the
room he was standing in—apparently a combina-

tion library and parlor—was a pleasant surprise.
The furniture was upholstered in mahogany-colored
leather, well lived in and equally well cared for. One
wall contained recessed bookcases which—Logan
noted—were devoted to a wide variety of subjects:
nineteenth-century English novels; Latin classics in
translation; a few recent whodunits; biographies;
and numerous books on sailing, architecture and
design, and the history of computing. The books
were not just for display: Logan pulled a few from
the shelves and found them to be lovingly read.
Several displayed marginal glosses in Strachey's
small, meticulous hand. The Edwardian trappings
of the mansion had been tastefully accentuated
in this room by a hundred additional touches—
vintage sconces, Astrakhan carpets, oil paintings
of the English romantic school. There was an old
mechanical doll; a vintage wooden radio; a worn
sextant—apparently, Strachey was a collector of
antique technology. A rolltop desk sat in one corner, with several old fountain pens lined up at one
side. Another corner was monopolized by a Stein-
way Model B, its glossy black finish shining in the
mellow light. The room exuded the warm, welcom-
ing feeling of a London gentleman's club from the
turn of the last century. It had taken money to create this atmosphere—Olafson said money wasn't a
problem for Strachey. But it had taken more than
that: it had taken time, and patience, and loving
care. It was subtle; it was refined; it was delightful.
Logan could imagine himself living in a place such
as this.

He moved through the rest of the apartment. It was not especially large—a dining room, a compact but expensively supplied kitchen, a bathroom, a bedroom—but each space displayed the same care and consideration as the library had. Nowhere did Logan find any evidence of Strachey's work: that was left in his office, down the hall. Rather, these rooms were devoted to private relaxation with the man's many avocations: sailing, art, industrial design.

Logan had spent almost the entire afternoon in Strachey's office, going through his papers, notes, manuscripts, sometimes on his own and sometimes with the assistance of Kim Mykolos. It had been as expected: there were clear signs that the pace of Strachey's research had been slowing. But as Mykolos had told him, the man had been in essence sealing the cap on a lifetime career, and greatly enjoying the process. Nowhere among the man's various notes and writings was there any indication of disappointment: just quiet satisfaction at having made significant accomplishments in his field. Logan now felt certain that, whatever might have prompted Strachey's suicide, it had nothing to do with the twilight of his career.

There had also been several large folders in the office relating to the West Wing renovation, and—feeling overwhelmed—Logan had packed these up and sent them back to his own rooms for later examination. He had then gone to speak with Lux's doctor in residence. The two spent twenty minutes going over Strachey's physical and psychological history. As Olafson had indicated, all tests and examinations showed Strachey to have been in excellent health for a man of his age, emotionally stable, with no indications of either preexisting conditions or future complications.

Now he returned to the parlor. He'd held out mild hope that Strachey had kept a diary or private journal, but there was no sign of any. So instead he reached into his duffel, removed the video camera, and made another tour of the apartment, filming each room. Replacing the camera, he took out a small notebook and a rectangular device about the size of a police radio, with a control knob centered at the bottom and a large analog gauge monopolizing the top: a trifield natural EM meter. He made yet another tour of the apartment, carefully watching the needle of the meter and making occasional jottings in his notebook. Finally, he pulled another handheld device from the duffel, studded with knobs, toggle switches, and a digital readout: an air-ion counter. He took several readings, but found the air ionization to be no different from that of the other areas of the mansion he'd sampled already.

His eye drifted around the room, stopping at the antique radio. It was a cathedral-style tabletop model of rose-colored wood. Absently, he turned the power knob to the on position. Nothing happened. Curious, he picked up the radio, turned it over in his hands, opened the back. There was a jumble of old brown and yellow wires and machinery, but the vacuum tubes had been replaced with what at a brief glance appeared to be more modern equipment. He shrugged, replaced it on its shelf, and turned away.

Placing the tools and the notebook back in the duffel, he glanced around again, selected the most comfortable-looking armchair—judging from the nearby book stand and the well-used footrest, Strachey's favorite chair as well—settled into it, closed his eyes, and waited.

At quite a young age, Logan had discovered he was an empath—someone with a unique, almost preternatural ability to sense the feelings and emotions of others. At times—if those feelings were strong enough, or if the person had resided in one place for a sufficient length of time—Logan could still sense them even after the occupant had departed.

He sat in the chair, in the dim amber light, emptying himself of his own feelings and preoccupations and waiting for the room to speak to him. At first, there was nothing save a vague, dissociated sense of security and comfort. This was not surprising: there were clearly no smoking guns, no hidden skeletons, no emotional issues, that would have prompted Strachey to . . .

And then something odd happened. As Logan sat there, eyes closed, relaxed, he began to hear music. At first it was soft—so soft it was barely audible. But as he waited, growing attentive, it began to grow clearer: lush, deeply romantic.

This had never happened before. As a sensitive, Logan was used to receiving emotional impressions, strong feelings, occasionally bits and pieces of memories. But never any sensory stimuli such as music. He sat up in the chair and opened his eyes, looking around, to see if perhaps the music was coming from an adjoining set of rooms.

Immediately, the music stopped.

Logan got up, shut off the lights, then returned to the chair. Once again, there was nothing at first. The sense of comfort was gone; so was the music. Gradually he began to be aware that, instead of the well-being he'd felt earlier, he now felt a faint—very faint—sense of uncertainty, perplexity, unease.

And then the piano music returned: once again, softly at first, then louder. The lush, romantic melody was still there—but as Logan listened, it slowly changed. It grew strange, haunting, maddeningly complicated: long rushes of rising arpeggios in a minor key, played faster and faster. There was something disturbing and ineffable in the music—something interwoven into the complex passages, almost below the threshold of comprehension, that seemed to Logan, as he listened, to be almost diabolical.

And then, along with the music, he began to smell something—a smell that was somehow part and parcel of the music itself—an increasingly strong and nauseating reek of burning flesh. A memory came to him suddenly, or perhaps it was precognition: an old house, flames billowing ferociously from its windows. . . .

Suddenly, he jumped up from the chair. His mouth had gone dry, and his heart was hammering in his chest. He staggered through the darkness to the light switch, snapped it on, then leaned against the wall, gasping in breaths, shaking his head to clear away the terrifying music.

Within a few minutes his breathing had returned to normal. Gathering up his duffel and slinging it over a shoulder, he stepped out of the door and into the hall—reaching inside to switch off the lights again—and then, locking the door, pocketed the key and made his way back down the elegant corridor to his own rooms, careful as he did so to keep his mind as blank and as empty as possible.

10

The Grounds and Infrastructure Maintenance Center was a hangarlike outbuilding in the eastern shadow of the mansion, sitting amid a minicampus of other, smaller structures. Although its facade was cleverly designed to imitate that of Dark Gables, its huge sliding doors and flat roof betrayed its true nature.

Jeremy Logan stepped through an employees' entrance and found himself in a cavernous space. To the far right was a veritable battalion of landscaping and earthmoving equipment: commercial mowers, chippers, Kubota tractors, Ditch Witch trenchers, and half a dozen more esoteric pieces of gear were lined up, gleaming and ready for use. Behind them were two repair bays with a large attached parts section. In the bays, Logan could make out mechanics in jumpsuits performing operations on disassembled machinery. In the middle of the maintenance center were several long, massive industrial shelves, stretching from the concrete floor to the ceiling and containing pallets full of every imaginable item necessary to keep the complex running, from light switches to PVC pipe to circuit boards to plumbing fixtures to office accessories, all carefully labeled. Next came an extensive machine shop. Finally, stretching along the left-hand wall of the maintenance center, was a small cluster of cubicles, staffed with workers typing at workstations or speaking into telephones. Logan walked up to the closest worker and asked directions to the office of Ian Albright. He was pointed toward a set of exposed metal steps set into the nearest wall.

Albright's office was small but functional. One wall was entirely of glass and looked out over his maintenance domain. Albright himself was middle-aged and roundish, with a drinker's red nose and a cheery disposition. "Have a seat, then," he said with a laugh, perching himself on the edge of a desk covered with work orders, invoices, and memos. "Dr. Olafson said to expect you." Albright spoke in a working-class London accent that Logan found refreshing after the somewhat stifling academic atmosphere inside the main house.

"Thanks," he said as he sat down. "I have to confess, Mr. Albright—"

"Ian, if you please."

"I have to confess, Ian, I'm not exactly sure what your job description is. One person referred to you as the 'infrastructure supervisor.' Another as the 'site manager.'"

Albright threw back his head and laughed. "That's a lot of rubbish, that. I'm just a glorified super—with a whacking great council house to look after." And he indicated the Lux headquarters with a westward wave of his hand and another laugh.

The man's laughter was infectious and Logan found himself smiling. He was suddenly reluctant to change the mood. "Actually, I'm here to talk to you about a former resident of that particular council house."

"Oh? And who might that be?"

"Willard Strachey."

Immediately, the smile fell away from Albright's face. "Oh," he said again, in a distinctly subdued tone of voice. "Terrible bit of business."

"Yes, it was."

"He was a good one. Not like some, mind you, who treat me and my mates like groundskeepers and won't give us the time of day. He was always polite, Dr. Strachey was. Always had a kind word."

"I've been asked by the board to look into the circumstances of his death."

"Right. Terrible bit of business," Albright

repeated, then leaned forward conspiratorially. "How much do you know?"

"About?"

"About his manner of death."

Logan hesitated. "Just about everything."

Albright nodded. Then he whispered: "*It was me as found his . . .*" He fell silent and pointed to his own head. "Trimming the verge at the time, I was, down near the East Wing, banking the soil and adding some plant food." He grimaced, reliving the moment. "Been told to keep my mouth shut about it."

"I think that's a very good idea. Morale's low enough as it is." Logan paused a moment. "Up until recently, how would you characterize Dr. Strachey's frame of mind?"

"Beg pardon?"

"What was he like? Withdrawn, contemplative, friendly, moody?"

Albright considered this a moment. "Do you know the expression 'Snug as a bug in a rug'?"

"Of course."

"Well, that was Dr. Strachey. Don't think I've ever seen a man better fitted for his line of work—or more suited temperamentally, like."

This jibed so closely with what others had said that Logan decided that in the future he'd stop asking the question. "I'd like to talk to you about the West Wing, if I may."

Albright looked at him curiously. "The West Wing? What about it?"

"Well, can you tell me its history? Why has it

been closed down for so long?" During Logan's own tenure at Lux, the subject of the West Wing had rarely come up; it was almost as if it had never existed.

"Can't say as I know for sure. It was in pretty constant use through the sixties and seventies— that's when I came on staff, in 1978. But by that time the Fellows were starting to complain."

"Why?"

"Well, it was just getting . . . down at the heels, like. Offices and labs were small and cramped— not to mention very confusing to get around, what with no central connecting corridor. And when the East Wing renovation was completed in 1976, and everyone saw how much nicer the quarters were over there, they started asking for transfers. The staff was smaller then, and the main structure and the East Wing could accommodate just about everyone. So the West Wing fell into disuse. It was shut up completely in 1984."

"Why?"

"There just didn't seem any reason to keep only a handful of blokes working in there. Waste of electricity. Besides, it was overdue for a lot of repair. The heating and plumbing systems were out of date. And so they just closed it up."

"Until recently," Logan said.

Albright nodded. "What with the new Fellows and research associates, I guess they needed more room."

"And they assigned Dr. Strachey to oversee the redesign."

"Yes. Along with Miss Flood."

"The architect." Logan had spent a few hours the night before going over Strachey's memos, charts, and blueprints for the redesign, and the name Flood Associates had appeared again and again. "And were your men going to take on the actual reconstruction?"

"Oh, no. They'd handle the finishing work, the plumbing and painting and HVAC. But this was to be a big job, a first-class job. You need professional builders for that—and specialists, as well."

"Specialists?"

"For stonework and the like. Dr. Strachey had some pretty grand designs for the place."

"But you were involved yourself, I assume?"

"Primarily in terms of arranging the construction schedule with the general contractor."

"Did Strachey seem to enjoy the work?"

"Funny you should ask that," Albright said. "I'd have thought he'd have disliked it. Being torn away from his beloved equations and whatnot. And at first he did seem to be on the fence about things. But from what I could see, he grew more and more fascinated with the work. The *design* work, mind you—he wasn't interested in knocking down walls or putting up Sheetrock. But the look of the place—now, that was something else. See, the West Wing is sort of like an old luxury liner. There's beauty under the rust—you just have to know how to look for it. And Dr. Strachey knew how to do that. He had a thing for architecture, he had."

"Was construction ready to get under way?"

"Under way?" Albright laughed. "The demolition's been going on for over a month."

"Did he hire the workmen himself?"

"That he did."

"I see." Logan thought for a moment. "It all seems pretty quiet at the moment. I suppose they've stopped temporarily because of the tragedy. And of course they'll need to find someone to take Strachey's place."

"Oh, they've stopped, right enough. But it's not because of Dr. Strachey's death."

Logan looked at the site manager. "Excuse me?"

"A few days before he died, Dr. Strachey put a stop to the work himself."

"He did?"

"He did and all. Sent the workers packing."

"Did he give a reason?"

"Something about problems with structural integrity."

Logan frowned. "But I thought the West Wing was sound."

"I'm no engineer. But I'd lay odds that it is."

A pause. "Could I talk to some of these workers?"

"Doubt you could find them. They were paid off, all scattered to the four winds now."

"Really? You mean, after all the work of assembling them, they were just dismissed?"

"Yes."

Odd. "Was Strachey planning to hire a structural engineer to inspect the wing?"

"Can't say. I'd imagine so."

Logan thought back to the paperwork he'd gone through the night before. He'd seen nothing referring to this sudden development.

"This general contractor you mentioned. How can I contact him?"

Albright thought a moment. "He worked out of Westerly. Let's see . . . Rideout. Bill Rideout. He probably has most of the working files."

"I'll get in touch with him." Logan paused thoughtfully. "Thank you for your time, Mr. Albright," he said after a moment. "You've been most helpful."

"I'll see you out." And—hoisting himself off the edge of his desk—Albright opened the door and led the way down the metal staircase.

11

It was eleven o'clock on his third evening at the think tank when Logan—duffel slung over one shoulder, rolled blueprints and plans and printed schedules under his other arm—walked down the main first-floor corridor of Lux. It was a weeknight, the dining room had closed its doors well over an hour before, and there were no scheduled lectures in the plush-chaired, velvet-bedecked Delaveaux Auditorium that evening. As a result, the associates and Fellows had—true to form—all retired to their various rooms for the night. Save the occasional passing maid or member of the cleaning staff, Logan had Lux's public areas to himself.

Late that afternoon, he'd made a detailed tour of the East Wing, noting the extensive changes that had resulted from the midseventies renovation. While it retained much of the grandeur of the main massing of Dark Gables, it had clearly been designed to be a more utilitarian space: recessed fluorescent lighting had replaced wall sconces, and—in the offices and labs, at any rate—the gothic moldings and other ornamentation had been largely removed, creating a cleaner, more functional—if less visually interesting—look. Externally similar in shape and size to the West Wing, it had three stories and a single basement, as compared to the main building's four stories and multiple basement levels.

Based on the plans Logan had looked over, Willard Strachey and his architectural partner had a completely different idea for the remodeling of the West Wing. In its initial realization, the wing had been the most eccentric of Edward Delaveaux's conceptions. Logan had peered at old black-and-white photographs of the West Wing, taken in the months directly before and after Lux bought the mansion, and he could picture it now in his mind. On stepping in from its grand entrance, the visitor had been confronted with a large, oval, and comparatively stark gallery stretching up unimpeded three stories to the roofline. This was devoted to a series of standing stones—two huge menhirs at one end, surrounded by a henge of liths. Delaveaux had purchased the relics, whole, from a mysterious and very old site on Ambion Hill near Market Bos-

worth, Leicestershire. The original purpose of the
standing stones was unknown—it was thought to
have been a site for prehistoric burial ceremonies—
and Delaveaux's purchase and subsequent wholesale removal of the megaliths in 1888 caused a
furor in England that, legend went, precipitated
the founding of the National Trust. Early on, Delaveaux had enjoyed giving costume parties in this
space, whose perimeter he'd furnished with divans,
ottomans, and chaise longues. In later years, after
the deaths of his wife and son, he had apparently
held séances in it. Galleries ran along all four sides
of the second and third levels of the open space.

The ring of standing stones took up perhaps the
first quarter of the West Wing. Beyond it had lain
a confusing welter of spaces: three stories' worth
of galleries, workrooms, art studios, music salons,
specialized libraries—literally dozens of interconnected chambers, each designed to indulge one of
Delaveaux's numberless pastimes, hobbies, and
avocations. According to rumor, it was the building and fitting out of this strange wing that finally
exhausted the onetime millionaire's funds.

When Lux had taken over Dark Gables, one
of the first things they did was to fill in as best
they could the second and third floors, retrofit-
ting the—to them—wasted space with offices and
laboratories. Their options were limited, however,
since the massive liths had been incorporated into
the mansion's foundation. When it came to the
labyrinthine series of chambers that lay beyond,
Lux had opted for the simplest solution: remov-

ing all of Delaveaux's detritus and simply assigning the empty rooms as work spaces for various Fellows. But this was a stopgap solution: in order to reach one's office, people would often have to walk through the offices of various other members of the staff and faculty: an inconvenience for all concerned. "Very confusing to get around," Albright had observed. No wonder people had been eager to find new digs once the East Wing reconstruction was completed.

Willard Strachey's plan to address the vast welter of rooms was to tear down walls and gut nonstructural elements in order to create two parallel corridors running north to south. Off each corridor, modern offices and labs would be built. The original decorative elements, windows, and wood veneers would be retained and reused wherever possible.

Logan realized that his feet had taken him all the way to the end of the central first-floor corridor. Ahead, two wooden doors blocked his way. Before them was a velvet rope, hanging from brass stanchions and holding a large sign, which contained the symbol of a hard hat and the message CONSTRUCTION AREA. AUTHORIZED PERSONNEL ONLY.

Logan had signed a long series of documents for Dr. Olafson absolving Lux of any obligation or responsibility in the case of personal injury, and he had carte blanche to roam the entire campus. Glancing over his shoulder and finding the wide corridor behind to be empty, he stepped past the velvet rope, pulled a key from his pocket, unlocked the doors, and stepped inside. It was very dark, and the air smelled of sawdust and joint compound. Closing the doors and fumbling in his duffel, Logan pulled out a flashlight, snapped it into life, and swiveled it around. Locating a bank of light switches, he flicked them on, one after another.

He found himself in a small vestibule, apparently a kind of front office for the entrance to the West Wing. The furnishings were all covered with protective drapes, and the wooden floors were hidden beneath multiple layers of drop cloths. They gave the space a strange, anonymous feel. There was only one exit—a large, doorless arch directly to the south—and after finishing his reconnoiter Logan moved through it.

He paused a moment to put down his duffel and page through the working blueprints and reports he had brought with him. Based on the construction schedule, the first job would—naturally enough—be the demo. One team of workmen had been tasked with demolishing the fixtures in preparation for a full-scale rebuilding. A second team of workmen had been given the rather more delicate job of tearing down certain non-load-bearing walls on the second floor to make way for what had been termed in the architectural specs "lateral corridor A" and "lateral corridor B"—the two new hallways off which the redesigned office and lab spaces would be constructed. The rest would follow later.

Stepping into the space beyond the vestibule, Logan found himself in darkness once again, the only light being that which filtered in from the front office. He looked around, found another bank of lights, and turned on the switches. Nothing: clearly, the electricity had been turned off for the purposes of demolition. Switching the flashlight back on, he found he was standing in a seemingly roofless space. There were additional drop cloths on the floor, but here they had been wadded and twisted this way and that by the passage of numerous booted feet, and Logan could see the heavy dust that lay on the floorboards beneath. On all sides, ancient stones rose up around him: Delaveaux's ceremonial henge. Hemmed in by walls, the liths seemed even larger than they actually were. Logan let his flashlight shine on them, angling its beam up toward the ceiling far above. They were rough-hewn, dark, tapering slightly toward their top edges. What events, good or ill, had they witnessed? Had they seen Richard III die in the nearby battle that marked the fall of the Plantagenets? Or older ceremonies, profane and dark? There was something about these silent sentinels that Logan found unsettling, and he was careful not to touch them as he moved on.

Beyond the standing stones, a corridor led deeper into the wing. Logan moved down it until he reached a staircase, which he ascended. The second floor was a confused jumble of half-destroyed offices. Bare lights dangled from cords. The dust was heavier here, but it was primarily plaster dust, caused no doubt by the wholesale demolition of walls and nonstructural elements to make way for Strachey's two parallel hallways. Standing where he was, Logan could make out the rough outlines of what must be lateral corridor A. It was visible, not so much from what had been built but from what had been torn away: a long, gaping hole, ripped out of offices and storage rooms and corridors, heading due south into the dark.

With the aid of his flashlight and a compass, Logan consulted the work orders for the construction. The demo work for lateral corridor A was to come first, to be followed later by corridor B.

He moved ahead slowly down the unfinished corridor, swinging the flashlight left and right. He was uncomfortably aware that he was in a construction zone; some of the half-destroyed walls and slanting ceiling beams were clearly less than stable. Not only was he without a hard hat, but he was investigating a space that had just been declared structurally unsound.

He continued south for perhaps twenty yards, peering around with his flashlight, before his way was blocked by two tarps hanging from the ceiling to the floor, one blocking his way ahead and the other to the right. They had been nailed into place, and a hastily scrawled sign was fixed to the closest that read: HAZARDOUS AREA—OFF-LIMITS.

He paused in the dust-heavy darkness, considering. Then, pulling a penknife from his pocket, he cut a small hole in the tarp ahead of him, thrust his light into it, and peered through.

Clearly, this was where the demolition work had stopped. Beyond lay rooms that, though dusty and long abandoned, had not yet been touched.

What was it about this spot that had suddenly convinced Strachey the wing was unsound?

Lying on the floor in front of the tarp wall was a small gold mine of equipment: nail guns, sledgehammers, compressors, a portable generator. It was almost as if the workers had dropped their tools and run.

He hesitated a moment. Then, turning, he shone his light over the tarp that blocked his way to the right. Once again, he took a penknife to it, then peered through the tear that resulted. To his surprise, there was no opening or corridor beyond—but instead a bare wall.

This was odd. Logan could understand why Strachey would bar entrance to an area that might be unsafe. But why cover a wall?

Carefully, he pulled the tarp away from the nails that fixed it in place and pinned it back, exposing the wall beyond. It was clearly old, dating back to the original construction of the West Wing. Workmen had removed some of the wallpaper and plaster, exposing the old laths.

In the middle of the wall, at approximately chest level, a ragged circle of plaster, roughly the size of a fist—or the head of a sledgehammer—had been set into the lath, like a plug in a dike. Logan examined it with his flashlight, then scratched at it with his fingernail. It was fresh plaster, only recently set. It could not have been applied more than a few days previously.

Using the tip of his knife, Logan worked away at the edges of the plaster patch, easing it away from the surrounding matrix of lath until it fell out, landing at his feet. Where it had been was now a hole in the wall, black against black.

Bending forward, Logan shone his flashlight at the hole and peered into the cavity beyond. Almost immediately, he went rigid.

"What the *hell*?" he muttered under his breath.

He snatched the flashlight away, almost as if he'd been burned. Then he stepped back: one step, another.

For a long time he stood, staring at the ragged circle of black. And then—laying his flashlight on the ground so that it illuminated the wall—he pulled a sledgehammer from the pile of equipment. Hefting it, he tapped it gently against the wall a few times. Then, taking a firmer grip on the handle, he struck the sledgehammer against the lath surrounding the hole.

A spiderweb of cracks appeared, and a rain of plaster chips fell to the ground.

Again and again, Logan hammered at the wall, but cautiously, calculatingly, knocking away the old construction, creating a passage just large enough to duck through.

After about ten minutes of work, he'd extended the space from the preexisting hole down to the level of the floor: a black maw about four feet high and two feet wide. He put the sledgehammer down and wiped his hands on his sleeves. He paused a moment in the darkness, listening. He'd been as quiet as he could, but a sledgehammer was not a delicate instrument. Nevertheless, there was no sound of voices, no calls or cries—this far from the occupied areas of Lux, his work had gone unnoticed.

And now he picked up his flashlight, moved toward the opening he'd made, bent low, and then disappeared into the hole.

12

Beyond lay a room. As Logan played his flashlight around it, he saw it had been a laboratory of some kind. There was a single worktable, surrounded by straight-backed chairs, on which sat a few old-fashioned pieces of equipment. A much larger device—waist-high and even more mysterious in appearance—sat in the middle of the floor.

The room was not large—perhaps twenty feet square—and was constructed of the same tasteful cast as the rest of Lux. An elegant fireplace was set into one wall. A few pictures in antique frames hung here and there, but they were not like the pictures seen elsewhere in the mansion: one frame

held a Rorschach inkblot; another a painting by
Goya. An old-fashioned percolator sat on a corner
table. A vintage phonograph stood on a stand in
one corner, with a large brass amplifying horn fixed
to its top and a hand crank on one side. A stack of
78s in paper sleeves was set on the floor beneath
it. Beyond the worktable was a stainless-steel dolly
containing a row of what appeared to be medical
instruments: forceps, curettes.

In the beam of his flashlight, Logan could see
a metal bar fixed to one wall, from which hung
bulky suits made of some heavy metal, perhaps
lead, with fanlike joints at the elbows, wrists, and
knees. Their helmets had faceplates into which thin
grilles had been set. The bizarre uniforms looked
like alien suits of armor.

He made out, above the wainscoting near
his feet, an old-fashioned electrical socket. On
a whim, he pulled a circuit tester from his duffel
and plugged it in. A green light came on. Odd that
this room should have electrical power, when the
spaces he'd just passed through did not: perhaps
Strachey's crews shut off the power only to rooms
they were actively demolishing.

Except for a pile of plaster chips and pieces of
lath caused by Logan's forced entry, the room was
spotless. No dust had accumulated on any of the
surfaces. It was like a time capsule, hermetically
sealed.

Stranger still—and Logan only now became
aware of this fact—was that the room had no
apparent means of entry. He shone his flashlight

carefully around the walls, but could see no breaks in the polished wood to indicate a doorway of any kind.

What kind of a room was this? And what on earth had it been used for?

Logan took a step forward, then stopped abruptly. Something—some sixth sense or instinct for self-preservation—warned him that he proceeded at his peril, that there was danger here. For a moment, he stood absolutely still. And then he began backing out; but slowly, quietly, as if not to disturb some slumbering thing. He bent down slightly, feeling his way through the hole he'd created. Then—replacing the tarp over the wall as carefully as he could—he made his way stealthily back through the ruins of the West Wing, flashlight licking over the broken surfaces as he went.

13

"My God," Olafson said. He looked around, shocked surprise distorting his patrician features.

It was the following morning. Immediately after breakfast, Logan had tracked down the director and brought him here, making the laborious journey through the West Wing's unfinished litter of construction, down lateral corridor A, beneath the tarp, and through his rudely constructed entrance into the secret room.

"So you had no idea this place existed," Logan said.

"No."

"Or what it might possibly have been used for. Or why it was kept secret."

Olafson shook his head. "If this didn't appear to be some kind of laboratory, I'd have guessed it predated Lux's ownership. The original builder, you know, was famously eccentric."

Logan nodded slowly. Hard as it was to believe, it appeared that—for many decades—Lux academics and scientists had worked and studied and experimented here in the West Wing . . . never knowing that, all the time, a secret room had lain hidden in their midst.

"Good lord," Olafson said, following the beam of Logan's flashlight as it settled on the heavy, armorlike metal suits that hung from the projecting bar in one corner. "What on earth could have gone on in here?"

"You're the director," Logan said. "I realize there's not much to go on. But does anything you see here suggest projects that may have been undertaken during Lux's early years at Dark Gables?"

Olafson thought a moment. Then he shook his head. "No." He hesitated. "I don't see any door. How did you find this room, exactly?

"That tarp had been carefully nailed over the exposed lath, along with this." Logan reached outside, picked up the scrawled sign that read HAZ-ARDOUS AREA—OFF-LIMITS. "I noticed a fist-sized hole in the lath, recently plugged with plaster. It aroused my curiosity. So I investigated."

"And you said Strachey had just sent the workmen away," Olafson murmured. He looked around again. "Do you suppose he was the one who made that hole, discovered this room?"

"He'd be an obvious choice. But then, why seal it up again, send the workers away on a pretext?" Logan pointed to the sign. "Does this look like his handwriting?"

"Impossible to say, given the block letters."

"Want to hear something else interesting? I tried contacting the general contractor. William Rideout, based in Westerly. All I got was an answering service. It seemed that Mr. Rideout has abruptly retired, and is currently traveling, exact location unknown."

Olafson took this in. He seemed about to speak, but then he simply shook his head.

Logan let the sign slip to the floor. "Who here could tell me more about the West Wing?"

"Ironically, Strachey would have been your man. He's been living and breathing the place for the last six months." Olafson paused, as if considering something. "Look here. We'd better not tell anybody about this place—at least, not until we have a better idea of what its purpose was and why it was boarded up."

"And I'm going to examine the original blueprints in Strachey's office. I'd like to see how this room relates to its surroundings—and figure out if the West Wing houses any other secrets we should know about." Logan glanced at the director. "There's something else. At dinner the other night, Roger Carbon told me that I should be asking about 'the others.'"

"The others," Olafson repeated slowly.

"I mentioned it to Perry Maynard, but he sidestepped the question."

A frown crossed Olafson's face. "Carbon is a brilliant psychologist, but he can be rather a divisive influence." He hesitated. "Before Strachey's death, there were a few reports of . . . ah . . . rather odd incidents involving some other residents here at Lux."

"Odd how?"

"Nothing all that alarming. Certainly nothing anywhere near what happened to Will. Hearing voices, seeing things that weren't there."

Nothing all that alarming. "When was this, exactly?"

Olafson thought for a moment. "A month ago, maybe. Six weeks, at most."

"And it went on for how long?"

"A week or two."

"How many were affected?"

"A handful. We didn't think there was a connection. And we didn't want you to start barking up the wrong tree."

"Can you get me a list of names of the affected personnel?"

Olafson frowned. "Now, Jeremy, I really don't think—"

"I can't afford to ignore any leads. And this sounds like a lead to me."

"But . . . well, I doubt those involved would want others to know."

"Carbon knew."

Olafson hesitated again. "And I'm sure they'd be disinclined to talk about it. It's . . . I imagine it's a little embarrassing."

"I've had plenty of experience dealing with embarrassing experiences. I'll let them know they can rely on my utmost discretion." When Olafson didn't reply, Logan continued. "Look, Gregory. You brought me here. You can't ask me to open an investigation and then tie my hands."

Olafson sighed. "Very well. But I'll require your utmost tact. Lux's reputation as a conservative, serious-minded institution is its most important asset."

"So I'm told."

"Well, then. I'll see about furnishing you with a list." Olafson took another look around in the reflected beam of the flashlight, disbelief once more settling over his features. Then he turned and, without another word, allowed Logan to lead the way out of the shadow-haunted chamber and back toward the tenanted regions of Lux.

14

Late that evening, Logan returned to the room. He waited until, once again, most of the activity at Lux had subsided for the night; it was highly unlikely of course that anybody else would be in the West Wing, but he didn't want to take any chances.

He unpinned the tarp, tucked it aside, then ducked through the opening he had made previously. In one hand, he held a flashlight; in the other, a large, tungsten barn door lamp of the kind used on movie sets, which he had borrowed from a mystified Ian Albright. He placed it on its collapsible stand in one corner, then ran the cord to an outlet beneath the worktable. Returning to the lamp, he snapped it on. The space suddenly was flooded with brilliance. He wanted—needed—that brilliance for the kind of minute examination he now planned to undertake.

The danger he had sensed upon first crossing the threshold of the forgotten room had not gone away. But—under the eight hundred watts of luminescence provided by the stage lamp—it maintained its distance.

Under one arm was a set of rolled papers. Logan let his duffel slip from his shoulder, placed it on the worktable along with the flashlight, then placed the rolled papers beside them and smoothed them out. These were original blueprints of Lux, which he had appropriated from Strachey's office that afternoon. He leafed through them until he located the plans for the West Wing. Within a small rectangular box at the bottom were the words DELAVEAUX RESIDENCE. M. FLOOD, ARCHITECT. 1886.

The oversized blue sheet was dense with lines, measurements, and tiny technical notations, but little by little he managed to decipher it. Mentally, he compared the original state of the wing with the new conception that Strachey and his workmen had been assembling. It was clear that the room he had discovered was not in the blueprints. In fact, it appeared that the space he was currently standing in had been designated, at least in part, as a stairwell. That meant one of two things—either the room had been retrofitted into the wing after the mansion's initial construction . . . or the plans had been redrafted with the specific intention of hiding the room's existence.

He rolled the blueprints up and put them aside.

Under the pitiless glare of the light, things he had not noticed before now became visible. A round disk was set flush with the ceiling, decorated with elaborate chasing—no doubt it covered the hole left by a previously installed chandelier. Had this room once been part of a larger, more elegant space? While five framed pictures remained on the walls, there were three bare spots where other objects had once hung—betrayed by the slight yellowing of the paint beneath. While he had originally believed the room to be spotless, he now made out the remains of ash in the fireplace grate.

He stepped into the middle of the room, turning his attention to the large central device. He walked around it slowly several times, examining it curiously. It was unevenly shaped, as long as a coffin and almost twice as high, with appendages of an unknown nature sprouting from its sides and its top. Each appendage was hidden beneath bulging, carefully fitted pieces of protective rosewood, fixed and locked into place like old sewing machine covers, so that it presented a uniform, monolithic surface of polished wood grain.

One end of the device was wider than the other, covered partly by a metal plate screwed onto its surface. About four feet beyond, Logan noticed that the roman numerals I through VI had been etched into the floor.

The narrower end was covered in yet another piece of wood, monolithic, edged in metal, and locked in two places to the main housing. Logan ran his fingers over one of the keyholes. As he did so, he noticed there was a small brass plaque screwed into the wood, just below the locked section. It was tarnished and age-darkened, but he could make out two words on it, one at each edge: BEAM and FIELD. There was no clue as to what these referred to.

Searching, he found two other plaques, smaller, and screwed into place near the bottom of the device. One read ROSEWELL HEAVY INDUSTRIES, PERTH AMBOY, N.J. and the other—on another section—read ELEKTROFABRIKEN KELLE AG. Plucking a digital recorder from his jacket pocket, Logan dutifully notated all this.

Putting the recorder away, he analyzed the room with both a trifield EM meter and an air-ion counter. He jotted the readings in a small leather-bound notebook for later comparison to other readings he'd taken in Strachey's rooms and various locations around Lux.

Now he moved over to the light and switched it off. Total blackness was the result. He felt his way back to the large, mysterious machine, sat down on the floor with his back to it, cross-legged, and closed his eyes, waiting to see if the room had anything to tell him. He was curious, and a little apprehensive, as to whether there would be a repeat of the strange and sinister music he had heard in Strachey's apartment.

At first there was nothing, save the faint aware-ness of lurking danger. And then, gradually, the sense of unease and disquiet he'd felt in Strachey's rooms returned, along with a feeling of confusion. And then, quite suddenly, there it was again—the haunting, maddening passages of music, harsh and malevolent, washing over him in waves of sinister minor-key arpeggios, any sense of calm romantic beauty now utterly gone.

Logan leapt to his feet and rushed back to the light, almost knocking it over in his haste to turn it on again. And then he stood there, breathing hard, the disembodied music still echoing in his mind.

This was strange. Most strange indeed.

He walked slowly around the room, not look-ing at anything in particular, until his heart had slowed and his breathing had returned to normal. At last, when he felt himself again, he continued the investigation.

Above the worktable was a row of book-shelves, all empty. Beside it was a filing cabinet. Logan opened each drawer, only to find all of them empty as well.

Had this laboratory been planned and built, but then abandoned before any work had actually begun? If so, why all the apparent secrecy? On the other hand, if research of some sort *had* been con-ducted here, and then brought to a halt, why hadn't this odd device been removed and destroyed, along with, apparently, all the books and papers?

Returning his tools to the duffel, he now removed something else: a small rubber mallet in the shape of a triangle, of the kind doctors use to test reflexes. Ear to the wall, he made a slow, careful circuit of the room, tapping the mallet against the wall every now and then, listening for the telltale echo that would betray a hollow space or a hidden door. He knew there had to be an entrance—whoever had built and worked in this place had not entered the way he had. But nothing was forthcoming. He replaced the mallet with a sigh. Had this room been entered via the floor or ceiling? No—that would have been ludicrous.

It seemed the answer would have to wait.

Now, adjusting the angle of the lamp somewhat, he began to examine the ash he'd noticed in the fireplace. It wasn't, as he'd initially assumed, wood ash. Rather, it appeared to be the remains of carefully burned paper. Stretching out a hand, he grabbed a handful of ash and let the tiny, curled bits of blackened paper sift between his fingers. Then he raised the fingers to his nose. The charred smell was faint though detectable, but this meant nothing—the papers could have been burned the day before or five decades before.

Near the rear of the fireplace, he found a few items that were not quite as carefully burned. There were half a dozen bits of paper, each with a few decipherable letters. Most contained too few letters to be of any use—mere fragments—but as he sat down he carefully put them to one side nevertheless. Of more interest were the remains of an old photograph: perhaps one of the pictures that had been removed from the walls. While most of it had been burned away, the bottom edge still remained. He could make out a portion of a desk, apparently the worktable that still stood in this room. A few pieces of paper were visible on it, along with some journals or periodicals, all too blurry to be readable.

Behind the desk stood three people in lab coats. Only their torsos were visible; everything higher in the camera's field of view had been burned away. Logan put this to one side, too.

The final piece of recoverable paper appeared to be a memo. It had been typed on a manual typewriter, and was obviously many decades old. It was badly burned and faded, but—taking a seat at the worktable and peering at it very closely—Logan was just able to make out one fragment: "Project Sin."

Project Sin. The page had been burned away along the right edge, and the second word was evidently incomplete.

Or was it?

Just at that moment, Logan froze. His instincts, which he had learned to trust without question, had suddenly gone off five-alarm, dumping adrenaline into his bloodstream. What was it?

And then it came again: what sounded like the stealthy tread of a foot, the faint creak of a floorboard. It seemed to be coming from beyond the wall—the wall *opposite* that from which he had entered the room.

Logan stood up quickly—too quickly. The chair he'd been sitting on fell backward, crashing to the floor.

He remained utterly motionless, listening intently. For a long moment, all was silence. And then came what he thought was the soft patter of steps, quickly receding.

Grabbing his flashlight, he ducked out of the hole in the wall and hurried down the hallway, moving as quickly as he could through the confusion of deconstructed offices, abandoned equipment, and intersecting hallways, trying to make his way over to the far side of the wing. After five minutes of fruitless searching, he stopped, breathing hard. He turned off his flashlight and listened in the dark. There was no sound, no light to betray the presence of another. The West Wing appeared utterly deserted.

Turning the flashlight back on, he began making his way—more slowly now—back to the forgotten room.

15

The elevator doors whispered open onto a dimly lit basement hallway. Jeremy Logan knew that—as with several other areas of the mansion—Lux's underground complex was strictly off-limits to visitors, day researchers, and even some part-time staff. As a result, it did not need to maintain the rococo elegance of the more public spaces. The hallway in which he found himself, for example, had walls of dressed stone and a curved ceiling faintly reminiscent of the Roman catacombs. The air was pure and chill, however, with no smell of damp or niter.

He glanced at his watch: quarter after one in the afternoon.

The discovery of the forgotten room, along with its overpowering foreignness and mystery, had affected him more than he'd initially realized. He had awoken that morning with an uncharacteristic sense of listlessness, as if he did not know what to do next or where to turn. Newport, however, was possessed of a remarkably comprehensive public library, and a visit to it after breakfast—in particular, to its microfiche and DVD collections—had dispelled his feelings of doubt. If he did not know precisely what to do next, he at least had the germ of an idea.

He'd never been in the mansion's basement during his tenure at Lux, and there were no signs indicating which way to go, so on a whim he headed left, past the base of the mansion's central staircase, lacking in these subterranean depths its skin of polished marble. Within a hundred feet he was brought up short by a door of gleaming steel—a remarkable anachronism in this Poe-like space—with a single thick window of tinted Plexiglas, punctuated every few inches by small round holes set into an otherwise featureless surface. A sign on the door read RESEARCH LABORATORIES: AUTHORIZED PERSONNEL ONLY. Looking through the window, Logan made out a long hallway of exceptionally modern, high-tech design, lit by recessed fluorescent panels. Closed doors with airbrushed labels lined both sides of the hallway, receding into the distance. It looked like the laboratory complex of a research hospital, save the fact that it appeared to be utterly empty.

There was a keyed panel beside the door, and a card reader, but no phone or buzzer for admittance. Somehow, knocking didn't seem appropriate. Logan knew that Lux kept its most modern labs here in the basement—not only did this sequestration preserve the antique feel of the other floors, but the building's status as a historic structure made it a requirement. With a shrug, he turned away from the polished door and decided to try his luck in the other direction.

This yielded better results. After passing the elevator again and following the passage around a bend, he arrived at an open door with a sign that read ARCHIVES. Beyond the door, the walls and ceiling fell away, revealing a most impressive space bathed in bright yet pleasingly mellow light. Row after row of filing cabinets ran from front to back in achingly regular lines, but they were spaced far enough apart to forestall any sense of oppressiveness. At the far end, Logan could just make out another, smaller door, with what looked like a security station beside it. He stepped inside. Decorative wooden columns carved with encircling grape vines marched in serried ranks down the walls of the room. On the ceiling was an elaborate trompe l'oeil painting of Bacchus reclining in a glade, wineskin on his lap, his tresses and limbs being caressed by what appeared to be maenads.

Just inside the door, an elderly woman was seated at an official-looking table. A nameplate on one side of the desk read J. RAMANUJAN. She ran her eyes up and down Logan, lips pursing with an expression he could not decide was appraising or disapproving.

"May I be of assistance?" she asked.

"I'm here to research some of Lux's early files," Logan replied.

"ID, please."

Logan rummaged through his jacket pockets and produced the card that had been provided him during his initial processing. The woman looked at it.

"This is a temporary card," she told him. "I'm very sorry, but temporary staff are not allowed access to the archives."

"Yes, I know," Logan said, half apologetically. "That's why I was given this, as well." And he slipped out a letter on Lux stationary. It was written by Olafson, overriding Logan's temporary status and giving him unrestricted access.

Ms. Ramanujan read the letter over, then handed it back. "How can I help you?"

Logan slid the letter back into his jacket. "I'm not sure, exactly."

The woman frowned in confusion. "The researchers and scientists who use the archives are always looking for something specific." Picking up a clipboard from her desk, she turned it toward him. It contained blank document requisition forms. "Before I can be of assistance, I'll need to know the particular project or assignment you wish to research."

"I fear the nature of my research is rather . . .

amorphous. Unfortunately, I can't be more specific until I actually investigate the files."

This was clearly outside the archivist's purview. "If you can't give me a project title, or even a name, perhaps you can provide a time frame? A particular month, say, during which the work took place?"

Logan nodded slowly. "That might work. We could start with the thirties."

"The thirties?" Ms. Ramanujan repeated.

"The nineteen thirties, yes."

The woman's face went strangely blank. She picked up the ID card, which she'd placed on the desk, looked at it, then replaced it on the polished wood. After a moment, she looked up again. "Dr. Logan," she said, "there are records chronicling over eleven thousand research projects here. The total number of documents attached to those projects approaches two and a half million. Do you expect me to retrieve"—she did a quick calculation—"some two hundred thousand documents for your perusal?"

"No, no," Logan said quickly.

"Then what do you suggest?"

"If I could just do my own, ah, browsing through the stacks, it would probably give me a better indication of what I'm searching for—and perhaps very quickly, as well."

There was a pause. "Researchers are not normally admitted to the stacks themselves," the woman said. "Especially temporary researchers. It is most unusual."

In response, Logan let Olafson's letter peep out again from his jacket pocket.

The archivist sighed. "Very well. You may use that table over there, if you need to. But take no more than five folders from the stacks at a time. And *please* be careful when you refile them."

"I will," Logan assured her. "Thank you."

Over the next three hours, Logan—under the watchful gaze of the archivist—moved back and forth between the stacks and the research table, thick folders in hand each time. He opened the folders and scanned them quickly, scribbling observations into a small notebook with a gold pen. At first, his investigations took him all over the large room. But later, he narrowed his concentration to a much smaller area. Now his examination of the folders became more studious, his reading slower. At last he put the final set of folders away, and—instead of doing additional reading—moved from stack to stack, gazing into various drawers, all the time making notations in his journal as if tallying something. Finally, he put the notebook away and returned to the archivist.

"Thank you," he said.

Ms. Ramanujan inclined her head as she returned his ID card.

"I have a question. Extensive as these files are, there doesn't seem to be anything more recent than 2000."

"That is correct. These archives contain only files of closed or inactive research."

"Then where is the more recent documentation kept?"

"Some of it, of course, is kept with the scientists doing the research. The rest is in archive two, beyond that door." And she pointed toward the far end of the room.

"I see. Thank you again." And Logan turned away, heading in the indicated direction.

"Wait—" the woman began. But Logan was already moving quickly toward the back of the room, his footsteps echoing on the marble floor.

At the back of the vast space—as he'd noticed upon first entering—was a security station, blocking the door beyond. A lone man in the garb of Lux's security staff sat at a desk within it. He stood up as Logan approached.

"May I help you?" he asked.

"I'd like to examine the recent archives," Logan said, nodding toward the door.

"Your ID, please," the guard said.

To save time, Logan presented not only the ID but the letter from Olafson as well.

The guard examined them, then handed them back. "I'm sorry, sir, but you have insufficient privileges to access archive two."

"But this letter from Dr. Olafson—"

"I'm sorry, sir," the guard repeated in a firmer tone, "but only persons with a level-A access or greater are permitted past this door."

Level A? Logan had never heard of such a thing. In fact, during his time at Lux, he hadn't been aware of any access levels at all. "But—" he began, taking a step forward.

In response, the guard moved to block his progress. As he did so, Logan caught sight of a nightstick and a can of Mace snugged into the man's heavy service belt.

"I see," Logan said slowly. Then he nodded, turned, and made his way back through the stacks and into the basement corridor beyond.

16

It was quarter to seven when Logan knocked on the door of the director's inner office.

"Come in," came the disembodied voice from beyond.

When Logan stepped inside, Olafson was standing before a small mirror, adjusting his tie.

"Your secretary's gone for the day," Logan said. "Oh, I'm sorry—were you on your way to dinner?"

"It can wait." Olafson shrugged into his suit jacket, then took a seat behind the desk. "You've got something?"

"Something, yes. And I need something—from you."

Olafson spread out his hands, palms up, as if to say *I'm at your disposal.*

Logan placed his duffel on the arm of one of the chairs arranged before the desk, then sat down. Opening the duffel, he pulled something out: a badly charred piece of paper inside an envelope. He handed it to Olafson, who scrutinized it carefully.

"I found that among a pile of burned papers in the forgotten room's fireplace," he said.

Olafson continued to look at it. "It seems to be three men in lab coats, standing behind a worktable."

"Not *a* worktable. The worktable that's still in the room. You can tell by that deep scar in the wood, near the left corner."

"Even so, it's impossible to identify the people. The images have been burned away from the chest up."

"That's correct," Logan replied. "But the photo can tell us something nevertheless." Reaching into his duffel again, he took out a piece of paper, folded it in half, and held the bottom half up for the director to see. It was a bright, cartoonish picture of an exaggeratedly rotund man standing on the deck of a ship in heavy seas—wearing a blue double-breasted yachtsman's jacket, white shorts, and a beanie—gazing bemusedly down at an obviously seasick woman lying beneath a blanket on a deck chair.

Olafson squinted at it. "What about it?"

Now Logan unfolded the top half and let Olafson see the paper in its entirety. The logo of a magazine, *The New Yorker*, was emblazoned across the top of the sheet, along with a date: July 16, 1932.

"The Newport library has an excellent periodical collection," Logan said. "They wouldn't let me bring the actual issue, but they did make a color Xerox of the cover for me."

"I don't understand," Olafson said.

"Take a closer look at the burned photograph. Notice those letters and periodicals sitting on the desk? They are all too blurry to make out—*except* for the magazine cover featuring a porcine man in an odd yachtsman's uniform. Look closely; you can just make it out. It's obviously not a cover from a slick such as *Colliers, Life,* or the *Saturday Evening Post*. In fact, it looked to me like a quintessential *New Yorker* cover." He put the paper back in his duffel. "So now we have a *terminus post quem* for the work being done in that room. It was in use at least as late as the summer of 1932."

"I see."

"And that puts to rest any question about who was using the room. *Lux* was using that room—in addition to, or instead of, the mansion's initial owner. And speaking of the owner: I checked the original blueprints for Dark Gables in Strachey's office. They did not include the forgotten room." Logan picked up the charred fragment of photograph and returned it to his duffel. "Have you heard of something called Project Sin?"

"Project Sin?" Olafson frowned. "No."

"Please think carefully. 'Sin' may well be just the beginning of a word. No Lux project of that name comes to mind?"

When Olafson shook his head, Logan pulled another glassine envelope—this one containing the bit of burnt memo he had also recovered from the fireplace—and handed it to Olafson.

The director looked at it a moment before returning it. "Doesn't ring even the remotest bell."

"I wasn't able to find anything about any such project in your archives, either—although my search was as exhaustive as possible. I did discover something, however. Something quite interesting."

Olafson poured himself a glass of water from a decanter on his desk. "Let's hear it."

Logan sat forward. "I've discovered what I think is a gap in your records."

"What kind of gap?"

"When I was investigating Lux's archives earlier this afternoon, I found files relating to certain projects that were gathering steam in the late twenties and early thirties. Interesting but seemingly unrelated projects on such subjects as exotic qualities of electromagnetic radiation; on the classification of chemicals in the brain; and on the attempted isolation and analysis of ectenic force."

"Ectenic force?" Olafson repeated.

"Yes. That's especially interesting, isn't it? 'Ectenic force,' otherwise known as ectoplasm, was the substance believed to be emitted by spiritual mediums during séances, for purposes such as telekinesis or communicating with the dead. It was studied rather intensively in the late nineteenth century, but interest waned after that." He paused. "Why would scientists at Lux have revived such a study?"

"I can't imagine," Olafson said. "Surely the files themselves must have given you an indication."

"Therein lies the problem. While the files gave clear indications that these projects, and a few others, were gaining traction over the course of several years, there was a remarkable paucity of hard data on any of them—the names of the scientists involved, specifics on the nature of the work, data from experiments or tests or observations. Other files in the archives, by comparison, were stuffed full of information."

Logan sat back again. "The files in question share another commonality. They all cease abruptly around the same time—early in 1930."

Olafson rubbed his chin. "Do you have a theory?"

"I have the beginnings of one. I'll get to it in a minute. But let's return to the gap in your records. I did a comparative analysis of the amount of data in the Lux archives between 1920 and 1940. It was a quick-and-dirty analysis, but it nevertheless seemed clear to me that the years between 1930 and 1935 have less archival material than the rest. Sometimes a little less; sometimes rather more."

Olafson looked at him, saying nothing.

"So: my hypothesis. There were several projects under way at Lux in the late 1920s that, around 1930, merged into a single project. This project continued until 1935, when—for whatever reason—it was suddenly abandoned."

"And you think this was the so-called Project Sin," the director said.

"Made visible by its very absence," Logan replied. "Because in 1935, Lux's records resumed their normal volume. I believe that whoever removed those files also sealed the secret room."

"Which—I assume—you believe was the location for that project's research?"

"What other assumption can I make?"

For a moment, a strange look came over Olafson's face. Instantly, Logan sensed what it was: the look of a man who had just fitted two pieces of a puzzle together.

"What is it?" he asked quickly.

Olafson did not answer immediately. Then he roused himself. "I'm sorry?"

"You've just thought of something. What is it?"

Olafson hesitated. "Oh, nothing. I'm just trying to absorb all these deductions of yours, that's all, get them straight in my mind."

"I see. Well, I'd like to ask you a favor. Could you get me a list of all the Fellows who were working here at Lux from, say, 1930 to 1935?"

"A list," Olafson repeated.

"As I told you, all the names of the scientists had been redacted from the files. If I could learn who was involved, perhaps I could work backward and discover more about the actual project."

"I'm afraid that would be quite impossible. We don't keep any such list—never did. Some people have reasons to keep their work, and their time at Lux, to themselves. If somebody wants to add their period at Lux to their curriculum vitae, that's their business . . . but we make it a point never to broadcast it."

Logan looked speculatively at him for a moment. Throughout the conversation, the director had proven singularly unhelpful.

"In any case, I don't see what any of this has to do with Strachey's death," Olafson went on. "And that, after all, is why I summoned you here."

Logan took a new tack. "I wasn't allowed into archive two," he said. "I was told something about level-A access. What is that? I thought I had unrestricted access to Lux's records."

It took Olafson a moment to parse this sudden change in subject. Then a slightly chagrined look came over his face. "I'm sorry. You have access to ninety-five percent. But there are a few recent projects, still ongoing, that deal with extremely sensitive kinds of work."

"Work so sensitive it requires a dedicated guard?" Logan asked. "I thought you told me you had a—what was the phrase?—skeletal security force."

Olafson laughed a little uncomfortably. "Jeremy, just because we won't work for the military doesn't mean there aren't projects at Lux that don't have their . . . classified aspects. It's something you had no experience with during your tenure here, and you have no reason to concern yourself with it now. The vast majority of Lux's work, while of course proprietary, doesn't fall under that rubric. Fellows working on current projects have the option of keeping their files in archive two. Will Strachey didn't avail himself of that option—as you've seen, he was the most open of men, kept all his files in his office. Like almost everyone, yourself included, Strachey had level-B access. Level-A access is restricted to those few working on high-security projects."

When Logan didn't reply, Olafson continued. "Really, Jeremy, there's no connection between any classified work going on here at Lux and Will's death. None at all. And he wouldn't have wanted it any other way."

For a long moment, Logan didn't say anything. Then he nodded.

The director put his hands on his desk. "Well. Anything else?"

"Do you have that list I requested earlier? Of, ah, 'affected personnel.'"

"Yes." Olafson unlocked a drawer of his desk, reached in, and withdrew a sealed envelope, which he handed to Logan.

"Just one thing more. Did Lux ever do any radio research in the early part of the century?"

Olafson thought a moment. "I don't think so. I've never heard of any. Why?"

"Because I found a vintage radio in Strachey's rooms. Well, it looked like a radio from the outside, anyway. I thought maybe he'd picked it up around here from some abandoned project."

Olafson chuckled. "Will was always collecting

strange bits of antique technology and mechanical curiosa. You must have noticed examples of it in his rooms. He loved to haunt flea markets for the stuff." He shook his head. "It's funny, really, because as brilliant as he was with software, he was terrible with anything mechanical or electrical. It was all he could do to screw in a lightbulb or sail his beloved boat." He stood up. "Well, despite everything, I've worked up an appetite. Shall we go down to dinner?"

"Why not?" And picking up his satchel, Logan let Olafson usher him out of the office.

17

Pamela Flood leaned over the drafting table in her office, both elbows resting on an overlapping assortment of plans and schematics, completely absorbed in the west elevation of a building she was sketching. Although, like almost all modern architects, she rendered her final drawings via software—her own choice was AutoCAD Architecture—Pamela preferred doing her initial sections for a project by hand, allowing ideas to flow naturally from the point of her pencil. And this was a very special project—the renovation, from footing to roofbeam, of an old cannery on Thames Street into a condominium complex. She had always wanted to do more commercial work, and this might well lead to a series of—

She suddenly realized that—thanks to her absorption in the sketch and the *Birth of the Cool* CD playing in the background—she hadn't noticed the doorbell ringing. Straightening up, she left her office, went down the passage beyond, through the parlor of the rambling old house, and into the front hall. She opened the door only to look into the gray eyes of a tall man with light brown hair, who, judging by his face, was perhaps forty years old. It was a nice face, she thought: reflective, with sculpted cheekbones and the faintest hint of a cleft in the chin, the skin smooth in the rays of the late morning sun. It looked vaguely familiar, somehow.

"Ms. Flood?" the man said, handing her a business card. "My name is Jeremy Logan. I wondered if I could have a few minutes of your time."

Pamela glanced at the card. It read merely DR. JEREMY LOGAN, DEPT. OF HISTORY, YALE UNIVERSITY. The man didn't look all that much like a history professor. He was a little too tanned, with a slender but athletic build, and he was wearing a bespoke suit instead of the usual hairy tweeds. Was this a potential client? And then she realized she was leaving him standing on the doorstep.

"I'm so sorry. Please come in." And she ushered him into the parlor.

"This is a very attractive house," he said as they sat down. "Did your great-grandfather design it?"

"As a matter of fact, he did."

"The Victorian lines are refreshingly unique

among so much Colonial and Italianate architecture here in Newport."

"Are you a student of architecture, Dr. Logan?"

"To quote a line from an old movie, 'I don't know a lot about anything, but I know a little about practically everything.'" And the man smiled.

"You must know a lot about history, at any rate."

"The problem with history, Ms. Flood, is that it keeps on happening whether you want it to or not. At least a Shakespeare scholar, say, can go about his or her work fairly confident that new plays aren't going to turn up."

Pamela laughed. The man might be charming, but she had a condominium to design. The initial plans were due to be submitted in just two weeks. "How can I help you, Dr. Logan?"

The man crossed one knee over the other. "As it happens, I'm here about your great-grandfather. His name was Maurice Flood, right? An architect like yourself."

"That's right."

"And, among other grand residences, he designed the Delaveaux mansion in the mid-1880s. The mansion that came to be known as Dark Gables."

At this, the slightest tickle of alarm coursed through Pamela. She did not reply.

"Now, of course, home to Lux."

"Are you in residence at Lux, Dr. Logan?" Pamela asked guardedly.

"Just temporarily."

"And what is it you want, exactly?"

Logan cleared his throat. "Since your great-grandfather was the architect of the mansion, and since this house was his office and residence—as, I believe, it is now yours—I was curious as to whether the original plans for the structure were still at hand."

So that was it. She looked at the man with sudden suspicion. "And what would your interest in the plans be?"

"I'd like to examine them."

"Why?"

"I'm afraid I can't go into specifics, but I can assure you that—"

Pamela stood up so suddenly that the man stopped in midsentence.

"I'm sorry, but the plans aren't available."

"Is there some way in which they could be secured? I'd be happy to wait—"

"No, there is no way. And now, I'd appreciate it if you would leave."

Dr. Logan looked at her curiously. He stood up slowly. "Ms. Flood, I know you were involved in—"

"I'm very busy, Dr. Logan. Leave. *Please.*"

The man continued to look at her for a moment. Then he nodded his thanks, turned, and walked through the front hall and out the door without another word.

18

It was just past four in the afternoon as Logan walked along the long fourth-floor corridor of the Lux mansion. Midway down, he turned toward two glass-paned doors that opened onto a lavishly appointed parlor. He stepped inside and glanced around. An elaborate tea service had been set out on a linen-covered table: rows of china cups, a tray of wheatmeal biscuits, a large stainless-steel urn full of tea. The tea was invariably Darjeeling, and the parlor was invariably empty; at this point in the afternoon, all the denizens of Lux were fully absorbed in their respective scholarly pursuits, or at least pretending to be, and too busy to stop for tea. And yet it was still laid out, day after day, year after year, too ingrained a tradition to be changed.

Logan slid a few sheets of folded paper from his jacket pocket—the list Olafson had provided for him—and reviewed it briefly. Currently, Lux had eighty-two scholars in residence; seventy assistants to support them; an administrative staff of fifty-four; and an additional thirty cooks, guards, groundskeepers, dogsbodies, and assorted others who kept the place running. Out of this roughly two hundred and forty people, Olafson's list numbered five.

Logan reread the single-paragraph dossier of person number three: Dr. Terence McCarty. Then, replacing the list in his pocket, he looked around the room. The wall opposite the double doors was covered by a series of richly brocaded curtains. He approached the curtains, then followed them to the far corner of the room. A door was set into the wall here, small and almost hidden behind the last curtain. Opening the door revealed a narrow, dark passageway. Logan walked down this to a second door, which he opened in turn.

It led to a revelation: a sprawling rooftop terrace ending in a balustrade of worn marble. Beyond were magnificent views of Lux's lawns and gardens, and, beyond that, the perpetually furious sea, hurling itself endlessly against the rocky beach. The mansion fell away on both sides, leading at last to the long, dependent wings, east and west, that pointed toward the coast.

A series of round glass tables and wrought-iron deck chairs were arrayed across the faded brick. Only one of the chairs was occupied: a man in a brown suit, with a shock of black hair and piercing blue eyes, sat in it, staring back at Logan, a wary expression on his face.

Logan took another moment to admire the view. Then he walked over and took a seat beside the man.

"You're Dr. McCarty?" he asked.

"Call me Terence."

"I had no idea this place existed."

"No one does. That's why I suggested it." The man frowned briefly. "I know who you are, Dr. Logan. As you might guess, I'm not especially keen on this meeting. But Gregory pressed me to agree. He said it was for the good of Lux. When he put it like that, what was I to say?" And he shrugged.

"Let me set you at ease, then," Logan replied. "I'm looking into the details of Will Strachey's death. Before it took place, a few other residents of Lux reported—shall we say—some anomalous occurrences. I'm not going to tell you who they were, or what they experienced, just as I wouldn't tell any of them about you. What you tell me will be kept in strictest confidence. It won't be published, it won't be repeated. If, as you say, you know who I am, then you can appreciate that my job entails a great deal of discretion. The details of what you tell me won't go beyond these rather beautiful surroundings."

As Logan spoke, the man named McCarty continued to eye him closely, the look of wariness slowly easing. When Logan fell silent, McCarty nodded. "Very well. Ask what you want."

"First, I'd like to know a little more about what you're doing here at Lux."

"I'm a linguist."

"I'm told it's an interesting profession."

When McCarty added nothing more, Logan said: "Can you be more specific?"

"What does my work have to do with our conversation?"

"It may be useful."

McCarty shifted in his chair. "You said you would be discreet."

"Completely."

"Because I've heard horror stories of cleaning ladies, bribed to collect trash from offices and labs and deliver it off campus. Not here at Lux, you understand, but at other think tanks and institutes. There's a lot of competition out there—too many researchers, not enough ideas."

"I understand."

McCarty sighed. "Basically, I'm studying whether or not code talking—the use of little-known languages or dialects to transmit secret information—can be applied to digital cryptography."

Logan nodded.

"Specifically, I'm comparing relatively well-known languages such as Navajo and the Philippine dialect of Maranao to truly obscure languages like Akurio and Tuscarora, each spoken by only a handful of people. I'm trying to determine whether the grammars, syntactical qualities, and other factors of such languages can be efficiently rendered into an encryption system that doesn't rely on prime numbers, substitution, or the other digital schemes common in today's cryptography."

"Sounds fascinating. But I'm surprised Lux doesn't object."

"Why?"

"Because it seems to me that such research, if successful, could be used by the military. Such a coding system could potentially be weaponized."

McCarty smiled thinly. "Anything can be weaponized, Dr. Logan, and it's naïve to think otherwise. But the fact is, if my work is successful, the algorithms would form the basis of proprietary microchips—*proprietary,* to be patented jointly by Lux and myself—for use in such things as routers and cellular phones. Forget the military; forget conventional warfare. The Web is the real danger. It's notoriously porous. Identities are stolen, bank accounts emptied, credit cards maxed out—and that's just for individuals. Power companies, the core routers on the Internet backbone, air traffic control—not to mention the kind of classified government protocols that keep our nation safe: none of these are nearly as secure as they ought to be.

That's a huge problem for me. And for the Lux board of directors, as well."

Logan nodded again. It truly did sound like fascinating work. *To be patented jointly by Lux and myself.* Fascinating—and potentially highly remunerative.

McCarty waved a hand. "But surely that's enough about me. Let's get on with it."

"Very well. Why don't you tell me about the, ah, event in your own words."

McCarty fell silent. He was still for so long that Logan began to fear he'd changed his mind. Then he sat up in his chair and pointed. "Do you see that rock formation, there, beyond the Japanese garden?"

Logan looked in the indicated direction. He saw a large black boulder with a smooth top, surrounded by a few smaller ones, rising out of the lush emerald grass. They lay in the late afternoon shadow of the West Wing.

"I used to sit out there and think, after lunch, on warm days. It was quiet, peaceful. I'd stare out at the sea, think about what I had or had not accomplished that morning, collect my thoughts in preparation for the afternoon."

Logan nodded. He was careful not to take out his digital recorder or worn leather notebook.

"My work is important to me, Dr. Logan. During the day, I'm totally absorbed in it. I'm not the kind to daydream or procrastinate. But one day, I found myself staring out at the sea. Just staring.

I don't know exactly how long it went on. Then I started rather abruptly. 'Spacing out,' for want of a better term, just wasn't the kind of thing I did. But I shrugged it off. And then, the next day—the very next—it happened again. Except this time, I was aware of it. I simply could not take my gaze off the ocean. It was as if everything around me went dim and still. It must have lasted at least ten minutes."

"When was this, exactly?"

"Maybe six weeks ago. A Tuesday. I ascribed it to lack of sleep, preoccupation. I was doing some rather difficult analytical work at the time. Anyway, I didn't go back to the rock for a few days. But then, at the end of the week, I did." McCarty went silent again, looking off in the direction of the rocks. "It was a Friday. I'd missed the place. And this time . . . this time . . ." He swallowed. "It happened again. Only it was worse. Much worse. I didn't just want to stare at the ocean. I wanted to walk down to it. Walk down to the sea, walk into the sea, and *keep on walking* . . . I stood up. It was a terrible feeling. I knew what I was doing, I didn't want to do it, but I could not help myself. It was like a strange compulsion." Beads of sweat were springing up on McCarty's forehead, and he brushed them away with the back of a hand. "And there was a voice, too. A voice in my head—that was not my own."

"What did it say?"

"It said: 'Yes. Yes. Go. Go, *now.*'"

McCarty drew in a shuddering breath. "I took a step toward the sea. Then another. And then—I don't know how I managed—I was able to master it. Not completely, but enough. I turned and dashed my hand against the rock. More than once." He raised one hand, displaying knuckles still bandaged. "The pain helped. And then I . . . I yelled. I yelled to keep the voice out of my head, make it go away."

He lapsed into silence once again for several minutes before going on. "And then it was gone. Just like that. The whispering voice. That horrible need to drown myself. It was as if some iron will that had taken over my mind and my body was suddenly exorcised. I've never felt anything like it in my entire life. It was dreadful. Dreadful. I took a deep breath. Then I looked over and saw two people in the Japanese garden, staring at me."

Logan nodded. That was how the incident had become known: McCarty was observed beating his hand against the rock and yelling at the top of his lungs. He suddenly had an unpleasant thought. "Incidents" with five people at Lux had been reported. He'd talked with three of those so far, including McCarty. Only one had actually spoken to the Lux doctor about it; the others had been seen by witnesses. How many others, he wondered, might have experienced something strange, but had not been overseen, or had not chosen to report the incident?

"And that was it?" he said aloud.

"That was it."

"There were no further recurrences? No voices, no compulsions, no feeling of being possessed against your will?"

"No. Nothing. But I've never been back *there*." McCarty nodded in the direction of the rocks. "And I never will."

"Plenty of other nice places around Lux for a postprandial meditation."

"That's true." McCarty turned toward Logan, fixing him once again with his gaze. "There's something else you should know. I also have a medical degree. In fact, I practiced medicine for half a dozen years before going back for a doctorate in linguistics. I graduated from Johns Hopkins Medical School with the highest marks in my class. I did my residency at one of the busiest hospitals on the East Coast, on the surgical track. To call it a brutal experience is putting it mildly. Of the fifteen residents that started with me my first year, six dropped out. Another four switched hospitals. Another committed suicide. Another fell asleep at the wheel, exhausted, and died going off a bridge. Only three of us made it through. And do you know what? During all four years of residency, the only time my pulse went over sixty was when I was using a treadmill in the gym. I'm a tough, hardheaded son of a bitch, Dr. Logan. I don't get stressed; I get focused. And I don't scare easily. Remember to mentally clip that factoid to the story I just told you."

"I will."

"Are we done?"

"We're done." Logan looked around again. "Mind if I sit here awhile, take in the scenery?"

"As long as you don't talk."

"And ruin such a pleasant view?" Logan settled back in his deck chair. "I wouldn't think of it."

19

Logan liked the Blue Lobster the moment he stepped into the bar. It was pleasantly dark, beer fragrant, and unpretentious. Unlike many of the fussy, trendy restaurants in town, its bill of fare—scrawled in chalk on a blackboard hanging over the bar—consisted of only four dishes: fish and chips, cheeseburgers, lobster rolls, and clam chowder. The establishment was situated on the second floor of the Newport Commercial Fisherman's Cooperative. It was just six o'clock, and through the west-facing windows, fishing boats could be seen chuffing up to the wharves, ready to unload the day's catch.

As his eyes adjusted to the dimness, Logan saw the person he'd come here to meet: a slender woman in her early thirties, with long brunette hair, dark eyes, and a heart-shaped face. She was sitting at one of the heavily scarred wooden tables overlooking the wall of windows. She stood up as he approached, smiling a little shyly, or perhaps— Logan thought—with chagrin.

Pamela Flood. She had called not an hour before, using the cell number on the card he'd given her, apologized for her curtness that morning, and asked whether she could buy him a drink.

They shook hands and sat down. A barmaid came over, with a weathered face and arms muscular enough to have spent a decade or two before the mast. "What'll it be?" she asked him.

Logan glanced over at what Ms. Flood was drinking. "Another Sam Adams, please."

"You got it." And the woman walked off into the gloom.

"Thanks for coming," Pamela Flood said. The smile had not left her face.

"Thanks for inviting me, Ms. Flood."

"Please. Call me Pam. And I want to apologize again for the way I practically threw you out this morning."

"It's all right. I've been thrown out of better places." And they both laughed.

His beer arrived and Logan raised the glass. "So architecture runs in the family."

"My great-grandfather and grandfather were architects. My father was a lawyer."

"Don't tell me—the family pariah."

"Something like that." She laughed again. "I was building houses out of Legos at age two. Spent my entire childhood growing up around building plans and plats and construction sites. It never entered my head to do anything else." She took a sip of her beer. "Look. Almost as soon as you left this morning, I began feeling like a complete idiot. And then a few minutes later I realized where I'd seen your face before—on the cover of *People* magazine—and felt even worse. So I thought the very least I could do was buy you a drink, tell you why I acted the way I did, and find out what it was you came to see me about."

Logan sipped his beer. "I'm all ears."

"It's just that . . ." She hesitated. "Well, you aren't the first person to come around, wanting to see those blueprints."

"Really?" Logan sat up. "Tell me about it."

"It was about six months ago. The doorbell rang and I answered it. There was a man standing outside. I knew right away he wasn't a potential client."

"How?"

"When you've done as many building projects as I have, you just know. Anyway, he started in asking about the original plans for Lux. Said he would pay money, quite a lot of money, for a look at them. Something about him gave me a bad vibe. I said the plans weren't available anymore. But he wouldn't leave, wouldn't take no for an answer. Just stayed on my doorstep, asking where they were, how he could get them, demanding to know who he needed to pay. For a minute I thought he was going to force his way in and search the house. Finally, I closed the door in his face."

"Did he say who he represented?" Logan asked.

"He gave me a business card. Some firm I'd never heard of, Iron Fist or something. I think I threw it into the trash first thing."

"What did the man look like?"

She thought for a moment. "I can't give you many specifics. It was late winter, he wore sunglasses and a hat, and he kept the collar of his coat up around his neck. About your height, but beefier." She paused to take another sip of her beer. "But it was his behavior more than his appearance that gave me the creeps. He was just short of threatening. I almost called the cops—but what hard evidence did I have? And then, for a couple of weeks afterward, I had this strange sensation I was being followed. Nothing I could be sure about—just a feeling."

"And that's why you gave me the bum's rush. Can't say I blame you."

"But everything's been normal for months now. He never came back. I had no reason to act that way."

The nearby panes of glass shivered under the blast of an approaching boat horn. "Why don't you tell me why you want to see the building plans for Dark Gables?" she asked. "I mean, they have copies of the plans at Lux. They're the ones we worked from in refitting the West Wing."

Logan rolled the glass between his hands, stalling for a little extra time.

"Does it have to do with Will Strachey's death?" she prompted.

Logan looked at her quizzically.

"You must know that I worked with him on the plans for the West Wing revision."

"Yes."

"A tragedy. He was such a nice man."

"How was he to work with?"

"Great. Except that he became something of an enthusiast. He wanted to understand every last architectural detail."

"How did he seem to you over the last several weeks?"

"I couldn't say. I haven't seen him in almost three months."

"Isn't that unusual? I mean, you worked with him on the refitting of the wing."

She shrugged. "Once the major structural work was complete, he brought in a general contractor to oversee the day-to-day details. So, anyway: what does this have to do with poor Willard's death?"

"I can't comment on that, except to say that my interest in the plans is only tangentially related." He paused. He could make something up, of course. But, though he barely knew Pamela Flood, instinct told him that the truth—or at least a subset of the truth—would probably yield better results.

"It's rather sensitive," he said. "Lux is a very private outfit."

"Oh, I'm good at keeping my mouth shut. You'd be surprised how many secrets people want built into their houses."

"As it happens, that's exactly what I'm looking into—a secret. You see, we've stumbled upon a very unusual architectural detail inside the mansion."

Now it was her turn to look quizzical. "A *de*tail?"

"One that's remained hidden for years. It isn't shown on any of the blueprints in the Lux files. So naturally I was curious as to whether your great-grandfather—who probably kept a more complete set of plans—could shed any more light on things."

"A detail," she said again. "How mysterious." She finished her beer. "Tell you what. Fact is, I *do* have my great-grandfather's files—including the original plans and specifications for Dark Gables. If you can come by the office sometime—say, the day after tomorrow—we can look them over together. How about it?"

Logan drained his own glass. "Just name the time," he said.

20

"Yes, I saw him," Roger Carbon said. "It's no secret."

"When was this, exactly?" Logan asked. The two men were sitting around a table in the capacious lab suite that Dr. Carbon shared with another scientist.

"Perhaps ten minutes before he died, as near as I can make out. It was in the first-floor corridor, not far from the central staircase. Under escort, as I recall."

"Being taken to the visitor's library," Logan said, more to himself than Carbon. He'd already spoken to the guards who'd undertaken this—they knew nothing of value. He glanced at the evolutionary psychologist. "Did he say anything?"

"He was too busy frothing at the mouth."

This was in exceedingly bad taste, but Logan didn't rise to the bait. He was near the end of the list of Lux employees and Fellows whom he'd planned to interview about Strachey, and—knowing it wouldn't be pleasant—had put Carbon off to the end. "That made you one of the last to see him alive."

"I suppose so."

"Roger, I wonder. You're a psychologist. Do you have any theories about what might have happened to Dr. Strachey?"

"I'm an *evolutionary* psychologist. I'm not a diagnostician."

"So you refuse to even hazard a guess as to the underlying cause?"

Carbon expelled a put-upon sigh. "Very well. To put it in the most technical of terms: Willard went barmy."

Logan frowned. "In the most technical of terms."

"It happens, you know. Perhaps more frequently to brilliant scientists than to others. Even brilliant scientists who are—shall we say—past their prime."

"Speaking of that, Perry Maynard told me it was you who advocated for Dr. Strachey to be put in charge of the West Wing renovation."

Carbon did not reply to this. He merely rubbed his Freud-like beard.

"You seem to enjoy meddling in the affairs of Lux residents," Logan said.

"If you're referring to my efforts to get you ousted, that was nothing personal. Your work was pseudoscience, smoke and mirrors, below Lux's standards. In the case of Willard, I saw a piece of slowly vegetating human matériel that could be put to better use."

"Why the West Wing?"

"Why not? It was a job that needed doing. Although, had I known he was about to crack, I wouldn't have suggested it." He shook his head. "All that nattering about 'voices in the dark.'"

Logan glanced up. "When was this?"

"When he went past me, of course."

"I thought you told me he didn't say anything."

"He didn't say anything to *me*. He was just raving."

Logan looked at him speculatively.

"You don't think *I'm* responsible, somehow? What—you think Willard blamed me for putting him in charge of the West Wing . . . a resentment that eventually pushed him over the edge? Ludicrous."

"I didn't say that," Logan replied.

"If you're looking for a scalp to collect, go chat up that Grecian assistant of his. She's had her eye on his chair from her first bloody day in the place."

"I already have." Logan stood up. "Good day, Roger."

"Close the door on your way out," Carbon

said, rising as well, turning his back, and heading for his desk. "And don't slip on any ectoplasm."

As Logan was leaving, a woman appeared in the other doorway of the suite. "Dr. Logan? Do you have a minute?"

"Of course." Logan stepped into a lab on whose large desk sat no less than three computers and four flat-panel monitors. A nearby rack contained at least half a dozen blade servers. "Good lord. Do you work with them, or repair them?"

The woman smiled. Then she closed the door and gestured Logan to a seat. "I work with them. I'm an electrical engineer, with a specialty in quantum computing."

Logan nodded. The woman—whom he had seen once or twice at dinner—was young, very thin, with arresting raven hair and deep-set eyes. Her movements were sharp and abrupt, like a bird's. Although she was still smiling pleasantly, she seemed to be cloaked in an invisible veil of melancholy.

She sat down in a nearby chair. "I'm sorry. My name is Laura Benedict. I asked you in because I couldn't help overhearing your conversation with Roger. I wanted to apologize for his behavior."

"Thanks, but that really wasn't necessary."

"Roger is an exceptional scientist, but he's also like the schoolyard bully who never grew up. He still likes to pull the wings off flies.

"It sounds like he didn't get along with Willard Strachey."

"They certainly weren't the best of friends. But then, Roger rubs a lot of people the wrong way." She looked at him with her penetrating eyes. "Nobody's actually made an announcement, but I can guess why you're here. You're looking into Will's death, right?"

"Yes." Logan paused. "Did you say your name was Laura Benedict?"

The woman nodded.

"As it happens, you and Dr. Carbon were the last on my list of people to interview."

Laura Benedict looked at him inquiringly.

"Forgive me, but I have to ask. On the afternoon following Willard Strachey's death, you were seen on a bench overlooking the ocean, hugging yourself, rocking back and forth. The person who logged the incident said that at one point you stood up and walked toward the cliffs at the edge of the ocean. You seemed so . . . well, so distraught that they were about to call security. But then you returned to the bench, and . . ."

As Logan spoke, the woman's eyes filled with tears. She began sobbing, quietly at first, and then more loudly. It didn't take a sensitive such as Logan to see that the woman was grief stricken. Uncomfortable at the reaction he'd precipitated, Logan fell silent.

After a minute or two, the woman collected herself. "I'm sorry," she said, wiping her eyes with a tissue. "I thought I was over the worst of it."

"It's my fault," Logan said. "Had I known, I wouldn't have—"

"No," the woman said, sniffling. "No, I have to learn to deal with it." She got a fresh tissue, blew her nose with shaking hands. "There's no mystery. I was beside myself with grief. Will was . . . he took me under his wing when I first came to Lux. It can be a pretty intimidating place, you know; the brain-power here is almost incandescent." She smiled through her tears. "Will was so patient, so helpful. He was my mentor. No, more than that. He was like a father to me." Her hands began trembling again and she reached for another tissue.

"I didn't know him well myself, during my own brief tenure here a decade ago, but he always struck me as a kind and gentle person." Logan paused. "Do you have any idea what could have caused such a change in him?"

Laura Benedict shook her head, wiped her eyes again. "I hadn't seen much of him these past few weeks. I've been preparing a paper I'm present-ing at the next meeting of the Society of Quantum Engineering, and it's been consuming all my time. But he always had time for me—I should have found time for him. I keep thinking that if only I'd spoken with him, heard him out, that maybe . . . maybe . . ."

"That's survivor guilt talking. You mustn't think like that." Logan did not want to intrude on this woman's grief any longer. It was clearly still too raw. "One last question—and, again, I hope you'll forgive my asking. When you were seen walking toward the cliffs, were you . . . ?" Finding himself unable to frame the words, he fell silent again.

"Was I going to fling myself in? No. That's not me. Besides, I have a paper to present—remember?" Another smile, but it was a wan smile, as before.

"Thank you for being honest at a difficult time, Dr. Benedict." And Logan rose. "And thanks also for the words about Carbon."

Laura Benedict rose as well. Her eyes looked a little bruised and red, but at least they were now dry. "If he gives you any more trouble, let me know. For some reason, he's a pussycat around me."

Back in his rooms, Logan entered some notes on these two interviews into an encrypted file on his computer—a paragraph on Laura Benedict, several on Roger Carbon. Now that he had spoken to everybody on his initial list, he read over their brief dossiers one more time. Then he created a spreadsheet, also encrypted, and entered each name and a small comment on why they had been chosen for questioning. Then he sorted the names into various groups. One group, including people like Ian Albright and Kim Mykolos, comprised those who had worked with Strachey. Another group, which included Roger Carbon, consisted of people who had witnessed Strachey's strange behavior in the days leading up to his suicide. And then there was the final group: those, such as Terence McCarty, the linguist, whom Carbon had labeled "the others." There were five names in this last group. One was Laura Benedict, and Logan put an asterisk beside her name—her behavior had stemmed from simple grief.

The remaining four were interesting. Three were scientists in residence; one was an administrator. None had been eager to talk about their experiences, some less so than others. Two had reported seeing or smelling things that turned out either to be not there at all, or to be grossly different from reality. Three of the four said that they had briefly felt compelled to do unusual or uncharacteristic things. All four had heard music or voices, or a combination of the two.

Logan knew that paracusia, or auditory hallucinations, could be a side effect of many things: sleep disorders, psychoses, epilepsy, encephalitis. But the chances of four people in such a small sampling, all suffering such mental or physical illness, was vanishingly small. Besides, people with musical hallucinations almost invariably heard tunes they were familiar with, which was not the case here—Logan had made it a point to ask. Nor were the voices of the standard types: argumentative or narrative or the loud noises common with exploding head syndrome. Instead, the voices all four had heard were *whispered*.

"Visions" and "strange compulsions" were terms that had come up frequently. All the incidents had begun six to eight weeks earlier. In all four cases, the people were aware that the phenomena, the aberrant behaviors, were not normal; and in all of the cases, the phenomena had ceased

abruptly—usually, weeks before Strachey's death—
and not returned.

There was one other commonality—one that
was of particular interest. Cross-checking his notes
on the four individuals, a pattern emerged. All four
who'd been affected either lived or worked in the
vicinity of the West Wing.

The West Wing. It was, Logan sensed, bound
up inextricably with the circumstances of Strachey's
death. And now, he thought he was beginning to
understand why.

21

Late that same afternoon, Logan steered his Lotus Elan coupe from Carroll Avenue right onto Ocean, downshifting smoothly as he made the turn. What had started out as a foggy, drizzly day had turned at least temporarily bright and warm, and Logan had the hardtop's windows down: the breeze coming in from Hazard's Beach on the left filled the car with a deliciously salty smell.

While Lux could provide just about everything in the way of edibles—their meals were first-rate, and a small café was open from 10 a.m. to 8 p.m. if anyone grew hungry in off hours—they did not serve PG Tips tea, a habit he'd developed while doing graduate work in England and never been able to shake. So he'd driven into town to pick up a box, and a few toiletries, from a gourmet food market on Pelham Street.

Now, as he drove back toward Lux, his thoughts returned to what Carbon had said about Kim Mykolos. *If you're looking for a scalp to collect, go chat up that Grecian assistant of his. She's had her eye on his chair from her first bloody day in the place.* This directly contradicted what Kim herself had told him about her relationship with Strachey. Odd . . .

He was forced to slam on the brakes when a dark SUV pulled out of a side street and onto Ocean Avenue directly in front of him. Frowning, he suppressed the urge to give the vehicle a blast of his horn. The driver was almost undoubtedly a tourist—judging by the glacial pace at which the vehicle was moving, the occupants were either lost or else taking in the sights. And the sights were admittedly stunning: the road was running nearer the sea here, and was rising to the highest point on Ocean Avenue, almost one hundred feet above the beach.

Leaving the Elan in second gear, Logan's thoughts went back to Carbon. His instincts told him that Kim Mykolos had been genuinely upset and shaken by Strachey's death. Those weren't the behaviors of somebody gunning for his job. And she herself had indicated there was no tension between them, no strain in their relationship.

The SUV was still ahead of him. Maybe it wasn't taking in the sights, after all—perhaps the driver was having mechanical problems. The vehicle would slow down, speed up abruptly, then slow down again. At this rate, instead of getting back to Lux in one minute, it would take him ten. Logan drifted into the oncoming lane to look for any approaching traffic, but the road angled to the right up ahead and he couldn't get a good enough view to pass. He settled back into place behind the bulky vehicle to wait.

Carbon might be a first-rate bastard, Logan thought, *but why would he lie about such a thing? Was he trying to deflect my attention? If so, why? And then again, Strachey did attack Mykolos right before he killed himself.* That did add some possible weight to Carbon's accusation. . . . But no, he decided; it just didn't feel right to him.

Now the SUV had pulled over to the side, at an angle, still partially blocking the lane. As Logan came to a stop behind it, the driver's window slid down, and a gloved hand emerged, waving him on. With a reciprocal wave of thanks, Logan moved out into the other lane, ready to depress the clutch and shift into third. . . .

Just as he did so, the SUV, which had been idling, suddenly roared into life, veering directly toward him. Logan's heart began to race and he downshifted, braking in order to tuck himself back behind the SUV—but the dark, slow-moving vehicle was still lumbering sideways toward him, at speed now, as if with a stuck accelerator pedal. In another second it would impact his small sports car, push him off the road.

In desperation, Logan veered off to the narrow left shoulder. The Lotus spun on the sandy shoulder, tires shearing sideways. Out of control now, it hurtled toward the rocky cliff edge and Logan got a stomach-churning view of the long drop to the boulder-strewn breakers below. Heart hammering, he spun the wheel in the opposite direction to the turn. He felt a sudden dip as the left rear wheel dropped onto the rocks at the very edge of the cliff. Downshifting into first, feathering the brakes, Logan desperately gunned the car forward. At the last moment, the rear-wheel drive gained traction and the Lotus half lurched, half leapt back onto the shoulder. He killed the engine and sat there, breathing heavily, a faint cloud of sand and dust falling all around him.

A red mist that had fallen over his eyes slowly cleared. Logan glanced left again, at the dizzying, one-hundred-foot drop to the ocean just beyond the shoulder. Then, heart still thudding in his chest, he looked down the road. The plodding SUV was just barely visible ahead, at a gentle curve in the road. Then it turned onto a side street and disappeared from view.

22

It was nine o'clock in the evening when Logan rose from the desk in his quarters on Lux's third floor and walked over to the nearest window. The bad weather had finally won out over the good and a storm had settled over Newport. Swollen clouds scudded before the moon, and sheets of wind-driven rain beat against the panes of leaded glass.

He stared out at the storm-lashed ocean—pounding fiercely against the coastline—for several minutes, lost in thought. Then he turned back to the desk. It was covered with notes he had taken following various interviews, along with brief dossiers on a dozen of the scientists and administrators at the think tank: Roger Carbon; Terence McCarty; Perry Maynard; Laura Benedict, the quantum computing expert. Life, he had learned, had been especially unkind to Ms. Benedict recently: in addition to losing her mentor, she was doubly bereaved—her grandfather had died of cancer a few years before, and not long after she'd been tragically widowed. Her husband, an aviation enthusiast, had died in a midair crash with another small plane during a storm—perhaps a storm not so different from this one.

He flipped through the pages on his desk for a minute, then pushed the folders aside. Beneath them was another: a file on Kim Mykolos. He'd made a point to sit at her table that evening for dinner, and had found that—when the conversation did not turn to Strachey, obviously still a painful subject—she was witty and charming, an excellent conversationalist. She had also borne out the fact that Strachey had, in fact, been like a father to Laura Benedict. Logan's empathetic instincts assured him of what he'd already deduced: that, whether out of misapprehension or spite, Carbon was wrong about Kim—she had not been after Strachey's job.

Turning to his computer, he brought up his encrypted spreadsheet on "the others" and reviewed it one more time, just to be sure. But there had been no mistake in his deduction.

He paused, looking at the screen, for several minutes. Then he turned off the computer. It was time.

Picking up the printed phone directory for Lux, he turned pages until he found the number he wanted: Dr. Olafson's private quarters. Picking up the phone, he dialed.

It was answered on the third ring. "Olafson."

"Gregory? It's Jeremy Logan."

"Jeremy. I penciled a note on my calendar to call you tomorrow morning, discuss your progress."

"That's why I'm calling. I wondered if I could drop in for a few minutes."

There was a pause. "Now?"

"If you're not otherwise occupied."

The sound of shuffling papers came over the line. "Of course. I'll be expecting you."

"Thanks." Logan hung up the phone and, without bothering to grab his satchel, quickly exited the room.

23

Olafson lived in a large suite of rooms at the far eastern end of the Lady's Walk. He answered the door, not in his usual dark suit but in a V-necked cashmere sweater over khakis. A tumbler of whiskey, poured neat, was in one hand. "Ah, Jeremy," he said, shaking hands. "Come in."

"Sorry for the short notice," Logan said. "But I didn't see why this should wait."

Olafson led the way down a corridor and into the living room. In stark contrast to the mansion's Edwardian appointments, the director's rooms—as the abstract expressionist paintings in his office could have hinted at—were furnished in Bauhaus style. Chrome and leather chairs of smoothly curved and polished tubular metal were offset by glass-topped tables and strange, ziggurat-styled bookcases straight from the Marcel Breuer school. Large windows set into both the east and south walls offered dramatic views of the storm.

"Scotch?" Olafson said, heading toward a wet bar.

"A couple of fingers, thanks."

Olafson picked up another tumbler, splashed some Lagavulin into it, then brought it over to Logan and ushered him to a chair. He took a sip of his scotch, waiting for Logan to begin.

"The first stage of my work is complete," Logan told the director. "I've reviewed all the reports and dossiers, watched the surveillance videos, done a thorough background investigation on Strachey, reviewed his work, spoken with everyone who interacted with him during the last seventy-two hours of his life. I've done everything, followed every avenue, a standard investigation would encompass."

"And?"

"And I agree with what you told me when I first arrived five days ago. Willard Strachey was a man who had everything to live for. He'd had a highly rewarding career and was looking forward to an equally rewarding retirement. This was not a man who would commit suicide—and, as you said, he was a man whose temperament would be utterly opposed to such an act." He sipped his drink. "Something happened to Strachey in the last few weeks of his life. Something that changed him utterly, that forced him to kill himself, and to do so immediately. And I've become convinced that something has to do with his work in the West Wing."

"The West Wing," Olafson repeated.

"Specifically, with the secret room. There's a connection—I know there is. But in order to learn what it is, if I'm going to learn what happened to Strachey . . . I need to know the purpose of that room."

The room glowed with the livid glare of lightning; a moment later, there was a sudden crack of thunder.

Olafson frowned. "I don't know, Jeremy. That seems a bit of a stretch to me. What could his work on the renovation have to do with his suicide?"

"Strachey had the keys to the wing. He'd been working for months on its redesign and restoration. He knew it better than anyone else. And don't you remember that small, hammer-sized hole in the wall of the room? It had been plastered over. You said it yourself: that means *he might already have discovered it.*"

Slowly, Olafson put his drink down on a nearby table. "That's right. I did say that."

"I told you I've done everything a standard investigation would cover. Now, it's time for me to undertake a nonstandard investigation."

"And what does that entail?"

"Learning the riddle of the forgotten room."

"Riddle," Olafson said. "Interesting word."

"But that room is nothing *but* riddles. What

was its purpose? Why doesn't it appear on the architectural plans? Why was it secret in the first place? And why did Strachey happen to kill himself when he learned—or was about to learn—of its existence?"

Olafson didn't answer.

"There's something else. 'The others' Carbon spoke of—the Lux residents who had been seen, in recent weeks, acting in an uncharacteristic or unusual manner—they told me of seeing, hearing, or smelling things that weren't actually there. They spoke of strange compulsions—in one case, a suicidal compulsion. But the most interesting fact is that the four individuals all either lived, or worked, in the shadow of the West Wing."

"Are you sure of that?" Olafson asked.

"I've double-checked my observations. I'm sure."

Olafson reached for his drink.

"If I'm going to solve this mystery, I need your permission to shift my focus: to the West Wing and, in particular, the forgotten room."

Olafson took a long sip from his drink. He sighed. Then, slowly, he nodded.

"I'm also going to need an assistant."

Olafson frowned. "What?"

"I'm a historian, an enigmalogist—I'm not a mechanical engineer. I need somebody who possesses skills I don't have if I'm to stand any chance of unlocking this riddle."

"But we agreed the existence of the room was to be kept secret."

"I know. But the more I've thought about it, the clearer it's become that I can't solve this alone."

This was followed by a brief silence.

"I don't know, Jeremy," the director said at last. "Strachey's death was bad enough, but that room . . . it must have been sealed for a good reason. We can't afford any stain on Lux's escutcheon."

"I've heard that speech before. And I'm aware of how delicate the situation here is. But this is the only chance you have of learning what happened to Strachey."

Logan watched as the director went silent, thinking. "It would have to be somebody on whose discretion we can utterly rely."

"I'll vouch for her utmost discretion."

"Her?" Olafson said in surprise. "You've got somebody in mind already?"

"Kim Mykolos. Strachey's assistant."

"Why Mykolos? I mean, she's not even a Fellow, for heaven's sake."

"She's the perfect choice. She knows Strachey's work better than anyone—and, with all the workmen scattered to the four winds, that goes for his work on the West Wing as well. She's up to date on the people and politics of Lux—and she's honest enough to give me straight answers. But most important, one of her specialties is reverse engineering. And I need someone who can help me 'reverse engineer' that room."

"Jeremy, I'm not sure I can sanction that," Olafson said. "I doubt if the board would approve."

"Does the board know about the forgotten room?"

"No, of course not."

"Well, they don't need to know about this, either."

"But we're such a private, insular organization . . . involving Mykolos would go against all our principles of compartmentalization and secrecy."

"Doesn't suicide go against Lux's principles, as well?"

Olafson didn't answer.

"As I said—it's the only way you're going to get the answers you seek. And don't forget: I'm here because you *don't know* what happened to Strachey, or why. Look at those other four, and what happened to them. Can you afford to just wall up the West Wing and look the other way? Who knows what else might happen in the future? You'd be turning your back on a ticking bomb."

Olafson sighed. "If you put it that way, I guess I have to agree."

"Thank you, Gregory."

The director looked around the room a moment before settling his gaze again on Logan. "When do you plan to start?"

"First thing tomorrow." And Logan drained his drink.

24

As Logan was returning to his own room on the third floor, another resident, in a small set of rooms in a far section of the second floor, was pacing restlessly. The lights were out, and the only illumination came from the flickering tongues of lightning beyond the mullioned windows.

After several minutes, the pacing stopped. The person, apparently coming to a decision, walked over to the phone, then dialed a number with a 401 area code.

The call was answered on the first ring by a gravelly baritone. "Operations. Abrams."

"You know who this is, right?"

"Yes," the man named Abrams said.

"You were responsible for what happened today, weren't you? That run-in with Logan on the road."

"How did you learn about that?"

"I heard him talk about it at dinner. Besides, it's hard to keep anything private in a place like Lux. But that's beside the point. Are you crazy, doing a thing like that?"

"But he knows about the room. You said it yourself. If he pokes around in there, it could ruin everything."

"What would ruin everything is your killing him right in town. That's not what we agreed. He's too high profile. You'll only raise suspicion. You might even wreck my cover."

"Logan is an unknown variable in the equation. We can't afford to let him remain at Lux."

"He won't learn anything. I've been too careful for that."

"That's a chance we can't take," said the man named Abrams. "The stakes have grown too high. If only he'd waited a few more days before—"

"Well, he didn't. We have to play the hand we've been dealt. Look—no more going behind my back. No more making any rash decisions without consulting me. Otherwise . . . otherwise, I'll back out. Take the item elsewhere."

"You wouldn't be that foolish. You're in it too deep."

"Then you listen. We're going to do this *my* way. I believe Logan thinks what happened was an accident—and it's a good thing for you that he does. If he gets suspicious, he's going to become ten times as dangerous as he already is."

"So what, exactly, is 'your way'?"

"Logan is my problem—let me deal with him. I know just what to do."

"You're going to . . . ?" The voice on the far end of the line trailed off.

"Precisely."

"Don't wait too long. The clock is running, and we don't have much time."

"That's why I'm going to act fast." And with a sharp click, the call was disconnected.

25

"This is weird," said Kim Mykolos. "Seriously weird." She was standing in the middle of the forgotten room, staring around in slack-jawed fascination.

When Logan had let her in on the secret—after securing the necessary promises of utter confidentiality—the young woman's reactions had been first disbelief, then shock, and then consuming curiosity. Leaning against the worktable, Logan watched as she moved around, peering at this and that, reaching out to touch something, then quickly pulling back her hand as if afraid of being burned.

The tungsten lamp stood in a bare corner, providing a strong illumination but also splashing deep, jagged shadows against the far wall. Turning toward the worktable, Logan opened his duffel, pulled out a video camera, and then a portable music player, which he placed beside the unknown implements and turned on. The calmly syncopated rhythms of *Jazz Samba* wafted quietly over the room.

"And you say that whatever research was going on in here stopped abruptly in the midthirties?" she asked.

Logan nodded.

"And the room was sealed off and remained forgotten to this day?"

"So it seems. And all the notes and records of whatever went on here have apparently vanished from Lux's files."

"What about Dr. Strachey? Did he discover this room before . . ." Her voice trailed away.

"I don't know for sure. But it's quite possible."

Mykolos pulled herself away from her examination and glanced over at Logan. "So why me, exactly? How can I help?"

"You were his assistant. You've got a background in computer logic, in reverse engineering. I need a mind like yours if I'm going to solve this room."

"Solve it?"

"Yes. I'm convinced that only by solving its puzzle will I learn why Strachey died. And besides, from a purely practical standpoint I need a second pair of hands." He hefted the video camera. "I want you to use this to document everything we do here."

Mykolos nodded slowly. "So how do we start, exactly?"

"I've given that a lot of thought. I think the most important thing is to understand the purpose of *that*." And he pointed to the oversized, coffin-shaped device of polished wood that sat in the center of the room.

"I was wondering about that. It looks sort of like a mystery machine on steroids."

"A what?"

"A mystery machine. Something from the old penny arcades. A big box of wood or metal, with question marks all over it but no obvious features—no handles, levers, knobs. You put in your penny and then kicked it, banged it, tried to figure out how to make it do whatever it did."

"Well, don't kick it, please."

Mykolos nodded toward the bulky metal suits that hung from a metal bar on the far wall. "What do you make of those?"

"I can only assume they're some sort of protective gear."

She walked up to the closest, took it gently by one wrist, and moved the arm up and down, watching as the fanlike elbow joints telescoped to accommodate the movement. "Protection from what?"

"That's what we're here to find out." He motioned her over to the central device, handed her the video camera. "You see those brass plaques screwed into the base, there and there? Those are manufacturers' imprints."

Mykolos turned on the camera and pointed it at the indicated plaques, filming both.

"I've looked into the names on those plaques. Elektrofabriken Kelle was a German electronics firm founded in Dresden in 1911. It has since merged with so many companies that its original purpose has become obscure. And in any case, all its records were destroyed in the firebombing of 1945. Rosewell Heavy Industries was an early manufacturer of sound and radio equipment. It went out of business in the fifties. I haven't been able to learn much beyond the fact that it made highly specialized equipment for industrial use."

Mykolos panned the camcorder slowly over the device. Then she thoughtfully caressed the appendages that sprouted irregularly here and there: gently curved panels of rosewood, carefully fitted and locked to the central mechanism, itself completely encased in wood. She walked over to the thick end of the device, looked at the roman numerals etched into the floor beyond. Next, she walked around to the narrow end and filmed the heavy wooden housing that was locked in place onto it. Lowering the camera, she pointed at the two words, BEAM and FIELD, etched into another brass plaque just beneath the cowling, raising her eyebrows at Logan as she did so.

"As good a place to start as any," he said.

Approaching, he examined a wooden keyhole set into the housing directly over the plaque. Plucking a flashlight from his duffel, he gave it an even closer examination. Then, pulling a set of lockpicks from his pocket and laying the flashlight on top of the housing, he started working on the lock.

"Odd skill for a professor of history," Mykolos said as she filmed the process.

"Don't forget, I'm an enigmalogist, too."

A brief silence settled over the room, broken only by the low sounds of samba. "What's with the Stan Getz?" she asked after a moment.

"I'll tell you if you promise not to laugh."

"I promise."

"I'm what's known as a sensitive. An empath. I have a knack—if you can call it that—for hearing things, sensing things, that people felt or experienced, whether in the present or in the past. This room is . . . unpleasant. I've been hearing music—hearing it in my head. Stan Getz helps me to tune it out."

"What kind of music?"

"Wild arpeggios, giant clashing clusters of notes, waves of sound. Unsettling melodies, almost insolently virtuosic."

"You could almost be describing Alkan."

Logan paused. "You mentioned him before. Wasn't he a favorite composer of Strachey's?"

"Charles-Valentin Alkan. Perhaps the strangest composer who ever lived. Yes, Willard was a huge fan. In fact, Alkan was the only composer other than Bach thematically and harmonically complex enough to interest him. I think it was his mathematical turn of mind."

Logan reapplied himself to the lock, and a second later there came a click as the last pin crossed the shear line. Straightening up, Logan placed both hands on the rosewood cowling and carefully lifted it. Beneath lay a row of buttons, with two knobs—one above the BEAM label and the other above the FIELD label—sporting matching antique VU meters and sets of switches. Everything was remarkably free of dust.

"What do you suppose all this means?" Mykolos asked, putting the camera aside and shaking out her jet-black hair.

"You tell me. You're the propeller-head, remember?"

For a moment, they looked at the controls in silence. "Do you see anything that looks like an on switch?" Logan asked.

"No. But I wouldn't look for one near these controls. I'd look on the side, below, nearer whatever machine powers this thing."

Logan hunted around the base of the wooden housing until he found a much smaller cowling attached to the near edge. Once again employing his lockpicks, he managed to remove it after about ten seconds of manipulating the pins. Beneath were two switches, one marked PWR and the other LOAD.

"Bingo," Mykolos said, looking over his shoulder, video camera once again in hand, eyes widening in excitement.

Logan reached forward to flip the power switch, then hesitated. "Should we?"

"Won't get any further if we don't."

Gingerly, he took hold of the switch, then flipped it into the on position. At first, there was nothing. Then there came a low humming, almost beneath the threshold of hearing. He placed one hand on the main housing. It was now vibrating slightly.

"Anything?" Mykolos asked as she filmed.

Logan nodded.

"What's that?" And she pointed to the LOAD switch.

"It probably connects a load from a voltage source."

"In other words, like throwing a car from neutral into drive."

"Basically, yes."

They looked at each other, then at the switch. Even more gingerly this time, Logan reached forward and placed the tips of his fingers on it.

"You think maybe we ought to put on those suits of armor first?" Mykolos said, only half joking.

Logan did not reply. He took a firm grip on the LOAD switch, flipped it into the active position.

Nothing happened.

"Broken," Mykolos said after a moment.

"Not necessarily. We don't know the function of all those switches and dials on the front panel. They probably do the real work. But let me see if I can get the rest of these cowlings off first."

Logan turned off the load switch, then the power switch. The faint vibration stopped and the device came to rest. Then, one after the other, Logan picked the locks of the two wooden housings fixed to the flanks of the device, and then, lastly, the metal plate covering the wide far end. Removing the two cowlings revealed complex gizmos of metal and rubber. One reminded him of a bulky, futuristic antenna; the other a kind of labyrinthine radiator, sporting two rows of horizontal tubes.

He shook his head. It seemed that each bit of progress they made with this strange device just yielded up fresh mysteries.

They bent over the antenna-like device. "What do you make of it?" Logan asked. "Does it ring any bells?"

"Look at this faceplate." And Mykolos pointed to a legend beneath the contrivance that read, in small letters: EFG 112-A. PATENT 4,125,662. WAREHAM ELECTRIC COMPANY, BOSTON. TOLERANCES 1–20 MG, .1–15 MT.

"'mG,'" Logan read aloud. "Do you suppose that's milligauss?"

"I think so. And I think 'mT' stands for microtesla."

"Then this thing is a . . ." Logan fell silent.

"A primitive electromagnetic field generator. And that"—she pointed at the lower section of the assembly—"is probably a rotatable pickup coil."

Logan took a step back from the machine.

"What is it?" Mykolos asked.

Logan did not reply.

"What is it?" she repeated, frowning.

"One function of such generators," Logan said at last, "is to detect changes in electromagnetic fields."

"Yes, I recall that from my electrical engineering courses. So?"

"In my line of work, they're used for a specific kind of electromagnetic change. Distortions caused by paranormal events."

Surprise, then disbelief, crossed Mykolos's face. "You aren't saying that this was a machine built to . . . to detect *ghosts*?"

"It seems possible. Interest in spiritualism and mysticism was big in the nineteen thirties, and—"

"Wait. You're creeping me out here." Now it was Mykolos's turn to take a step back from the machine. "You think this thing was created to detect ghosts . . . and was abandoned because it didn't work?"

"Perhaps," Logan murmured. "Or perhaps because it worked too well."

26

Pamela Flood's office was a large space in the rear of the old house on Perry Street. For a workroom, it was surprisingly elegant. While the antique drafting tables, framed and faded elevations, and technical volumes in old wooden bookcases gave testimony to earlier generations of architects, Pamela had refreshed and brightened the room with several feminine touches.

"Please take a seat," Pamela told Logan, motioning to a metal stool set beside one of the drafting tables. "Sorry there isn't anything more comfortable."

"This is fine." Logan took a look at the table,

noticed it contained a series of architectural sketches in pencil. "You still work the old-fashioned way?"

"Only for the first drafts. Got to keep up with the times, you know. I use a CAD-based software suite to make the customers happy, and I'm also learning BIM."

"BIM?"

"Building Information Modeling." She went over to a second drafting table, on which sat several old blueprints, tightly rolled. "I got these out of basement storage this morning. They're my great-grandfather's personal set of plans for Dark Gables."

"Can we examine the diagrams for the second floor of the West Wing?"

"Sure." Pamela sorted through the rolled sheets of paper, selected one, and brought it over to Logan's table, where she unrolled it. "I have to tell you, it was something of a struggle not taking an early peek at these."

"Without me, you wouldn't have known what to look for."

"Want to bet?" she asked, smiling. Logan couldn't help but notice that it was a genuine, and rather winning, smile.

He turned his attention to the blueprint. It was covered with the same crowded lines, measurements, and notes that the set in Strachey's possession had been. But as he refamiliarized himself with the warren of rooms and corridors, he was surprised to discover that—there, almost directly in the center of the floor—was the very room he had found. A corridor ran along its west wall; flues and mechanical spaces bordered its northern side; and rooms labeled GALLERY and ART STUDIO lay to the east and south, respectively. The room itself was unlabeled.

"Odd," Pamela said just a few seconds later, placing a finger on the very room Logan was examining. "This room has no doors. And no obvious purpose. It can't be a staircase—there are staircases here, and here, and another would be redundant. It's not structural, and it's not mechanical." She paused. "It's possible this is an unfinished blueprint . . . but, no, there's my great-grandfather's signature in the nameplate. How strange."

On the drive from Lux to Pamela's house, Logan had found himself in the grip of an internal debate. Now, the speed with which she had noticed the secret room made up his mind for him.

"I'm not going to swear you to secrecy or anything," he said, "but can you promise me that you'll keep this between ourselves?"

Pamela nodded.

"Absolutely between ourselves? No gossiping to friends or family?"

"I don't have any family. And I know how to keep a secret."

"Very well." Logan placed the tip of his finger gently atop hers, still resting on the sketched room. "*That* is the 'unusual architectural detail' I mentioned to you at the Blue Lobster."

Pamela's eyes widened. "It is? What is it, exactly?"

"You'll understand if I'm a bit short on details. Suffice to say that it is a forgotten room, unused—in fact, unknown—for more than fifty years. I discovered it myself during an inspection of the West Wing, when I was looking into why Strachey stopped work so abruptly."

He knew that Olafson would strenuously disapprove of involving Pamela Flood, even marginally. But he also knew there was a good chance—given her architectural knowledge, her family connection to the original design of the mansion, and her close working relationship with Strachey—that she could make a significant contribution.

Pamela was shaking her head. "Do you mean this room was hidden deliberately? What was its purpose? And why isn't there any means of ingress or egress?"

"I don't know all the answers yet, and they aren't germane to this conversation. I wanted to see your blueprints because I was hoping they might shed some light on the mystery."

Pamela glanced at the diagram for a moment before answering. "Well, they don't shed much. They tell us that, for whatever reason, the blueprints I worked from at Lux were modified from my great-grandfather's originals."

"And they tell us the room was, in fact, in existence during the life of the original owner. Presumably, Delaveaux himself asked that the room be built—he seems to have been an eccentric character, to say the least. But they don't tell us *why* the blueprints were changed. The structure itself wasn't—the room shown on this sheet is still there. I have to assume the plans were deliberately altered to conceal the existence of the room."

"But by whom? And why?"

"I'm hoping perhaps your great-grandfather has other documents in his files that could tell us why."

"I'll start digging right away." Then a new expression came over her face, as if a thought had just struck her. "Wait a minute. Do you suppose that man I told you about, the creepy one that came bothering me last winter, asking to see the original plans for Lux . . . do you suppose he knew about this room?"

"Not very likely." Privately, Logan thought that it might be, but he saw no reason to alarm the architect. "Do you think we could spend a minute or two looking over the rest of these plans? Just in case there are any other, ah, surprises."

"Of course." And Pamela turned to the stack of rolled-up blueprints.

Twenty minutes of careful examination turned up some eccentric spaces in the original mansion— a lion cage, a gymnasium modeled after a Roman bath, an indoor skeet-shooting range—but nothing as puzzling as the secret room.

"How long do you think it will take to look through your great-grandfather's papers?" Logan asked as Pamela began to put away the blueprints.

"Not long. A day at the most."

"Then maybe we can talk about it over dinner tomorrow night?"

Another—warmer—smile lit up Pamela's features. "I'd like that."

She led the way out of the deeper recesses of the house to the parlor, where they had first met just a few days earlier. "I'm particularly interested in why the room was built in the first place and, even more, how it was meant to be accessed," Logan told her.

"Right-o."

Logan opened the door and stepped out into the gathering dusk of evening.

"See you tomorrow," she said.

He nodded. "Looking forward to it already."

As he made his way back to Lux—a little more cautiously than usual, given what happened the last time he'd driven this route—Logan thought about what he'd learned . . . and what he hadn't. He was fairly certain that, at some point early in the twentieth century, the think tank had discovered the secret room and realized it was a perfect location for doing work that was, if not officially unsanctioned, at least so unusual that it should be kept from the rest of the staff. A device to detect ghosts would certainly fall under that category.

A device to detect ghosts. His thoughts wandered back to the strange device and its output in milligauss and microtesla. He'd told Kim Mykolos that electromagnetic field generators, such as this device apparently sported, could be used to do just that. What he did not tell her was his other suspicion: that the radiator-like device they'd discovered on the machine might be an EVP recorder. Such devices were used to monitor electronic voice phenomena. To the unbelieving, such electronic noises were thought to be banal radio transmissions. Researchers into the uncanny, however, felt it possible EVP recorders could capture voices of the departed. More than that: when replayed, such voices might be capable of inducing activity of a—put euphemistically—paranormal nature.

If this were true, the machine might not just have been built to detect ghosts—but to *summon* them, as well.

Was this, in fact, the case? Had paranormal entities—intentionally or unintentionally—been unleashed on Lux? Was this behind the recent strange behaviors, the ominous atmosphere . . . the death of Strachey?

He turned in at the security gate and, in the distance, saw the vast bulk of the mansion rearing up, backlit against the sinking sun, neither inviting nor hostile; simply waiting.

. . . At that same moment, the device in the forgotten room powered up; its throaty baritone hummed into life; and, moments later, a shadowy figure moved quietly away and the few lights that had been turned on in the deserted West Wing went dark.

27

Stifling a yawn, Taylor Pettiford walked into Lux's elegant dining room and looked around a little blearily. The room had been set up in the standard breakfast arrangement: long, buffet-style counters along one wall, while the rest of the room was filled with the usual round tables covered in crisp white linen.

Pettiford got in line at the buffet, grabbing a tray and a plate and helping himself to his favorite breakfast: freshly squeezed orange juice, black coffee, a Gruyère and fines herbes omelet from the attendant at the omelet station, three sausage links from one steam tray, five rashers of bacon from another, and a croissant from the overstuffed bakery basket. Carefully balancing the alarming load, he glanced around the room for a place to sit. There, at a table in the near corner, he saw his friend and fellow sufferer, Ed Crandley. He maneuvered his way over and plopped down in the seat beside Crandley.

"Another day in the salt mines," he said.

Crandley, mouth full of *pain au chocolat,* mumbled a reply.

Pettiford took a sip of coffee, a mouthful of orange juice, and then froze. There, across the room, was Roger Carbon: the reason he was so tired this morning. Carbon was sitting with the thin, birdlike Laura Benedict, the quantum engineer who shared an office adjoining Carbon's. Pettiford believed Benedict didn't especially like Carbon, and guessed she'd sat with him simply because she was too kindhearted to see him eating alone.

Roger Carbon. Lux, as everyone knew, was the country's most prestigious think tank. When, fresh from U. Penn with a newly minted degree in psychology, Pettiford had won a year's position as an assistant at Lux, he felt like he'd just won the lottery.

How little he'd known.

Actually, he thought as he downed the first piece of bacon, that wasn't quite fair. Lux had a reason for its sterling reputation, and a lot of excellent scientists and researchers passed through its doors, producing high-quality work. And many interns and assistants had pretty decent experiences there as well. Take Ed Crandley, for example: he had a good enough gig, working for a fair-minded, well-regarded statistician.

It had been Pettiford's own bad luck to catch Roger Carbon for a boss.

Upon arriving at Lux, Pettiford had been unprepared for a man like Carbon: unprepared for his withering sarcasm, his impatience and impetuousness, his quickness to find fault and seeming blindness to a job well done. Instead of handing Pettiford interesting assignments, or trusting him to help with the raw research, Carbon treated him the way a marquee Ivy League professor might treat his lowliest research assistant. Just the night before, Pettiford had been up until 2 a.m., cross-checking bibliographic citations for Carbon's latest monograph.

Ah, well. Shit happens. Pettiford polished off his second strip of bacon, his mood improving as his thoughts turned to plans for the upcoming weekend. Half a dozen of the assistants were going to converge on a popular singles bar overlooking the Newport boat basin. Such an outing was a rare thing—the volume of work, coupled with the way Lux frowned on intermingling with the local townspeople—and it had taken Pettiford a fair amount of time to put it together, wheedling, cajoling, promising to buy the first two rounds.

"You're still in for Saturday night, right?" he asked Crandley, with a leer and a nudge.

"Oh, yeah."

"You know, I haven't been out of this place in six weeks. I think I'm getting cabin fever."

"That's because you didn't bring a car."

"The orientation literature urged us not to, and—"

There was a commotion on the far side of the dining room—a raised voice, a burst of animated talk—and Pettiford looked up. It was the historiographer, Dr. Wilcox. He was standing up, burly and easily six feet four, hands outstretched, his tablemates looking on.

Pettiford shrugged. In a place that took itself as seriously as Lux, Wilcox was an anomaly: a laid-back guy with a flair for melodrama, even at times a ham. No doubt he was entertaining the table with something out of his endless fund of stories and off-color jokes. Pettiford speared a sausage link and turned back to Crandley.

"It's a conspiracy," he said, picking up where he'd left off. "That's what it is. First, they situate this place just far enough from town that you can't reasonably walk in. Then they suggest—strongly—that you don't bring your own transportation. They don't pay us much—such an honor to be here, and all that—so we're not likely to have the dough for regular cab fares. Get the picture? We're indentured servants."

"This paranoia is something new," Crandley said. "Maybe you ought to have a skull session with your pal Dr. Carbon over there."

"Are you kidding? Carbon? That would be

the last straw." And Pettiford shuddered in mock horror.

Suddenly, there was another commotion from the far side of the room—this one much louder. Pettiford looked over quickly. It was Wilcox again. He was shouting something, and Pettiford could tell instantly that this was no joke, no amusing anecdote: the historiographer's eyes were so wide that all he could see was the whites, and the froth that flew from his mouth flecked his generous beard with foam. There were gasps around the room; people rose from their chairs; one or two made for the exit.

Through his surprise, Pettiford began to make out what Wilcox was shouting. "Get them out!" he cried. "Get them out of my head!"

Wilcox's tablemates were now gathering around him, speaking soothingly, urging him to sit down again. Several people from other tables— friends, acquaintances, Wilcox was a popular fellow—approached. Pettiford looked on, frozen in place, sausage halfway to his mouth. Now Wilcox fell silent, allowing himself to be led back to his seat. He sat down, then shook his head, like a horse trying to drive off a determined insect. There was a moment of stasis. And then, abruptly, he leapt to his feet again, roaring, his seat tumbling away behind him.

"Get them out!" he shouted. "They're too sharp—they hurt. *Get them out!*"

Once again, a small crowd gathered around, trying to calm him. Easily freeing himself, the big man spun around, crying and roaring in obvious torment. He was now scratching desperately at his ears and, to his horror, Pettiford could see even at this distance flesh shredding under the man's nails, the blood beginning to flow from long gashes.

Suddenly, Wilcox darted away from the table and—fists drumming at his ears—looked this way and that. For a moment, his gaze locked with Pettiford's, and the assistant felt a stab of fear. Then Wilcox turned toward the long row of tables on which breakfast had been laid out. Shouting *"Out of my head! Please, no more voices in my head!"* he rushed toward the buffet. The waiters standing in position behind the offerings backed away nervously as he approached.

Wilcox ran toward the tables so violently, fists still pounding at his head, that the impact almost toppled the closest one backward. Everyone in the dining room except the frozen Pettiford was now on his feet, some rushing toward Wilcox, others running in the opposite direction. From the corner of his eye, Pettiford saw someone speaking frantically into a house phone.

Bellowing out increasingly inarticulate cries, Wilcox looked up and down the table, eyes jittering and rolling in his head. Then he darted forward, once again shaking off the well-intentioned hands of friends trying to restrain him, and grasped the steam tray holding the bacon Pettiford had helped himself to, not five minutes earlier. Batting the tray away with one swipe of his meaty paw, bacon flying in all directions, Wilcox grabbed the two small cans of jellied cooking fuel that sat flaming in the panel beneath. He scooped up one of the cans in each hand, roaring.

As he looked on, Pettiford suddenly had a dreadful, chilling premonition of what was about to happen.

The room was full of alarmed cries, shouts of dismay. But for the moment, Dr. Wilcox himself went silent. And then—quite deliberately—he jammed one container of canned heat into each ear. An instant later, he became vocal again: only now, the shouts of torment had been replaced with shrieks of pain.

Everyone had abruptly fallen back in shock and disbelief. Even the security guards who had come running into the dining room faltered, struck dumb by what had just occurred. Wilcox was lurching back and forth, purple gel flaming from both ear canals, his sideburns and beard catching fire as the fuel dribbled toward his jaw. Screaming ever louder, he slashed this way and that, sending plates of artisanal breads, jams, and marmalade flying away from the tables.

And then Wilcox stopped again. Not the screaming—that was now continuous—but his physical movement. It seemed to Pettiford, for whom the scene had now abandoned any semblance of reality and morphed into nightmare, that the man had seen something that caught his attention. Wilcox lurched forward once more, ears and beard still afire, and stopped before an industrial four-slice toaster. Bellowing at the top of his lungs, he plunged a hand into one of the four slots; depressed the machine's toasting lever, powering its element; and then—with his free hand—grabbed a nearby pot of steaming coffee and poured it directly into the unit.

Flames; a blue arc of electricity that rose like a single-colored rainbow above the serving table; a universal, room-wide cry of shock and horror, overridden by a single, larynx-shredding ululation of pain—and then the convulsing form of Wilcox was obscured by a rising pall of smoke.

Above all the noise, a sudden thud sounded to Pettiford's left. Crandley had fainted.

28

As the afternoon slowly slid toward evening, Logan remained in his third-floor office, poring over books of secret knowledge; transcripts of paranormal encounters; and the writings of famous occultists and mystics: Helena Blavatsky, Edgar Cayce, Aleister Crowley. He had tried, with only some success, to blot out the shocking events he'd witnessed that morning. He had also avoided going downstairs for lunch, which under the circumstances was being served in a series of conference rooms: given the public nature of what had happened, he was sure that the conversation would be about nothing else. Wilcox had occupied the suite of rooms right next to his own. He'd only spoken with the man a few times, but he'd struck Logan as bluff, hearty, and an utterly grounded individual.

Out of my head, Wilcox had said. *Please, no more voices in my head.* Logan thought back to Strachey's transcript: *It follows me everywhere. It is with me. In the dark.* Different words—and yet, in a chilling way, similar.

Logan put down the book he was reading and wondered whether he should pause to look into Wilcox. But no: Wilcox, in stable but serious condition at Newport Hospital, suffering from both chemical and electrical burns, was raving, incoherent, unresponsive to questions from either doctors or psychiatrists. Better to continue the investigation at hand—and continue it as quickly as possible. If he could discover what lay behind Strachey's breakdown, then what happened to Wilcox—and what, to a far lesser degree, had happened to several others at Lux—might be more explainable.

He picked up the book again: a 1914 volume titled *Chronicles of the Risen Beyond.*

About fifteen minutes later, he came across a passage that stopped him cold. He read it again, and then again:

> The apparition, which had been summoned
> by a complex set of rituals which I will not
> describe here, was undoubtedly malignant.
> Those who had been present (I was not
> among them) spoke of a terrible stench that
> assaulted the nostrils; an odd thickening

of the atmosphere, as if one was within a compression chamber; and, most noticeably, the sense of a malefic presence—a hostile entity, angered at having been disturbed and wanting nothing more than to harm its disturbers. One member of the group collapsed outright; another began shouting incomprehensibly and had to be restrained. But the thing of greatest interest was that the presence, once roused, did not dissipate, but seemed to remain in the chamber where it had first appeared. Indeed, even now—thirty years after the original event—its presence has been attested to by nearly all who have frequented the chamber (there are not many who have willingly done so). This small group includes myself, and I write this to give assurances that—for whatever reason—the entity remains in the room where it was first summoned.

Logan put the book aside. He knew from personal experience that certain places—houses, cemeteries, deserted abbeys—could be home to evil presences: shadows of people or things who had once dwelled there. The more evil the person, the longer the aura tended to remain after death. Some might consider such places haunted; Logan himself did not like the term. But he could not deny the unsettling, even chilling sense of menace he had experienced upon first entering the forgotten room—a sense that had persisted, to one degree or another, ever since. In fact, even now, far from the West Wing, he felt uncharacteristically nervous and irritable.

He'd told Kim Mykolos that the electronic field generator built into the strange device might have been a mechanism for detecting paranormal phenomena. Ghosts. The heavily redacted lines of scientific inquiry he'd found in the Lux files helped lead to such a conclusion. Since the radiator-like assembly built into the other flank of the device appeared to be an EVP recorder, was it indeed possible Lux scientists had, in the 1930s, attempted to summon a spirit from beyond the grave—and succeeded?

Logan rose from his desk and began to pace the room slowly. *Chronicles of the Risen Beyond* and dozens of other books like it gave accounts of such entities being summoned against their will—and then remaining in the immediate vicinity, angry, malevolent, unwilling or unable to return to the void from which they had come.

Was this the case with Project Sin?

If such a thing had happened—if the scientists had succeeded, and perhaps gotten more than they bargained for—it would explain a lot of things: the abrupt cessation of work, the sealing of the room, the careful culling of Lux's files.

And then, what of Strachey? If a malign presence had persisted in the forgotten room all these years, his breaking into the space would have been like stumbling into an invisible hornet's nest. Was it possible this was what had caused . . .

Another thought struck Logan. He'd found the room unsealed, broken into; exactly when was uncertain, save that the plaster which plugged the hole had been fresh. Others at Lux had seen things, *done* things, most recently the tragic events of that very morning. Could the forgotten room have been a prison—and, now breached, could whatever was inside have escaped into the mansion at large?

He moved past the large, ornate window of his office, pondering the question. As he did so, he stopped abruptly, frozen in place. He stared out through the leaded panes, jaw going slack.

There, on the lawn far below, was the figure of his wife. She was wearing a yellow sundress and a wide-brimmed straw hat, with a bandanna tied—as was her style—loosely around its brim. She was squinting against the sun, smiling, one hand resting on a cocked hip in the characteristic pose he remembered so well, the other hand waving up at him. The ocean breezes caught at the dress, worried the sleeves and the hem.

"Kit," Logan whispered.

His mouth went dry and his heart began to race. He blinked, looked away a moment, then glanced once again out of the window.

His wife, Karen Davies Logan, was still there. She was still smiling, still beckoning, her silhouette framed by the angry breakers, her long shadow pushed back by the afternoon sun across the verdant green lawn. She opened her mouth now, and cupped her hands as if to call out, and he heard, or thought he heard, her voice: *Jeremy . . . Jeremy . . .*

He looked away again, counted to sixty. Then— slowly—he looked back through the window.

The figure was gone. And no surprise: Kit had been dead more than five years.

Logan stared out the window for a long moment. Then, shakily, he made his way to the desk and sat down again. Unbuttoning the top button of his shirt, he drew out the amulet that he always wore around his neck and began to stroke it unconsciously. Something was happening to him; something he did not care to explore, or even admit. It was more than just a case of nerves. He'd begun hearing strange, faint, disquieting music— the music of Strachey's study, of the forgotten room—even when he was nowhere near the West Wing. He had awoken in the middle of last night, certain that somebody had been whispering to him, but he'd been unable to recall what was said. Ever since waking, he'd felt poorly. And now, this . . .

He sat at his desk for another five minutes, breathing slowly, letting his heartbeat return to normal. And then he rose and left his chambers. Perhaps a bracing walk around the grounds would help restore him to better form.

He could only hope.

29

Kim Mykolos was so busy with a minute examination of what they had begun to call "the Machine" that she did not hear Jeremy Logan enter the forgotten room. When he softly cleared his throat, she swiveled around with a brief, sharp cry, almost dropping the video camera.

"My God!" she said. "You scared me to death!"

"Sorry," he replied, setting his ubiquitous duffel down on the nearby worktable.

Mykolos peered closely at Logan. His eyes looked a little puffy and red, as if he hadn't been sleeping well, and his movements weren't the usual quick, deliberate ones she'd already begun to expect

from him. He seemed preoccupied, even anxious—
also uncharacteristic. Perhaps he was upset about
the events in the dining room that morning; she
had not been there to see Dr. Wilcox, but she'd
certainly heard about it. If so, it was understand-
able: the whole place was on edge. But in her brief
acquaintance with Logan, she hadn't pegged him as
the excitable type. Quite the opposite—which was
a good thing, given his line of work.

"So," she said, "you got my message?"

He nodded. "What do you have to report?"

She turned back toward the Machine. Since
they had first begun analyzing it, Logan had managed to remove several more cover plates, and it
now sprouted nearly a dozen devices, large and
small, mostly metal, with the occasional piece of
rubber hosing or Bakelite knob, all remarkably
preserved in the almost-hermetic atmosphere of
the room. The process had reminded her of peeling back the layers of an onion—removing each
one simply revealed something else. They had not
tried turning the device on again since that first
examination.

Mykolos switched off the camera and walked
around to what she thought of as the business
end of the device: the narrow side closest to the
hanging metal suits. She pointed toward the two
labels, BEAM and FIELD, and to the attendant
rows of buttons, meters, and knobs arrayed above
each. "Something about those terms, 'beam' and
'field,' has been bugging me from the beginning,"

she said. "As if they were familiar somehow. Then, just last night, it hit me."

"What did?" Logan asked, moving closer.

"I realized there might be an analogue in computer science."

Logan's eyes drifted down toward the bank of controls. "Enlighten me."

She considered how best to explain. "In an object-oriented programming language like Java or C Sharp, you have—in the simplest of terms—two kinds of variables, local and global."

Logan nodded for her to continue.

"Local variables have a scope limited to an individual function, embedded within a larger program. When that function is called, the local variable is created on the fly; when the function ends, the local variable ceases to exist. On the other hand, a global variable can be seen by all functions in the program."

She paused.

"I'm waiting for the punch line," Logan said after a moment.

"Well, I'm no electrical engineer, but think about it. Beam and field. Local and global."

"So you're saying . . ." Logan frowned, considering. "You're saying the Machine has two modes of operation?"

"Exactly. A local mode, very specific and sharply directed: a beam. And a broader, more general mode. A field. And I believe I've studied these controls enough to test my theory."

Logan did not reply. He looked from the bank of controls to her and back again.

Mykolos reached down along the side of the housing, where the primary switches were located. She flipped on the power, waited five seconds, then followed it with the load switch. Then she straightened and returned to the main set of controls.

"I'll start with the beam mode," she said, "since it would seem to be the more confined of the two." She could feel the big machine trembling slightly beneath the palms of her hands. She bent over the beam controls, snapped on a toggle switch marked MOTIVATOR, then another marked ENGAGE. And then she moved her hand to the rotary dial, which was inscribed with the numbers 0 to 10. At present, it rested at the zero setting. Slowly, she turned the knob clockwise to the 1 position.

The trembling increased slightly.

She turned the knob to the 2 setting.

The VU meter came to life, its needle jiggling rightward a few degrees, straining like a dog at its leash.

She moved the switch to the 3 setting. A deep, throaty hum began to emerge from the bowels of the Machine.

All at once, two very strange things happened. To Kim, the room seemed to grow abruptly brighter—not from any one particular light source, but from all around, as if God had suddenly turned up the sun. A curious noise, halfway between the buzz of an insect and the drone of a melancholy choir, began to sound in her head . . . and then she was roughly pushed aside by Logan. With a quick twist of the wrist, he reset the dial to zero. Then he toggled the switches off, bent down beside the device's flank, and turned off first the load and then the power. And then he rose again and looked at her. There was a strange gleam in his eye that almost frightened her.

"Why . . . why did you do that?" she asked, recovering her breath.

"I don't know exactly what the purpose of this device is," Logan replied, "but I know one thing— it's dangerous. We can't just go around messing with knobs and yanking levers without understanding it better."

"But you brought me in here to analyze and experiment, and how can I—"

"That was before I realized certain things," he interrupted. "Look, Kim. I have to establish two ground rules."

She waited.

"First: no experimentation without first clearing it with me."

"That's a given. Why do you think I just called you in here?"

"I understand, and I appreciate it. I'm talking about going forward. And the second rule is that, whenever you're in this room—or even *near* this room—you need to wear this." And, rummaging in his duffel, he pulled out something, which he handed to Mykolos.

She took it up curiously. It was an amulet of some kind: a thin hoop made of metal, copper by the look of it, into which a web of finely spun netting had been woven. Set into the web were several items: a few strings of colored beads; a tiny fetish, apparently of bone; and, at the center, half the shell of a miniature nautilus, cut through longitudinally to reveal its spiral of ever-diminishing camerae.

"What is this?" she asked, turning it over in her hands.

"Something of my own invention. It's a synthesis of several religions and beliefs: the healing beads used by Santería *espiritistas;* certain African hex wards; the dream catcher of the Lakota." Picking it up by the leather laces tied to its left and right sides, he placed it around her neck.

"Let me guess," she said. "A *ghost* catcher."

"I wouldn't put it quite that way," Logan said in his normal voice. Something—perhaps handling the amulet itself—seemed to have calmed him. "I'd call it the paranormal version of a bulletproof vest. But I suppose that 'ghost catcher' is as good a term as any."

She tied the laces together, tucked it beneath the fabric of her blouse. The amulet was scratchy and uncomfortable, and she looked at him closely, not bothering to keep the speculation out of her expression. "You do realize this is seriously weird."

"Perhaps. But it's the product of many years of research into some very arcane arts. It's kept me safe and sane—more or less, anyway." He loosened his tie and opened his collar enough to show her he was wearing one, as well. "Tell me something. Do you enjoy working on this little mystery of ours?"

"You know that I do."

"In that case, consider this amulet the price of the dance." He looked around. "I'm feeling a little beat. Can we pick this up again tomorrow?"

Mykolos shrugged. "Sure."

"Thanks. And—thanks for *that*." With a forefinger, he pointed at the now-invisible amulet. Then he smiled slightly, turned, and quietly left the room.

30

Logan approached the building—just a few steps off Thames Street—with significant doubts. It was small, almost swallowed up by the surrounding edifices, and painted a dingy green. The lone window was covered by a curtain, and above it was a weather-beaten sign that read JOE'S RESTAURANT.

Joe's Restaurant? Logan stopped short, giving the place another once-over. There was no menu fixed beside the door; nothing to reassure him that he, in fact, was not about to endure a most disagreeable dining experience.

And then, from around the corner, Pamela Flood came into view. She was dressed simply, in a red-and-white striped blouse and capri pants, and she had a bottle of white wine tucked under one arm. Seeing Logan, she broke into a smile. "Glad you found the place okay."

He glanced back at the underwhelming facade. "Actually, I wasn't sure I had."

Pamela laughed delightedly. "You just wait and see."

She led the way into a tiny restaurant that held six tables, all but one occupied. Immediately, a middle-aged bearded man in torn dungarees came over. "Miss Flood!" he said. "Nice to see you."

"Joe," she said with a smile and a nod, handing him the bottle.

"Your table is ready and waiting." And the man led them to the lone empty table and helped them into their seats.

Logan looked around. The small space was sparsely furnished, with nothing but a few prize fish mounted on the walls. The other diners were obviously local; there wasn't a tourist in sight. *No surprise there,* he thought.

He realized that Pamela was speaking to him. He stopped his survey of the restaurant and looked back at her. "I'm sorry?"

"I was just saying you look a little weary," she said. "And distracted."

"Sorry about that. Long day."

The man named Joe came back and poured them both glasses of Pam's bottle of Pouilly-Fumé. Then he took a step back and looked from one to the other expectantly.

"Know what you want?" Pam asked him.

"But I haven't seen the menu yet," Logan replied.

She laughed again. "There's no menu at Joe's."

Seeing Logan's confusion, Joe waded in. "Only thing on the menu is fish," he said. "Caught local today, prepared to your specification."

"I see," Logan said. "What kind of fish, exactly?"

Joe looked skyward, assembling a mental list. "Black sea bass, cusk, fluke, haddock, mackerel, halibut, pollack, shad—"

"Okay," Logan interrupted lightly, chuckling. The headache that had been gathering around his temples all day seemed to be receding. He gestured toward Pam. "After you."

"Fillet of haddock, please, Joe," she said immediately. "Poached in a court bouillon."

"Very good." Joe turned back to Logan.

"You did say, prepared to my specification?" Logan asked.

"Broiled, grilled, steamed, seared, sautéed, fried, baked, blackened, breaded, meunière, bonne femme, Provençal." The man shrugged as if this was just the tip of the iceberg.

"I'll try the sea bass," Logan said. "Grilled."

"Thank you." And Joe turned away.

"Interesting place," Logan said. He took a sip of the wine, found it excellent.

"Best seafood in New England," Pam replied. "But you won't find it in any guidebook or Internet dining site. We Newporters keep it to ourselves."

Logan took another sip of wine. "Speaking of Newport, what projects are you working on at present?"

Pam didn't need any further encouragement. Immediately, she began describing not only the project she was currently engaged in—the conversion of a Thames Street cannery into condominiums—but also her dreams for a large-scale waterfront renovation that would balance the needs of local inhabitants, tourists, commerce, and the fishing industry. It was an ambitious and interesting plan, and as Logan listened the last vestiges of his headache melted away. Their fish arrived—Logan sampled his sea bass, decided it was perfectly prepared—and the talk shifted to himself and how he had fallen into the odd, self-developed profession of enigmalogist. Pam was not only a good talker but a good listener; she laughed easily, and her laugh was infectious; and it wasn't until Joe had taken away their plates (no desserts offered) and brought cups of fresh coffee that Logan realized they had finished their dinner without ever bringing up the subject that had supposedly brought them together this evening.

"Well?" he said, lifting his coffee cup.

"Well what?"

"Now I know all about you, and you know all about me. And I'm all ears."

"Oh. Yes." Pam smiled a little impishly. "I did some digging around this morning through my great-grandfather's papers."

"And?"

"And I found some references to your secret room."

Logan put down his cup. "You did?"

Pam nodded. "It was added to the mansion at the request of Edward Delaveaux. Not only that, but Delaveaux was very specific. He had precise measurements, building materials, and even the location within the main massing of the West Wing."

"Any explanation as to why, or what it was to be used for?"

"No. It seems my great-grandfather asked, but was never told. But then, Delaveaux was famously eccentric. You know about his mini Stonehenge, of course."

Logan nodded. "Any additional architectural plans for the room? Specific blueprints or elevations that might shed more light on things?"

"No, just some rough sketches. But here's the thing." And she leaned forward conspiratorially. *"I think I know how to get in."*

"What? You mean, how to access it?"

She nodded.

"How?"

Pam hesitated. "I can't tell you that."

"Can't? Or won't?"

Another hesitation. "Well, maybe a little of both. But in order to show you how to get in, I'm going to have to come out to Lux and do it in person."

"Oh, no. Sorry, but that's out of the question."

Pam looked at him searchingly. "Why?"

"Lux is famously reclusive. They're not going to want an outsider looking into this—especially at such a delicate time."

"But I'm *not* an outsider. I consulted extensively with Strachey on the redesign."

"That's the problem right there. Strachey—and what happened to him."

The table went silent for a moment. Pam poured cream into her coffee, stirred. "I'm not being coy here," she said. "I don't know enough to tell you *how* to do it. Some of my great-grandfather's notes on the room's construction are a little confusing. I need to see it with my own eyes in order for those notes to make sense."

"Olafson's not going to want to okay this. He made a big enough fuss when I asked for an assistant."

"Just tug on your forelock and look put out. Like you're doing right now. It's quite becoming. I'm sure it'll do the trick."

Logan paused, realized he was in fact playing with a lock of hair, and immediately let go. Pam giggled.

He shook his head. He couldn't help but admire this woman's intelligence and tenacity—not to mention attractiveness.

"Okay," he said. "No promises. But I'll give it a shot."

And when they parted outside the restaurant, he kissed her good night.

31

It was a few minutes after nine the following evening when a figure flitted across the moon-washed greensward that led down from Lux to the ocean. Reaching the deeper shadow of the mansion itself, the figure kept to the darkness of the bushes as it made its way along the rear facade to a small door with a single light beside it. The figure paused a moment, then rapped quietly on the door.

It was opened immediately by Jeremy Logan, who stepped out into the darkness and closed it behind him.

The figure—Pamela Flood—came closer. She held a small leather briefcase in one hand. "Okay. I followed your instructions. Now I feel like an actor in a bad spy film. Just what was it you wouldn't tell me over the phone?"

"Just this. After thinking about it some more, I realized Olafson would either say no to your presence here, or else announce that he'd have to take it up with the board."

"I told you, he knows I worked with Strachey. What's the problem?"

"I didn't mention it at dinner last night, but there's been another incident."

"Incident?"

"Never mind the details, but everyone's on edge. And Olafson's a company man. We need to move forward, and I don't want to waste time wresting permission out of him."

"They'll have a record of my passing the security gate. They'll know I didn't come in by the main entrance."

"Only if they compare both sets of records. You're here on my authorization—if anyone asks, I'll say we were looking over some blueprints." Logan opened the door. "Let's go. If we pass anybody, try to look as if you belong here."

"Easier said than done."

Logan led the way down a narrow hallway, around a corner, along a dimly lit gallery, and into the central first-floor corridor. They made their way westward, Pamela clutching her briefcase.

A door opened in the corridor and somebody emerged—Terence McCarty, the linguist who'd told Logan he'd heard voices urging him to walk into the sea. He looked from Logan to Pamela and back again, a puzzled frown coming over his face. But Logan just nodded and continued walking down the passage. He could sense McCarty's eyes on his back. After a moment, he heard the man's footsteps, muffled by the carpeting, moving away in the other direction.

After what seemed an eternity, they reached the decorative doors at the end of the corridor. Logan stopped and looked back over his shoulder with what he hoped was a casual gesture. The long hallway was empty. Quickly, he unlocked the doors, ushered Pamela past the velvet ropes and through the doorway into the vestibule beyond.

When Logan closed the doors behind them, darkness immediately descended. He pulled two small flashlights from his pocket, turned one on, and offered the other to Pamela. "Be careful," he said. "There's stuff everywhere."

"I'm an architect, remember? I'm used to construction sites."

Carefully, Logan led the way down rubble-strewn passages and half-finished chambers to the staircase. Ascending it, he continued along the dim, tunnel-like lateral corridor A. Ahead, a faint glow was now visible.

Logan stopped at the tarp wall with the warning placard. Strong yellow light came through the tear in the rough material.

"Remember," he said. "You aren't to speak of this to anyone."

"Cross my heart."

Raising the tarp, Logan ushered her through the rude doorway and into the secret room. Kim was there, standing on the far side of the Machine. She looked at them.

"This is Kim Mykolos," Logan told Pamela. "She was Dr. Strachey's assistant."

"We've met," Kim said.

"I've told Kim why you're here," Logan went on. But Pamela had already stepped inside and was looking around.

"My God," she murmured after a moment. "What is all this?"

"That's our problem," Logan said. "Yours is to find the front door."

"Right. Right." She looked around for another moment, as if unable to tear herself away from the bizarre sight. Then she stepped toward the worktable, put her briefcase on it, opened it, and removed some paperwork: old letters, diagrams, and what looked to Logan like a few pencil sketches. Picking up each sheet in turn, Pamela studied it a moment, then glanced around the room, as if to orient herself. The process took about five minutes. Kim looked on silently, arms crossed, an unreadable expression on her face.

Finally, putting the last sheet back on the worktable, Pamela gave the room another careful scrutiny: walls, ceiling, floor, furnishings, equipment. As she did so, a smile slowly formed on her face.

She turned back to her briefcase, pulled out a notepad and a pencil. "We need to go upstairs," she said, picking up one of the papers.

"Why?" Logan asked, surprised.

"Light the way for me, will you? I won't have a free hand." And she pulled something else out of her briefcase: a small device, encased in a protective housing of bright yellow rubber, with a small backlit display and half a dozen buttons.

"What's that?" Logan asked.

"Laser distance measurer." And, holding it up, Pamela gestured in the direction of the improvised doorway.

The three made their way along the unfinished hallway, heading in the direction of the staircase. They made slow progress, Pamela stopping several times to measure distances with the handheld device and make notations on her pad. Reaching the staircase at last, they ascended to the third floor. Logan had not been here before and he shone his flashlight around in curiosity. The crews had not yet reached here—at least, the part of the floor not devoted to Delaveaux's disquieting henge of standing stones—and it was more or less intact. There was no furniture or equipment of any kind—it had obviously been removed in preparation for the renovation—and the old, richly textured wallpaper was frequently defaced by scrawled notations in white marker, no doubt indicating where demolition would take place.

Their progress was even slower here, as Pamela took frequent readings with the measuring device and labored over her notepad. Glancing at the pad, Logan saw that the architect had made remarkably careful sketches of both the second and third floor, and that she now seemed at pains to accurately overlay the third floor onto the second. Kim watched the proceedings from a few paces back. She had not said a word, and Logan sensed—for what reason he did not know—that there was some tension between the two women.

They had made their way across a landing, down a short passage, through two large chambers stripped of all furnishings, and into a larger hallway, before Pamela finally came to a stop. "There," she said, pointing to a door on the right.

Logan tried it. The door was locked.

A moment of consternation passed before he thought to try the key that unlocked the main doors to the West Wing. It turned in the lock, and he opened the door.

Beyond, the shadow of his flashlight revealed what had once evidently been a storeroom. There were no windows, since the room was situated well within the massing of the wing, and a few old boxes sat in a far corner, covered in dust. In the very center of the room—bizarrely—stood one of the large, marble Solomonic columns, with the familiar corkscrew pattern, that were an omnipresent feature in the architecture of Lux. It must, Logan realized, be a load-bearing structure, and tucking it away within a storage room was as good a way as any of concealing it.

Now Pamela slipped the notepad and distance measurer into a pocket, removed her flashlight, and approached the column. She examined it closely, then placed both hands on it, pressing here, feeling there. After several moments, there was an audible click.

Pamela turned toward Logan. "Your front door."

He looked at her in confusion. "What are you talking about?"

"*Ecce signum.*" And, raising her hands toward the column again, she opened it the same way someone might open an armoire.

"*Tu es mira,*" Logan murmured in turn, shining his flashlight toward the column in astonishment.

It was not—as he'd expected—a load-bearing member that stretched from foundation to roof. Nor was it made of marble. Instead, it appeared to be of metal, its exterior painted to resemble marble. Its two curved, full-height doors, hinges cleverly disguised, opened onto a hollow vertical cylinder with a round floor and a large wheel, such as one might find on the hatch of a naval vessel, set into the rear wall.

Pamela broke the moment of paralysis by stepping inside, shining her flashlight around, then motioning for the other two to approach.

Logan did so, stepping a little gingerly into the hollow column. A moment later, Kim did the same. There was barely room for all three.

Grasping small metal knobs on the insides of the two curved doors, Pamela pulled them tightly shut. The space became a closed cylinder again. Then she undogged a retaining bolt on the winch and gave it a turn.

An odd feeling came over Logan. And then he

realized what was happening: the "column" was descending through the floor in a gentle, spiral motion.

"It operates by weight," Pamela explained.

Sixty seconds later, their descent was stopped by a gentle bump. Pamela opened the doors again to reveal the brilliant white light of the forgotten room. She stepped out, Logan and Kim following.

The column had come to rest in the empty section of the room between the Machine and the back wall, close to where roman numerals had been etched into the floor. Pamela shut the doors again and pressed an almost invisible button on the column's flank. It began to ascend again, spiraling back up into the ceiling. Watching it, Logan realized that, in this case, the spiral design of the column was not just decorative; it operated in the manner of a corkscrew, working its way back up into the third-floor storeroom. When it stopped, it was flush with the ceiling: reduced to nothing more than the round disc with decorative chasing that Logan had always assumed covered a hole left over from a previously installed chandelier.

He stared at the ceiling for a minute. Then he turned to Pamela. "You must have known about this in advance," he said. "You can't have figured it all out just now."

Pamela laughed. "You're right."

"Well, then why the hell didn't you say something?"

"Because I wasn't sure. I came across plans for just such a device among my great-grandfather's papers. But they weren't filed with the Dark Gables documents, so I had no way of knowing whether or not it was Delaveaux who implemented them. That's why I needed to see this wing—and this room—to be sure."

"So how do we bring it back down again?" Kim asked.

"I don't know," Pamela told her. "No doubt there's a retractor, hidden away somewhere around here, probably spring-loaded as it winds down into the room."

Logan looked back again at the ceiling. He shook his head. To think that the answer had been there, all this time, literally right above their heads. Just another puzzle of the forgotten room.

"Amazing," he said. "Thank you. Pam, you've just earned yourself the best dinner in Newport."

"We already had the best dinner," she replied. "Joe's, remember?"

"The most expensive dinner, then." And he squeezed her hand. Kim, he noted, was watching them silently.

"Come on," he told Pamela, motioning toward her briefcase. "Get your things together and I'll see you to your car."

32

When he stepped back into the forgotten room, Kim Mykolos was standing on a stepladder she'd appropriated from some nearby work space, examining the decorative circle in the ceiling.

"I'd never in a million years have guessed the door to this room would be some kind of gravity-fed elevator," she told him. "Disguised as a structural column. I have to hand it to old Pamela."

"Is there some problem between you two?" Logan asked her.

Kim waited a moment before answering. "I didn't really like the way she interacted with Willard. Early on, anyway, when they were first dis-

cussing ideas for revising the wing. I got this feeling
that she was the architect, and he was only a computer scientist, and any design suggestions coming from him had to be taken with a huge grain of
salt."

So that's it? Logan asked himself. *Still protective of her old mentor . . . despite what Carbon's
been insinuating?*

"Amazing," Kim breathed, still examining the
circle that formed the base of the elevator.

Logan had to admit that it was. Perhaps, in
some way, this was a failure of his own. All this
time, he'd been thinking in two dimensions . . . forgetting that there was also a Z axis to be considered. It had been there all this time, in that dusty
room just overhead. . . .

Dust.

Suddenly, a thought hit him—a chilling thought
that arrived with a visceral punch.

"Kim," he said abruptly.

Hearing something in his tone, she turned
toward him immediately. "What is it?"

As she descended the stepladder, he scooped
up one of the flashlights, tossed the other to her.
"Come with me."

By the yellow beam of the lights, Logan retraced
the journey they had just made, up the stairs and
through the abandoned rooms of the third floor.
It was still fresh in his memory, and the path was
relatively easy to retrace. Within five minutes they
were back before the door to the storage room.
Logan unlocked it again, and—instead of stepping

in—probed the room with his light. There, in the center, was the large, decorative column. There, against the far walls, were the old boxes, covered in their mantle of dust.

Now he turned his light to the floor—to the space between the doorway and the column. It was thickly covered in overlapping layers of footprints.

Following his beam, Kim caught her breath. "My God," she said in a voice so low it was almost a whisper.

"I'd been so caught up in what Pam was doing, I hadn't noticed it earlier."

"What does it mean?"

Logan stepped into the room—to the far left, to avoid the herd path of footsteps—then knelt to examine them. There were a great many; too many to make out any individual prints. One thing he could tell, though—they were fresh.

He stood up again. "Somebody has been this way dozens of times," he said.

"How recently?"

"Very."

Now he walked up to the column itself. Reconstructing Pamela's actions from memory, he opened the two matching doors leading into the elevator itself. His beam swept the circular floor. This, too, was covered with the dust of multiple overlapping footsteps.

"But there's no dust in the room below," he said, almost to himself. "Barely a speck."

"I don't understand," Kim said.

In response, Logan stepped inside, then beckoned her to follow. Closing the doors, he undogged the bolt just as Pamela had done, gave the winch a turn, and the mechanism spiraled slowly down into the room beneath.

Logan opened the doors, stepped out, waited for Kim to do the same, then sent the device back up to the floor above. And then he examined the floor. There were faint tracings of dust from their own shoes—but nothing more.

He took in a deep breath. "It seems," he said, "that this room hasn't been abandoned for decades, after all. Somebody has been accessing it—very recently, too—apparently on a regular basis."

"You mean, all these years? Is it possible the room was never forgotten to begin with?"

"No. I believe the room was rediscovered—and not that long ago."

Kim stopped, taking this in. "Accessed on a regular basis. Do you mean, studying the room, as we've been doing? Studying the Machine?"

"Studying it . . . or *using* it." Logan looked around. "Isn't it surprising, when you think of it, that there are no books anywhere? No papers, files, notes? I'd always assumed the files had been removed; sealed away; or, God forbid, burned when the project was halted. But I'll bet if we brought a forensic analysis team in here, they'd discover that the paperwork had been taken out quite recently. Removed, with care taken to make the room look spotless, unused. But that same care wasn't taken with the third-floor entrance—they never guessed we'd find *that*." He glanced around—at the worktable, the empty file cabinet, the shelves without books. "There's only one logical conclusion: somebody, or some group, has begun to resurrect the old, abandoned research. And that same somebody stripped this room of evidence when Strachey and his workmen's approach threatened to expose its existence."

"You're scaring me," Kim said. "Because . . ."

"Because you're wondering if they stopped at just emptying the room," Logan said grimly. "You're wondering if they also stopped Strachey."

Kim did not answer this. She took a seat on the lowest tread of the stepladder and looked down at her hands.

"There's another possibility," Logan said after a long silence. "Dr. Strachey himself first discovered this room. He could have begun resurrecting the research himself. Maybe that's why he dismissed all the workers so summarily—he wanted time alone with it."

"Unlikely," Kim said. She was looking up now; looking at Logan directly. "Dr. Strachey was terrible with anything mechanical. He'd have been lost in here. Besides, from what you've told me, it seems he'd just discovered the room—or, at least, broken through its wall—before he . . ." She didn't finish.

"Yes. I know he wasn't good at mechanical things. But, Kim, that doesn't mean he didn't tinker with the Machine." *And,* he thought to himself, *become haunted by whatever he accidentally released . . . until he was driven insane.*

The room settled into a tense silence: Kim sitting on the stepladder, Logan leaning against the worktable, gazing off at nothing. Then, suddenly, he pushed himself to his feet. Quickly, he began moving along the walls, probing, prodding.

"What are you doing?" Kim asked.

"I think we've been looking for answers the wrong way," Logan replied as he continued probing at the walls. "We've approached this place as if it's a normal room. But it's not—and, given its contents, I should have guessed as much. But it took Pam's discovery to make me realize."

For a moment, Kim just watched Logan as his fingers moved around the walls, searching for a hidden seam, concealed button, anything that might yield up additional secrets. And then, wordlessly, she joined in, examining first the far wall, then the floor, and then the large central instrument itself.

Moments later, Logan joined in her examination of the Machine. And within a minute, he achieved success: pressing at the polished wood, just below the two manufacturer's placards, activated a hidden detent. With a click, a narrow, spring-loaded tray slid out into view. It seemed to be lined in lead.

"Kim," he said. "Take a look at this."

She came around from the far side of the Machine and knelt beside him. He slid his find back into the closed position—the rectangular lines of its front panel becoming totally obscured by the surrounding wood grain in the process—and then, with a press of his fingers, opened it again.

"Puzzles within puzzles," Logan murmured.

Inside the compartment were four smaller trays. Two were empty, while the others held identical devices. They were small, with a profusion of wires—some yellow, others brown—and contained three vacuum tubes each. Something about them looked familiar to Logan, but exactly what he couldn't determine. His headache had returned with a vengeance, and he was having difficulty in both concentrating and in ignoring the music that always seemed to sound in his head when he was near the forgotten room.

"Any idea what their function might be?" he asked.

"No. They appear to be receivers of some kind. But then again, maybe they're transmitters. The technology is very old."

Logan stared at the devices. There *was* something maddeningly familiar about them . . . and then, quite suddenly, it came to him.

He reared back, almost as if from a galvanic shock. *Oh, my God . . .*

Heedless, Kim carefully removed one of the devices—unlike the rest of the room, it was coated in a thin mantle of dust—and peered at it. "One way to find out what it does. Fire up the Machine and see what happens."

Logan looked at her blankly for a moment before replying. "I'm sorry?"

"Clearly, its function is related to the central machine—otherwise, why would it be stored in here? If we activate the Machine, perhaps I could find a way to connect this device to the field generator or the EVP recorder."

"No," Logan said.

Kim stood. "We could speculate and theorize until we're blue in the face. At some point, we're going to have to do some actual experimentation. I say, turn it on and let's observe the result. Otherwise, I've got—"

"*No!*" Logan said. He too was on his feet now, and—as if from far away—he realized he was shouting. "We're not going to do that!"

An abrupt silence fell over the room. Logan raised a hand, trembling slightly, to his temple. His headache had spiked abruptly.

"I was about to say," Kim went on, quietly and evenly, "that otherwise, I've got work—*real* work—back in my office."

Logan took a deep breath. He needed time, time alone, to think this through. "That's probably a good idea," he said quietly. "Let's call it a night."

Kim replaced the device into its tray and Logan hastily closed the drawer. Then, turning out the lights and closing the tarp behind them, they made their way out of the West Wing in silence.

33

"Let me get this straight," Olafson said. "You let Ms. Flood into the secret room."

Logan nodded. It was the following morning, and they were standing in the parlor of Willard Strachey's set of third-floor rooms. The curtains were drawn wide, yet the space remained dim: a large tropical depression had formed over Bermuda, and already clouds were starting to veil the coast as far north as New Hampshire.

"And this was *after* telling her about the room—*and* about Will Strachey—when you'd been explicitly told of the need for discretion." The director's face looked pinched, his lips pursed into an expression of extreme disapproval.

"I needed information, and she was the obvious candidate. Look. She's the great-granddaughter of Dark Gables's architect. She worked with Strachey on the plans for the redesign. She refused to help unless I gave her physical access to the room."

"My God, man! Didn't it occur to you that she was just using you, leveraging this request of yours as a way of getting into the room?"

Logan hesitated a moment. This had, in fact, not occurred to him. But he dismissed it as being alarmist.

Olafson shook his head. "I don't know, Jeremy. You've changed since you were last here. Maybe it's all the press you've received. I thought I could trust your circumspection in this matter. But you've far exceeded your brief, and I'm afraid—"

"It's a good thing I did," Logan interrupted. "Because I've made some discoveries. Troubling discoveries."

At this, Olafson fell silent. After a moment, he motioned for Logan to continue.

"We've discovered the doorway to the room—if you can call it a doorway. I'd have never found it if it weren't for Pam Flood." Briefly, Logan sketched out how the room was accessed by a manually operated elevator concealed in the storeroom overhead. "And on the heels of that discovery, I learned something else—that a person or persons unknown have begun making use of the room . . . and recently."

A shocked look came over Olafson's face. Unconsciously, his fingers went to the knot of his tie, smoothing it down against the crisp white of his shirt. "How recently?"

"Hard to say exactly. A few months, perhaps. Half a year. But, Gregory—*they knew we were coming.* That's why the room was spotless. That's why all the books and files had been removed. I think they've resurrected the work that was shut down three quarters of a century before. Resurrected it—and *refined* it."

"Could it have been Will Strachey himself?" Olafson asked. "I mean, he was the one who ordered the work stopped."

"I wondered that myself. In hindsight, it hardly seems likely, since he was in charge of the reconstruction project and could have found a subtler way to keep the room secret. But the fact is I have proof it wasn't Strachey."

"Proof," the director repeated.

Logan nodded. Then he reached into the pocket of his jacket, pulled out one of the devices they had discovered in the hidden tray the night before, and held it out. Olafson reached for it tentatively, as if it might bite. He turned it over in his hands once or twice, then handed it back with a look of mute inquiry.

Logan placed it on a side table. Then he turned toward Strachey's cathedral-style antique radio, picked it up, opened its back, and showed it to the director. "Remember my asking whether Lux ever did any radio research?" he asked. "Look inside."

Olafson peered in. For a moment, a confused

expression came over his face. Then his eyes widened as he made the connection. He looked over at the device sitting on the side table.

"That's right," Logan said. "They're the same—except that the one in the radio has been enhanced, updated, with an integrated circuit instead of vacuum tubes and a twenty-first-century battery instead of electric power. If you reach into the radio and turn the device over, you'll see for yourself. They've been installed on the underside—no doubt to be better concealed."

Olafson took a step back. "What does it mean?"

"I'll tell you," Logan said. "But I don't think you'll like it."

When the director did not reply, he picked the unit off the side table and went on. "Last night, while investigating the secret room, I found a holding tray for four devices just like this. Two were missing." He patted the radio. "One of those is in here."

"But *why*?"

"I don't know what the devices do, exactly. But I think that whoever was accessing the secret room put one into the radio and, knowing Strachey's penchant for antiques, gave it to him as a present. Also, knowing of Strachey's mechanical incompetence, they felt confident he'd never mess with the radio's innards, try to get it to work. Because the ironic fact is that it *did* work—at least, in the way our unknown friends meant it to."

"You don't mean . . ." and Olafson went silent.

"Yes." Logan waggled the device in his hand back and forth—gently. "I think one of these was used to prevent Strachey from continuing his work in the West Wing."

"And you think that thing is responsible for what happened to him?"

Logan nodded. "As I said, I don't know how it works—not yet. But, yes, I think it caused Willard Strachey's psychotic break." He slipped the device back into his jacket.

"That means we have a murderer here at Lux," Olafson said.

"Clearly, someone who believes the technology in that room is valuable enough to kill for." Logan closed the back of the radio and replaced it on its shelf. "My guess is that whoever is responsible was close to completing their research. They knew Strachey's demolition crews were only days away from uncovering the room. But they still needed to finish their work. Nothing else makes sense. If they weren't so close, why get rid of Strachey like that? No, they figured they needed just the amount of time it would take for Lux to recover from Strachey's death and assign somebody else to the renovation. By then, their research would be done and they'd be gone. They hadn't counted on . . ." And here he went silent.

"They hadn't counted on you," Olafson finished the sentence for him.

"When they learned I was here, this person—or people—must have guessed why. I believe it was then that the room was emptied of its contents—at least, those that were movable." Logan ran a hand through his hair. "Once or twice, those first nights examining the room, I felt certain there was someone nearby, listening, watching. No doubt it was the killer, trying to determine whether or not I'd discovered the space."

"If you're right," Olafson said after a moment, "then shouldn't we stake out the room? Have it guarded, twenty-four hours a day?"

"I considered that. It wouldn't work. As I said, the person, or people, know we've discovered the room. They would find a way, *some* way, to continue using its technology."

Olafson did not reply to this.

"What I can't understand is how this person learned about the old research. Obviously it's not one of the original scientists—they must all be deceased by now. My guess is that it's somebody at Lux who's been snooping around the files in archive two and came across the redacted Project Sin files accidentally."

"That's not possible," Olafson said in an odd voice. "First of all, I doubt there are any relevant redacted files in archive two. Even if there were, nobody could get access to them. Fellows are only allowed to file, or remove, folders directly related to their own work—we're very careful about that."

Over the course of the conversation, a parade of emotions had marched across the director's face: first anger, then disbelief, then shock, and now something that not even Logan could read. Something in it alarmed him. "What is it, Gregory?" he asked.

Slowly and carefully, like an old man, Olafson gripped the arms of a nearby chair, then lowered himself into it. "There's something I need to tell you, Jeremy," he said in a solemn voice. "If I do, I'll be breaking a solemn vow that's held for many decades. But I think you need to know. You need to know, but I don't know how to begin."

Logan took a seat across from the director. "Take your time," he said.

Then he waited, in the dim light of the parlor, for Olafson to speak.

34

After a few minutes, Olafson shifted in his chair, cleared his throat.

"Several days ago," he began, "you asked me if I'd known the forgotten room existed, or what it might have been used for. I told you I didn't know." Olafson hesitated again. "That's not true. At least, not precisely true."

All of a sudden, the director—whose eyes had been roaming the room as he spoke—met Logan's. "There's something you have to understand. When you showed up here in answer to my summons, I was in shock. I was completely overwhelmed by what had happened to Will Strachey—by what he'd done. There were things you said, things you asked me, that I didn't fully absorb at the time. If I *had* absorbed them, I might have forbidden you to examine that room. But I've had time now to reflect on what you've said. And I've had time to . . . remember."

Watching Olafson, Logan was suddenly reminded of their conversation in the director's office, before they'd gone down to dinner, when he'd told Olafson about Project Sin and the missing files, and of his suspicion that the forgotten room had been the location of some mysterious research. At the time, a look had come across the director's face: the look of a man who'd just come to a realization.

"Go on," Logan said.

"The fact is, you're quite right, Jeremy—more right than you know. Secret work was going on here in the late twenties and early thirties. I can't tell you the nature of that work, because I don't know what it was. But I know knowledge of the work was confined to just the small group of scientists undertaking it—and the director of Lux at that time. I do know the work was being conducted in an undisclosed location here, on the Lux campus. I think it's safe to assume that location was the secret room that you—and, I fear, poor Will—discovered."

The director rubbed absently at his chin. "I don't know any details. What I do know is that those few who knew about the work held out great hope for it; that it would prove to be a true boon to mankind. But as the nineteen thirties progressed, the mood of hope turned to one of concern. You know, of course, that Lux's charter prevents it from undertaking any research that could possibly be used to harm humanity."

Logan nodded. "So I assume this secret research began to lead in that direction."

"Yes. Or at least, the *promise* of that direction was there . . . should people have decided to act upon it."

"So the research was abandoned, permanently."

"Abandoned, yes. But not permanently. A decision was made to mothball the work—to seal it away, in essence—until such time when it could be reexamined, and a determination made as to whether technology had sufficiently advanced so the work could be accomplished *in such a way that it couldn't be retasked to harm humanity.*"

"A scientific time capsule," Logan said.

"In effect. To be reopened—or, at least, reconsidered—one hundred years later."

"And, no doubt, all paperwork, journals, and notes on the project were moved from Lux's central files to the forgotten room itself. That would account for the gaps in the record."

"Most likely. And then the room itself was sealed."

"No." Logan rose to his feet and began pacing. "I don't think it needed to be sealed. The only entrance was hidden inside a column in a disused storage room on the floor above. The secret room was, to all intents and purposes, *already* sealed off."

"In any case," Olafson went on, "the few scientists who had worked on the project took solemn oaths of secrecy and left Lux within months of the project going black. That much I know."

"What else can you tell me?"

"Not much. In my office there's a safe—a special safe. It contains a sealed dossier. In 2035, that dossier is to be opened, and a panel convened to determine whether the old research can be safely reactivated. When I took this position eighteen years ago, I was told—among various other things—about the existence of this dossier. It is the duty of each outgoing director of Lux, in fact, to brief the incoming director on it, and to explain the importance both of the dossier itself and of the year 2035."

"Passed down, in secret, from one to the next. The same way an outgoing president briefs the new one on intelligence matters, hands over the nuclear football."

Olafson grimaced. "I can't say I like the allusion, although that's it in a nutshell. But you see, Jeremy, I am *four directors removed* from the events that took place here in the midthirties. I was told about the secret work, about the dossier in the private safe, during the course of a five-minute conversation years ago. By the time Will killed himself,

I'd forgotten all about it—or, I suppose, more accurately, it never occurred to me that it might have any bearing on recent events."

"No," Logan said. "No, of course not."

"That's why I had no problem sanctioning your exploration of that room—and also why I didn't link its existence with Will's death. But given what you've discovered, given that device you just showed me . . . I don't think there's any doubt."

"I agree." Logan stopped pacing. "So let's go."

The director frowned in confusion. "I'm sorry?"

"Let's open the safe."

"You can't be serious."

"I'm perfectly serious."

"You don't understand." Now it was Olafson's turn to stand, alarm on his face. "By telling you this, I've already broken my oath as director of Lux."

"But the answers we need are in there, and—"

"Jeremy. I've told you this, I've voiced what no director has since 1935, to let you know that you're right. Secret work, dangerous work, was being done here, no doubt within the secret room. You're close to an answer now—I know it. Now I've provided you with the confirmation you need to keep you on the right course."

Logan, almost dazed by this sudden refusal coming on the heels of such an unexpected revelation, struggled with conflicting emotions. "Greg. It's your moral and ethical duty to show me the contents of that dossier."

Olafson shook his head almost sadly. "No. I've

already broken my oath as director. I'm sorry, but I can't compound that by breaking my promise to the Lux charter."

"Then more people are going to die," Logan said quietly.

35

It was one p.m. by the time Logan returned to his office cum apartment on the third floor. He'd spent the latter part of the morning restlessly wandering the grounds under a gunmetal sky, the violent beating of the Atlantic against the rocks a counterpoint to his own inner frustration. He'd considered, and then dismissed, a dozen ways to wheedle, cajole, or threaten Olafson into opening his private safe. In the end, he'd put the question aside and determined to get back to work, at least for the time being. Lunch was now in full swing, but the last thing he felt was hungry.

He looked around the office, then picked up the phone and dialed Kim's extension.

"Mykolos," came the reply.

"Kim? It's Jeremy."

There was a brief pause. "Yes?"

"I wanted to apologize for my outburst last night. It was uncalled for, and you didn't deserve to be on the receiving end."

"Apology accepted—if you'll explain what caused it."

Logan sank into the chair behind his desk. "I haven't been feeling myself lately."

"Yeah, you've been looking a little peaked, to say the least. But I'm guessing it's more than that."

"You're right." He hesitated. "Kim, those devices we found in the secret room last night—I think one of them was the cause of Strachey's death."

A sharp intake of breath. "Are you sure?"

"Almost positive."

"How?"

"You mean, what do they do? I don't know. But I do know this: it was Strachey's discovery of the room that indirectly led to his death."

"Jesus." There was a silence in which Logan could practically hear the gears turning in Mykolos's head. "Um, I almost don't want to ask this, but . . . if that's the case, why are we still alive? Why haven't we wigged out and killed ourselves, too? I mean, we've been messing around in that room, as well."

Logan had been afraid she would ask this question. He'd been wondering the same thing. He decided to give her the easier, less alarming reply. "I don't think the killer thought we'd discover the secret room—at least, not so quickly. But now that we have, and now that Olafson knows what's going on—yes, he does—I think the killer has gone to ground. But if you'd rather back off from the assignment, I understand completely—"

"No. No *way*. But you have to let me *do* something, for a change."

"Agreed. And that's the second reason for this call. I want you to go ahead and research one of the devices we found last night. Pull it apart, put an oscilloscope to it, reverse engineer it. Try to find out what makes it tick, what its relationship is to the Machine. I know it's a job and a half—after all, somebody removed all the operating manuals. But you're much better suited to it than I am. And, Kim—you must be extremely, extremely careful. Document everything with the camcorder. Work slowly. Treat the thing as if it were a live bomb."

"Don't worry, I'll be careful. In fact, I've had some ideas about that."

"Like what?"

"You know those hulking suits, hanging from the back wall of the room? The ones that look almost like armor?"

"Yes?"

"Well, I think they *are* armor. I think the operators of the Machine put those on before firing it up."

In retrospect, it seemed so obvious. "What led you to that conclusion?"

"Did you ever look at one up close? See the wire mesh set into the glass of the visor?"

"I noticed, yes."

"Well, it got me thinking. About microwaves."

"I'm sorry?"

"Didn't you ever look at a microwave that was heating something, stare in at the steaming food, and wonder why you weren't getting cooked along with it?"

"I always assumed there was some kind of barrier."

"Exactly. The reason you weren't harmed by the energy inside the microwave—one of the reasons, anyway—is the wire mesh in the faceplate of the window. It acts as a Faraday cage."

"A what?"

"A Faraday cage. An enclosure made of a conductive mesh that ensures the electrical voltage on both sides remains constant. It also blocks certain electromagnetic radiation, such as radio waves. Anyway, I think those suits act like reverse Faraday cages, keeping the radiation—and I'm sure we're dealing with some kind of radiation here—*out,* rather than in."

Logan considered Kim's words. "I'm just a historian. Still, it sounds plausible. I'll feel better knowing you're protected. But be cautious nonetheless. And keep the power level to a minimum, please: you may be wearing a Faraday cage, or whatever, but the rest of us here won't be."

"It's a deal. I've got plans tonight, but I'll get started first thing in the morning. I'll let you know how I make out."

Logan hung up the phone and was about to turn away when he noticed that the small red message light on its base was blinking. He picked up the phone again and dialed voice mail.

There was a single message. "Jeremy? It's Pam. Listen, I'm really looking forward to our dinner this evening. And, hey, I've been digging deeper into my great-grandfather's papers, and you won't *believe* what I've found." A pause. "Just kidding! I haven't found anything else. But I did find the business card of that creepo who showed up on my doorstep last winter. Turns out I hadn't thrown it away after all. I'll bring it with me. Anyway, the reservation for Sub Rosa is at nine thirty. I know it's kind of late, but if I hadn't been a local, we wouldn't have gotten in at all. It's a great place, you'll love it. And after dinner, maybe we can have coffee at my place?" A shy laugh. "So why don't you pick me up at quarter after, okay? I'll see you then." A click as the phone went dead.

As Logan hung up the phone a second time and rose from his desk, the world rocked briefly around him. He grabbed for the chair back in order to steady himself.

Over the past forty-eight hours, he'd been feeling steadily worse. The headaches were almost constant now, and strange new whisperings in his head—along with the demonic music—threatened at times to overwhelm him. Just the night before, he'd found himself sitting on the edge of his bed, playing with the penknife from his medicine kit—blade open—and unable to account for the last fifteen minutes.

Something would have to be done.

Taking a pillow from the bed, he placed it in the middle of the floor, then sat down carefully upon it in the *kekkafuza,* or full lotus, position of *zazen.*

In times of great agitation or emotional unrest, Logan relied on Zen meditation, along with his skill as an empath, to calm his mind. He had never needed it more than now.

He pulled out the amulet and looked at it briefly. Then he let it drop gently onto his chest and lowered his hands to his lap, palms up, right over the left, in the *dhyāna* gesture of meditation. He began breathing very slowly and deliberately: inhaling, exhaling, clearing his mind of all extraneous thought, focusing on nothing but the breaths themselves; imagining that, with each inspiration, he was taking in pure, cleansing air and that with each expiration he was ridding himself of physical and emotional poisons. At first, he counted the breaths; after several minutes, this was no longer necessary.

A sense of calm began to steal over him. The headache receded, along with the whisperings. But the music—the unsettling, devilish music—remained.

Now he tried isolating the music in his mind, compartmentalizing it, so that he could study it simply as a phenomenon, rather than as an intruder to be feared. With effort, he managed to slow it down until only one note sounded at a time. As each note sounded, he mentally introduced another, *opposite* note of his own creation. One at a time, as each new note intruded into his consciousness, he quite deliberately added another, attempting to cancel out the first.

Logan did this for perhaps ten minutes, trying as he did so to retain the sense of inner stillness at the heart of *zazen*. It was not a perfect process—he did not have the mental discipline for that—but when he rose again, his headache had temporarily receded, the whisperings were stilled, and—most mercifully—the music was quieter.

He tossed the pillow onto the bed; slipped the amulet back into his shirt; paused to take one more deep, cleansing breath—and then, picking up his satchel from the desk, opened the door and exited his rooms.

36

In the old, wood-timbered Victorian on Perry Street, Pamela Flood sat in the small upstairs space she liked to call her dressing room, self-conscious before a mirror, applying makeup. She rarely did this, and even tonight applied only the bare minimum, but it felt an effort worth making. She had no siblings, and after the death of her father she had the house—with its strange crooked corridors, its back stairs and somnolent rooms of obscure functionality—to herself. The benefit of this—perhaps the only benefit—was that she could assign any number of spaces to her personal whims: hence, the dressing room.

It was quarter to nine in the evening, just about her favorite hour, windows open to the cool night breeze and the sleepy residential street, quiet save the soft droning of insects. A glass of iced tea with a sprig of peppermint sat at her right elbow, and a Charles Mingus CD was playing.

She was looking forward to her date with Jeremy Logan, and to what would no doubt be a marvelous dinner. She was also looking forward—as she privately admitted with a faint tingle of anticipation—to what might happen afterward. It wasn't easy, meeting people in a place like Newport. In a resort town, you always felt like a bug under glass. She wouldn't allow herself to get mixed up with clients and, living here all her life as she'd done, she felt she knew all the eligible bachelors too well, as former schoolmates and current neighbors, to ever consider them romantic material. Tourists, or the dot-com billionaires who showed up to display their yachts and pretend to drop in on the Jazz Festival . . . ? Forget it.

That left a pretty small field of opportunity.

. . . What was that noise? A rap at the front door, perhaps?

She stood up, turned down the CD, and made her way to the head of the stairs, listening. But there was nothing. She glanced at her watch: Jeremy wouldn't be here for another twenty minutes, at least.

Look at her: nervous as a high schooler about to attend the junior prom. Even so, she had a habit of turning up music until it was just loud enough to miss the phone or the doorbell. Not good for somebody who relied on clients and referrals for her livelihood. She returned to the makeup table and turned up the volume again, just not quite so much this time.

As she sat down, she reminded herself not to forget to bring along the business card she'd promised Jeremy. After rediscovering it, she'd been careful to put it away where she'd remember it: the rambling house, with its piles of books, drafting paper, and architectural drawings, had a way of sucking things in and hiding them away.

As she began applying lipstick, her thoughts turned again to Logan. Funny how her first impressions of him had been so colored by suspicion and alarm. And then, after learning who he was, she'd gone to the Blue Lobster, determined to meet but not to like him. That, she knew in retrospect, was probably a reaction to his high profile: her New England puritanism would never allow her to date somebody who'd been on the cover of *People*, especially given a profession so tailor-made for publicity as his. But despite everything, he'd won her over. Not that he'd tried—and maybe that was part of it. No: he'd come in with no attitude, friendly, modest, even self-deprecating, a little reserved when it came to discussing his own work. And he was entertaining, in a droll sort of way. The fact that he was good-looking only helped wear down her natural defenses.

But it wasn't until their dinner at Joe's that she'd really begun to take him seriously. She couldn't quite put her finger on it. He was clearly intellectual: you got the sense that, every time he spoke, a lot more thought had gone into his reply than you could glean from just the words. What you saw on the surface was just the tip of a very intriguing iceberg. But there was more than that: it was the way he looked at you when you spoke, almost as if he comprehended your feelings better than you did yourself—and as a result she had never felt judged that evening . . . only *understood*.

At least, that's how it had seemed to her. And she felt certain that, after a long candlelight dinner at Sub Rosa, she'd know for sure whether . . .

Was that a bump she'd just heard? Standing once again, she turned off the CD. It seemed to have come from downstairs. But then, with the music on, she couldn't be sure—it might have come from the street.

She stood in the dressing room, listening. She glanced at her watch again: still not quite nine. There had been a rash of burglaries over the past few months, but they'd always taken place in the early hours of the morning.

As she hesitated in the soft golden light, there came another noise: the squeak of an old floorboard somewhere in one of the rooms below.

Pamela took a quick, appraising glance at herself in the mirror: Jeremy didn't seem the type to just let himself in, but she wanted to look good just in case. She glanced around for her cell phone, found it, held it at the ready—also just in case.

She returned to the landing, descended halfway

down the stairs. "Jeremy?" she called out. "You know it's bad form to enter a woman's boudoir without getting an invitation first."

No answer.

Now she descended the rest of the stairs and walked past the parlor, past the dining room, turning on lights along the crooked passages until she reached the kitchen. Here she stopped and frowned. The back door was open. That was odd. Newport was a friendly place, but she knew enough to always keep her doors locked after dark.

She closed and locked the door. Then she glanced at her cell phone, made sure the 911 speed dial was ready, and moved silently into the kitchen, switching on the light as she did.

Everything seemed to be in order: the new refrigerator; the old stove that her mother had made so many wonderful meals on; the kitchen table, the day's mail at one end and the single place setting at the other. It was just as she'd left it after cleaning up from lunch.

It was then that she smelled smoke.

It was faint, but acrid, and she'd learned to take that smell seriously. The wiring in the house was very old, but she'd put off updating it because of the cost. One of the fuses was probably overheating. Because of the power-hungry equipment in her office, she'd put in a couple of 20 amp fuses into the 15 amp circuits. Since the fuses were the old T type, this was possible. She knew it was potentially dangerous, but she'd only had problems once, and ever since she'd been careful not to run the office equipment while the air conditioner was on. There didn't seem too much load running in the house that evening. But just to be sure, she'd check the fuse box and replace any 20 amp fuses with those of correct size. She didn't need to be warned three times: next week, she'd bite the bullet and get an electrician in for an estimate.

Preoccupied with these thoughts, she had opened the door to the basement, preparing to open the fuse box that was set into the wall at the top of the stairs. Then she stopped, rooted in place by shock.

A fire was raging in the basement: black smoke roiling furiously up the stairs, yellow tongues of flame curling and darting toward her in a way that, despite the violence, was almost caressing. As she watched, a second gout of smoke and flame suddenly appeared by the wiring junction on the far basement wall.

She whirled around, fumbling with the phone, preparing to call the fire department. As she did so, a dark figure darted out from behind the pantry door and wrapped a tweed-clad arm around her head, immediately cutting off her screams. Pamela's arms shot up reflexively and her cell phone went shooting across the room.

The figure began dragging her out of the kitchen, away from the windows and deeper into the house. For the briefest of instants, Pamela was too surprised to struggle. But then she began to fight in earnest, yelling through the fabric that pressed over her mouth, biting, beating at the figure with her fists.

For a moment, the fury of her attack seemed to surprise the intruder. The grip loosened and Pamela twisted around, preparing to counterattack. But just then, a damp cloth was jammed hard against her mouth and nostrils. A sour chemical stench assailed her. Blackness began crowding in from the corners of her vision. She twisted again, kicking desperately, trying her utmost to cry for help, but with every intake of breath her limbs grew heavier and more stupid.

One lurch at a time, she was dragged farther away from the back door, and freedom. The last thing she saw before darkness overtook her was an orange tracery of flame, now eating its way across the kitchen wall, consuming the old wooden house with incredible speed.

37

Jeremy Logan maneuvered his vintage Lotus along Ocean Avenue, the sea breeze ruffling his hair. It was a fine evening; the sun had set, and the still-gathering clouds high in the darkening sky were suffused with a pink afterglow. He felt better than he had in days. No doubt he had Pam Flood, and their impending date, to thank for that.

"You'd like her, Karen," he said, speaking to his dead wife, whom he imagined was sitting in the passenger seat beside him.

This was a habit he'd fallen into—talking to her now and then, when he was alone—and after the shock of unexpectedly *seeing* her on the expansive Lux greensward the day before, the imaginary interaction was something he was eager to have returned to a pleasant, controlled basis.

He turned onto Coggeshall Avenue and headed north, toward downtown. "She doesn't have your subtle wit," he went on, "but she's got your spunk and a self-possession I think you'd approve of."

Sirens were sounding in the distance. Logan glanced at his watch: quarter after nine. He'd be there in just a couple of minutes now.

He drove on, the tall, manicured hedges that lined both sides of the road forming leafy walls in the gathering darkness. Ahead, in the sky, the afterglow was brighter now; more orange than pink. "I find myself letting down my guard with her," he said. "And there's something else—she's made me realize, quite unconsciously, that life can be pretty lonely. Even when you're juggling two careers."

Abruptly, he fell silent. What, exactly, was he trying to say to Karen—and, by extension, to himself?

Coggeshall turned into Spring, and the road narrowed a little. The charming old houses grew denser. Ahead on his right, he could just make out the vast, genteel lines of the Elms.

The sirens were louder now, urgent *blatt*s overlapping in a hysteric fugue. He could make out a column of smoke ahead, roiling upward. As he stared, he realized that the bright orange glow illuminating the undersides of the clouds wasn't afterglow anymore: it was the reflection of flame.

He drove on, past Bacheller Street, past Lee

Avenue. The shrieks of sirens grew louder still. And then, quite abruptly, he could go no farther. The way ahead was blocked by police cars and emergency vehicles.

Pulling the Lotus up onto the curb, he got out and began walking. Now he could hear voices: cries, shouts, barked commands.

Some instinct told him to run.

The entrance to Perry Street was cordoned off, and a crowd was gathering: gasping, pointing, stretching to see past the police cars. Heart racing now, Logan ducked behind an ambulance, skirted the cordon, and began running once again down the street. A moment later, he stopped abruptly.

The charming old Victorian house was consumed by flame. Huge tongues of fire were licking out of every front window—first floor, second, round attic oriel—blackening the wood even as he stared. He took a step forward, staggered, took another. He could hear the crackling of flames, the groan of timbers. It was almost as if the house were moaning in pain. He could feel the heat even at this distance. Three fire trucks were parked outside, jets of white water pouring uselessly onto the conflagration. He'd never seen a fire so furious, so angry. Smoke stung his eyes, dried the back of his throat to chalk.

Another rending of timber; the old structure gave out a scream.

Suddenly, without thinking, Logan dashed forward, making for the front door. He ran ten feet before being restrained by a policeman.

"No!" Logan said, struggling furiously.

"It's no good," the cop said, tightening his hold.

Just then, the roof of the house collapsed in an inferno of sparks. Embers, ash, bits of fiery matter rose in a mushroom cloud of ruin. And—as the policeman relaxed his grip—Logan collapsed as well, sinking slowly to the pavement, staring on in grief and horror, the death of the house reflected on his face in streaks of yellow, orange, and black.

38

Early morning light streamed through the windows of Gregory Olafson's spacious office, illuminating the dust motes that hung in the air. Olafson was bent over his desk, scratching out a note with an expensive fountain pen on cream laid paper. While he was quite comfortable with computers, he still preferred to send personal memorandums by hand; he found more attention was paid to them that way.

As he was writing, he heard the door to his office open and somebody step in. Without looking up, he said, "Ian, I would appreciate it if, when my secretary isn't yet in, you would knock before entering."

A voice replied: "Ian?"

Olafson glanced up quickly. Jeremy Logan stood in the shadows just inside his office, one hand still on the doorknob.

"Ian Albright," he said. "Maintenance chief. He's due here for a meeting about the approaching storm. It's strengthened into a hurricane, Hurricane Barbara, and we have to take precautions against—"

Logan held up a hand to interrupt. "You need to open that safe," he said.

Olafson blinked. "I'm sorry?"

"You heard me, Gregory. We have to see what's inside."

"I thought I was quite clear about that," Olafson said. "Opening that safe prematurely would be breaking my promise to the Lux charter. Going against seventy years of compliance."

"And I think *I* was quite clear. If you refused, more lives would be lost." And Logan approached Olafson's desk.

Now Olafson saw Logan clearly for the first time. The enigmalogist's clothes and face were streaked with what appeared to be soot, and his eyes looked red and raw, as though he hadn't slept at all. Though he appeared exhausted, his mouth was set in a firm, determined line. Olafson quickly connected the dots. "Good God. You aren't implying that last night's disaster—that the fire at the Flood residence . . ." He fell silent as the soot on Logan's clothes suddenly made sense.

"Do you think it's a coincidence, Gregory?

Strachey, the calmest of men, abruptly going psychotic and killing himself. The general contractor
for the West Wing job, retiring suddenly immediately afterward, current whereabouts unknown.
And Pamela. Pamela told me she'd been harassed
months ago by somebody trying to get their hands
on the Lux blueprints. Now, she helps us discover
how to access the room . . . and the very next evening, she's killed."

"In a tragic accident."

Logan waved a hand as if to brush off a pesky
insect. "I don't believe that. And neither should
you."

Olafson took a deep, even breath. "Jeremy,
you're talking about a conspiracy."

Logan nodded slowly.

"I'm sorry, but I find that absurd. I know you
were fond of Pamela Flood, that much was obvious, and I feel truly awful about what's happened,
but you can't simply transfer—"

Logan quickly approached the desk, leaned
over it. "It's your *moral duty* to open that safe."

Olafson looked at him without replying.

"First Strachey, then Wilcox, and now Pam
Flood. How many lives are going to be ruined, or
cut short, before we get to the bottom of this?"

"Jeremy, I think that's rather—"

"*I* might be the next to die. I'm the logical
choice, after all. It's quite possible one attempt has
already been made on my life. How would you feel
if the next one was successful?"

"There's no reason to think that what's in the safe will—"

Logan leaned in still closer. "Pam's blood is on your hands. *Your hands.* You brought me in, Gregory. You asked for my help. And now we're going to see this goddamned thing through. I'm going to learn what's in that safe if I have to dynamite it myself."

A silence descended over the office. For a long moment, neither man moved. Then, with a quiet sigh, Olafson picked up the phone, dialed an internal number, waited for the south London accent of the answering party. "Ian? Dr. Olafson here. Can we push that meeting back an hour? Right. Thanks." Then he hung up the phone and his eyes swiveled back toward Logan's.

Reaching into a pocket for his key ring, he selected a small brass key and fitted it to the lower left drawer of his desk. He unlocked the drawer, then opened it, revealing a dozen hanging files. He let his fingertips drift over them until he reached the last. Inside was a single tabbed folder, unlabeled and brown with age. He removed it, placed it on his desk, and let it fall open.

Within was an envelope, also unlabeled. It was closed with dark red wax that had been impressed with the Lux seal.

Olafson picked up the envelope. Then he glanced at Logan once again. The man looked back at him, his expression now blank and unreadable. Finally, taking a deep breath, Olafson slid one fin-

ger along the back of the envelope, breaking the
seal.

Within was a single piece of light blue paper
containing three numbers: 42, 17, and 54.

Now Olafson swiveled his chair around so
that he faced the back wall of the office. Below the
abstract expressionist paintings, a smaller, framed
photograph hung on the dark wood: a formal por-
trait of the first director and all the Fellows, dating from 1892—the year Lux was formally named.
Olafson grasped the right edge of the frame and
pulled gently. It swung away from the wall, hinged
along the left side rather than hung from a wire.

Behind lay the combination dial of a small
Group 2–style safe.

Holding the piece of blue paper in his left hand,
Olafson grasped the dial with his right. He gave it
several spins to the left, then slowed, making sure
to stop when the crow's foot was precisely at 42.
Next, he turned the dial to the right, making two
complete revolutions before stopping at 17. Then,
turning the dial to the left once again, he made
another complete revolution before stopping at
54. Finally, he turned the dial gently to the right
until he felt the bolt retract. Releasing the dial and
grasping the adjoining lever, he opened the safe.

Inside the small cavity beyond lay a thin dossier, one envelope placed atop it. Olafson lifted
them gingerly out and placed them on his desk.
Both were sealed in the same red wax.

Silently, Logan came around the desk until he
was hovering at Olafson's shoulder.

Now Olafson picked up the dossier, broke the seal, and looked inside. He saw a list of names; a few diagrams and photographs; a memorandum of some kind. Placing it back on the desk, he reached for the envelope, on which was written, in a bold hand: HIGHLY SECRET AND CONFIDENTIAL—TO BE OPENED ONLY BY THE DIRECTOR OF LUX IN THE YEAR OF OUR LORD 2035.

He broke the seal and removed the single sheet within, then held it up so that Logan could read it as well.

Newport, Rhode Island
December 30, 1935

To the Director of Lux, 2035:

You are no doubt aware of the circumstances under which this letter, and the attached précis and other assorted documentation, are being placed under lock and key. You are also undoubtedly aware at least in bold strokes of the research that has prompted such action, and which has of this date been abandoned.

Those few here at Lux who knew of it had high hopes for Project Synesthesia. As the work matured, however, it became increasingly clear that there was no certain way to divorce the beneficial effects of the project from the potentially destructive.

In the wrong hands, this technology could prove uniquely devastating. I have thus, with no small amount of regret, determined that it cannot now continue.

The benefits, however, are so intriguing that I have not ordered the destruction of all work to this point. Instead, if you are reading this letter, one century has passed since its writing. No doubt human science has advanced to a great degree. It is your task, therefore, to examine the details of Project Synesthesia and make a determination whether it can be brought to conclusion in such a way that no potential harm could befall the human race.

This letter, and the documents that accompany it, do not detail the project or its aims; the extensive records held in the West Wing laboratory itself contain all relevant data. Rather, it provides a degree of background information and explains how the laboratory itself is to be accessed.

It is now your job to choose—and choose very carefully—four members of the board to assist you. Preferably, they should come from a variety of scientific, philosophic, and psychological backgrounds. You as a group are to study the records stored in the laboratory, examine the research that has been accomplished so far, consider the current state of technology as it exists in your own time, and then convene—in secret—to discuss and, ultimately, vote upon whether the work should be taken up again. In the event of a deadlock, you yourself are to act as tiebreaker.

If your decision should be in the negative, I strongly recommend that all records, materials, equipment, and anything else related to the project be immediately and thoroughly destroyed.

I wish you good luck and Godspeed on this most vital of tasks.

Sincerely yours,
Charles R. Ransom II
Director
Lux

39

It was half past two in the afternoon when a quiet knock sounded on Logan's door.

He glanced up from his desk. "Come in."

The door opened and Kim Mykolos stepped in. She had a satchel slung over one shoulder and was holding a plate covered by a linen napkin.

"I didn't see you at lunch, so I thought I'd bring you a sandwich," she said, putting the plate on his desk. "Roast chicken with avocado, peach chutney, and watercress. I had one myself—they're not bad."

Logan sat back and rubbed his eyes. "Thank you."

She slipped into a nearby chair and regarded him intently for a moment. "I wanted to tell you how sorry I was. About Pamela, I mean."

Logan nodded.

"You know, I felt bad, talking the way I did to you about her. Now I feel even worse."

"You couldn't have known."

They sat in silence for a minute.

"Have you heard anything?" she asked a little awkwardly. "About the fire, I mean?"

"Preliminary investigation is ruling it an accident. Faulty electrical wiring, overloaded fuse box. Supposedly."

"You sound skeptical."

"I am. I was there. I've never seen a fire rage like that one did." He swallowed. "She never had a chance."

The talk died away again. Outside, Logan could hear hammering, the whine of a band saw. Work was already under way to prepare the mansion for Hurricane Barbara. In a matter of hours it had strengthened to a Category 2 hurricane off the Delmarva Peninsula and, if it kept racing along its current track, was forecast to make landfall somewhere along the southern New England coast late that evening. Lux was already putting together evacuation plans.

"What are you working on?" Kim asked, gesturing at the papers that littered his desk.

"Something I've been meaning to tell you about." Briefly, he described Olafson's secret safe, the hundred-year freeze, how he'd successfully convinced Olafson to give him the documents. As he spoke, the expression on Kim Mykolos's face—which had been an odd mixture of regret and embarrassment—slowly changed to intense interest.

"What a break," she said when he finished. "What have you discovered?"

"Not as much as I'd like. Unfortunately, the documents in the safe don't go into any detail about the nature of the work. The assumption was that, in 2035, the director would be able to peruse the reams of paperwork in the secret lab—paperwork we now know to have been deliberately removed."

"So what have the documents told you?"

"How to access the lab—which we'd discovered already, thanks to Pam. The names of the three scientists who were directly involved in the work. Oh, and the name of the venture: Project Synesthesia."

Kim frowned. "Synesthesia?"

"A neurological term for an unusual phenomenon where stimulating one sensory pathway causes the stimulation of a second. Tasting colors. Seeing sounds. It was a topic of great scientific interest in the early part of the twentieth century, but that interest died out long ago."

"Interesting." Kim thought for a moment, eyes far away. Then she turned back to Logan. "But what does it have to do with catching ghosts?"

"I was asking myself the same thing. I'm beginning to wonder if I was wrong about the purpose of the Machine." He shifted in his chair. "At least we now know where 'Project Sin' came from. It was clearly the nickname, or code name, for the work."

"Nickname," Kim nodded. "You mentioned the names of the scientists. Anyone I might have heard of?"

"I doubt it." Logan glanced over his desktop, picked up a sheet of paper containing three brief paragraphs. "Martin Watkins was the elder scientist on the project. From what I can gather, he spearheaded the work. He was an expert in physics. He died quite some time back, in the early 1950s. Apparently a suicide. Edwin Ramsey was his associate, a mechanical engineer. He died four years ago. The third was named Charles Sorrel, the junior man on the project. A medical doctor, specializing in what today would be called neuroscience. I don't know what happened to him—I haven't been able to track him down."

"And that's all you've learned?" Kim looked disappointed.

"Yes, save what I've been able to read between the lines. The work was obviously controversial and cutting-edge, which is why it took place in the secret room. But there's nothing in this dossier about why the work was abandoned—why it was considered dangerous."

Another silence fell over the room. Kim looked out the window, chewing her lip absently. Then she turned back.

"I almost forgot. I've made some progress of my own in examining those small devices we found in the room. A little progress, anyway."

Logan sat up. "Go on."

"Well, based on the components, I think they might be tone generators. At least in part."

Logan stared at her. "What? For what purpose?"

She shrugged. "I haven't gotten that far yet."

"What's their relationship to the Machine?"

"Can't tell you that either. Sorry."

Logan slipped the napkin off of the sandwich. "Doesn't sound very menacing."

"I know. I could be wrong. I'll keep working on it."

Logan picked up half of the sandwich. "A tone generator." He prepared to take a bite. Then a thought came into his head and he put the sandwich down. "That reminds me. I meant to ask if you could lend me some Alkan CDs."

"Great minds think alike." She rummaged in her satchel. "I have one right here." She handed the jewel case across the desk.

He glanced at the cover. "*Grande sonate 'Les quatre âges,'* by Charles-Valentin Alkan."

"A four-movement piano sonata. Real hairy one, too. It was Willard's favorite."

Grasping the CD, Logan rose from his desk and walked into the bedroom, Kim following. Beside the bed was an alarm clock with a built-in CD player. He slipped the CD into the loading slot, adjusted the volume. A moment later, the room became filled with precisely the music he'd first heard in Strachey's parlor: lush and romantic, yet at the same time seemingly possessed by demons;

full of complex passages that veered between major and minor, wickedly complicated, shot through with the rising arpeggios and chordal work he remembered so vividly. He took an instinctual step back.

"What is it?" Kim asked him. "You look like you've just seen a ghost—to coin a phrase."

"This is it," he told her. "The music I've been hearing in my head."

"What does it mean?" she asked. "You don't think the Machine's responsible, do you?"

Quickly, he shut the music off. "No," he said, returning to his office and sitting back behind the desk. "No, I don't think so. Recall my telling you I'm an empath? The first place I heard that music was in Strachey's study. If I was to speculate, I'd guess that the empath in me was picking up what Strachey *himself* heard—when he was becoming sick." He paused. "But there's something else."

"What?"

"When I first heard that music—in Strachey's study—I smelled something, as well. It was awful, like burning flesh."

"Alkan's music has weird effects on people. Some have claimed to smell smoke while listening to it."

Logan barely heard this—he was thinking. "Right before he died, Strachey said he was being pursued by voices. Voices that tasted like poison. And then Dr. Wilcox, at breakfast. He raved about voices in his head. Voices that hurt, that were too sharp."

"I wasn't there," Kim said. "Thank God."

"At the time, I assumed Wilcox meant the voices hurt because they were too shrill, too loud. But I don't think that's the kind of 'sharp' he meant. I think he could *feel* the voices."

Kim looked at him. "You're talking about synesthesia—aren't you?"

Logan nodded. "Smelling music. Tasting voices. *Feeling* voices."

Kim stood before the desk, considering this for a long moment. "I'd better get back to work," she finally said, in a low voice.

"Thanks for the sandwich," Logan replied. He watched her leave, shutting the door behind her. His eyes traveled to the sandwich, sitting on the white china plate. Then they moved to the sheet containing three paragraphs—the brief dossiers of the scientists behind Project Sin. After a moment, he picked up the sheet and began rereading it thoughtfully.

40

The Taunton River Assisted Living Community was a cream-colored three-story building on Middle Street in Fall River, Massachusetts. Logan parked in the lot behind the building, then—leaning into the howling wind—went through the front entrance and made a series of inquiries.

"That's him over there," a second-floor nurse said five minutes later. "By the window."

"Thanks," Logan replied.

"How did you say you're related again?"

"Distantly," Logan said. "It's complicated."

"Well, however you're related, it's nice of you to stop by, especially with this storm approaching.

Both his children are dead, and his grandchildren never visit. Shame, really—mentally, at least, he's still sharp."

"Thank you again."

The nurse nodded toward the box of chocolates in Logan's hand. "He can't have those, I'm afraid."

"I'll leave them at the nurse's station on the way out."

He walked through the large community room, past superannuated men and women watching television, playing cards, doing jigsaw puzzles, mumbling to themselves, or in some cases just sitting with vacant expressions on their faces. He stopped before a large picture window in the far wall. It overlooked Kennedy Park and, past the train tracks, the approach to Battleship Cove. A wheelchair was placed by the window, and in it sat perhaps the oldest man Logan had ever seen. His face was sallow and covered with an incredible tracery of wrinkles; the bony white knuckles that grasped the arms of the chair almost threatened to burst through the tissue-paper skin. Extreme age had shrunk and twisted his body into the shape of a comma. A tube of oxygen lay in the base of the wheelchair, and a nasal cannula was fixed in place. But the faded blue eyes that glanced Logan's way as he approached were as bright as a bird's.

"Dr. Sorrel?" Logan asked.

The man looked at him a moment longer. At last, he nodded in the faintest of motions.

"My name is Logan."

The old man's gaze dropped to the chocolates. "Can't have those," he said. His voice was like dry leaves skittering over broken paving stones.

"I know."

Sorrel's gaze rose again. "What do you want?"

"May I?" Logan pulled up a chair beside the old man. "I'd like to talk to you."

"Talk all you like."

Logan sat down. "Actually, I'd rather hear what you have to say."

"About what?"

Even though nobody was listening, Logan lowered his voice slightly. "Project Sin."

The old man went very still. The knuckles grasping the arms of the wheelchair turned even whiter. Slowly, his eyes left Logan's and drifted away. It took a long time for him to respond. Finally, the end of a tiny pink tongue emerged to wet his lips. He cleared his throat.

"Quite a storm brewing," he said.

Logan glanced out the picture window. The leading edge of Hurricane Barbara was approaching the city, and the trees in the park were writhing crazily in the wind, small branches and green clouds of leaves streaming away in contrails beneath an ominous sky. The streets were eerily deserted.

"Yes, there is," he agreed.

"What did you say again?" the old man asked.

"I said, I'd like some information about Project Sin."

"Can't help you with that."

"I think you can, Dr. Sorrel."

Sorrel's eyes rolled in his head, as if he was looking around for assistance.

"Don't worry," Logan said, keeping his voice low. "My visit is officially sanctioned."

"I'm ninety-eight. I'm an old man. My memory's not so good."

"I doubt if you've forgotten this particular project. But let me refresh your memory anyway. Project Synesthesia was undertaken at the think tank known as Lux, in Newport. It was halted rather abruptly by Lux's director, Charles Ransom, in the nineteen thirties. You were one of the three scientists involved, along with Martin Watkins and Edwin Ramsey. They're both dead. You're the only one left."

Sorrel's only response was a faint shaking of the head, whether through denial or palsy, Logan couldn't be sure.

"I—perhaps I should say we, since I'm working at the behest of Lux—know about the secret room. I've been inside. I've seen the equipment. And I know why your work was halted: there were fears it could be used in ways harmful to mankind."

Sorrel's head jerked in an involuntary spasm. He closed his eyes. The lids were so thin, Logan could almost see the irises beneath.

"Someone—we're not sure who—recently broke into the room. We believe they are trying to restart the old experiments. Based on their actions, I can only assume they're less interested in the beneficial aspects of your work than in the harmful ones. But they've taken away all the lab notes, all

279 • THE FORGOTTEN ROOM

the files. I need you to tell me just what you were
working on."

Still no response.

Logan reached into a pocket of his jacket,
withdrew an envelope, took out a folded sheet, and
showed it to Sorrel. It was a letter from Olafson, on
Lux stationery, giving Sorrel permission to answer
any and all of Logan's questions, without reservation. The old man scanned it with his eyes, hands
still clutching the arms of the wheelchair. After a
minute, he turned his head away.

"How did you find me?" he asked at last.

"It wasn't easy," Logan said.

There was a silence while the old man's lips
worked. "I made a vow," he said at last.

"So did Olafson, the current director. But he
broke it—and for good reason."

"I've kept that vow," Sorrel said, more to himself than to Logan. "All these years, I've kept it."

Logan leaned in still closer. "Dr. Sorrel," he
said. "Since the secret room was broken into,
two people have died. Others have been adversely
affected to a greater or lesser degree. Some are
experiencing synesthesia—tasting voices, smelling
music. I need to know what you were working on,
and the reason that work was stopped. Only you
can help me. There's no one else."

As Logan was speaking, the old man had gone
very still.

"Dr. Sorrel?" Logan asked.

No reply.

"Your help is vital. It's critical."

Still nothing.

"Dr. Sorrel?"

At last, the old man stirred. "Two eighteen," he said.

"I'm sorry?"

"Two eighteen. That's my room." For the first time, Sorrel lifted one of his hands and pointed toward a hallway. "It's down that way. We can talk in there."

41

Sorrel's room at Taunton River was quite large, but as spartan as a monk's cell. There was a hospital bed with a suite of vital monitors on the wall above it; a spare tank of oxygen; a single window looking out onto the roiling, ever-darkening sky. There was a tray table on wheels, a few magazines arrayed atop it. Logan was surprised to see recent issues of *JAMA*, *The Lancet*, and *Nature*, apparently well thumbed.

Logan moved the wheelchair to a position facing a small couch, then, closing the curtains against the ominous, distracting view, took a seat.

"Show me the letter again," Sorrel said in his breathy whisper.

Logan complied.

"Tell me about the deaths," Sorrel asked. "Please."

"One was a computer scientist, a longtime resident at Lux. He'd been tasked with restoring the West Wing, which has been closed for years. He suddenly became violent, hysterical—completely out of character—raved about voices in his head, some barely articulated threat to his well-being. It was unendurable, and he killed himself."

Sorrel winced as if in pain himself. "And the other?"

"A descendant of Lux's original architect."

"And you say there is a connection between these deaths?"

"I don't know for sure. I think so."

"You mentioned that others have been affected."

Logan nodded. "Hearing voices. Feeling dangerous compulsions." He took a breath. "Seeing people who weren't really there."

The old man looked away for a moment. "Could you get me a glass of water, please?"

Logan nodded, then rose and, exiting the room, headed for the nurse's station. He returned shortly with a plastic bottle of chilled water, which he opened and placed in a receptacle set into one of the wheelchair's arms. Sorrel lifted the bottle and took a long drink, hand shaking slightly, his Adam's apple bobbing in his scrawny, withered neck. He replaced the bottle, dabbed primly at his lips with the edge of his robe.

"I came in late to the project," he said. "Not long before it was shut down. I was very young. We all were, really. But I wasn't long out of Harvard Medical School, full of new ideas—new at the time, in any case." He shook his head. "I was brought in to see if there was any neurological or other medical way the . . . negative effects could be ameliorated."

"I assume you were unsuccessful," Logan said gently.

The old man went silent again for a few minutes. "That was many years ago. I've kept my oath—I've spoken of it to nobody—but of course over the years I kept up with developments in biology and psychology. After all this time it is hard for me to . . ." He paused. "To extract my later conjectures of what *could* or *should* have happened with what actually took place."

The man might be old, but he was remarkably lucid. "Just tell me about the goal of the project," Logan said. "In your own words."

Sorrel nodded once more, and then his gaze went far away, as if he was peering into the distant past—which, Logan realized, was precisely the case. He remained silent, giving the man space to remember. In his own mind's eye, Logan saw a procession of sepia-toned images: a group of men in seersucker suits and straw hats, standing and laughing on the front lawn of Lux; the same men, huddled together in a lab, engaged in some experiment; the same men yet again, sitting around a table, faces serious.

Finally, the old man shifted in the wheelchair. "It started as an accident, really. Martin had been experimenting with the effects of very high-frequency sound. What today would be called ultrasound." He looked at Logan. "You probably aren't aware of the impact certain infrasonic frequencies have on the human body."

"You mean, like the Coventry Haunting?"

Sorrel nodded in surprise. "Why, yes. Precisely."

This haunting had been a discovery by researchers at Coventry University: that extremely low-frequency sound, in the vicinity of 19 hertz, caused feelings of disquiet and dread. A side effect of this infrasound was a peculiar ocular vibration that triggered visions of a shadowy, ghostly apparition.

"Our work took place much earlier than that phenomenon, of course. Martin discovered that certain very *high*-frequency sounds had quite specific effects on human subjects."

"By 'Martin,' I assume you mean Martin Watkins, the physicist."

Sorrel nodded again.

"What was the frequency of the ultrasound?"

"I don't recall precisely. Not one that would ever occur in nature. Somewhere in the vicinity of one point five or one point six megahertz, I believe. That was Martin's bailiwick, not mine. It was a very precise frequency, and the level of sound pressure had to be exact in order for the phenomenon to occur."

"What phenomenon was that?"

"Unusual sensory manifestations. Odd, unpredictable behavior. Even, in extreme cases, what a psychologist would term 'dissociation.'"

"That sounds like a form of schizophrenia," Logan said.

"Exactly. Of course, schizophrenia was a relatively new term in the thirties. Many still referred to it as dementia praecox." Sorrel chuckled mirthlessly. "You know, people aren't that much closer to understanding schizophrenia today than we were when Roosevelt was president. No known etiology."

"At least it's treatable. With drugs like Thorazine. Clozaril."

"Yes. Thorazine was the first." Sorrel seemed to slip into old memories again for a moment. "The basic idea of the research was that if certain specific ultrasonic frequencies could *induce* such reactions—if the sound waves influenced the brain in a certain way—then logically there should be other sound waves—perhaps harmonic, perhaps derivative—that would have the *opposite* effect."

It was as if a huge piece of an invisible jigsaw puzzle abruptly slid into place. "Of course," Logan said. "If sound could be used to trigger schizoid behavior in a normal brain . . . why couldn't it be used to suppress such behavior in a schizoid brain?"

"That's it in a nutshell, young man—that was the start of what was initially called Project S. For obvious reasons, the research was kept secret—

the last thing Lux wanted was for word to leak out that they'd found a way to reproduce schizophrenic behavior. But nevertheless, spirits ran high. Martin and his partner, Edwin Ramsey, thought they could find a way to cure, or at least treat with great efficacy, a disease that had baffled mankind for ages. All they had to do was reverse Martin's initial work."

As he'd spoken, the light in the old man's eyes had grown brighter, and he'd become more animated. Now, however, he sank back in his wheelchair. "They tried everything. Different frequencies and amplitudes. Sound masking. Interference. They all but invented a revolutionary method of antiphasing—noise cancellation. Ultimately, they made some progress at mitigating schizoid behavior in afflicted people—but they were never able to eliminate the negative effects on everyone else." The man's eyes slid closed, and his head nodded. Then he started. "Did I say 'they'? I meant we. I was brought in, as a last resort."

"What did they hope you could bring to the table?" Logan asked.

"Some kind of medical key. Some biological answer to the problem."

"How did the sound waves work, exactly?"

"Exactly? I can't tell you that, any more than I can tell you what causes schizophrenia. That's the central problem. Believe me, I've spent more than my share of time thinking about it. Researching the possibilities—for my own amusement, of course." He nodded toward the magazines on the tray table. "As best I can tell, the high-frequency sound waves stimulated—in today's terms—serotonin receptors in the frontal cortex of the brain. Perhaps they acted on the raphe nuclei, as well." He sighed. "Ironically, the more Martin refined his machinery—the electromagnetic emitters, amplifiers and compressors, and transmission equipment—the more extreme the effects became. The hallucinations grew more bizarre, the behavior more erratic. Synesthesia became a common side effect. Toward the end, in fact, the work became known as Project Synesthesia. They were hoping, you see, that if nothing else, we'd be able to learn more about the inner workings of conditions like synesthesia and schizophrenia. But . . ." And Sorrel lapsed into another silence.

"You were closed down in 1935," Logan said.

Sorrel nodded. "Ransom, the director, became increasingly concerned that a device such as ours, which created hallucinations and unpredictable responses, could effectively short-circuit minds. My term, not his. He worried about the device being used to force people to see things that weren't real, hear voices that weren't actually speaking. Do things they didn't want to do. The last straw was when other scientists, working in the vicinity of our lab, began seeing and hearing things, acting oddly. Ransom said it went against the charter. Nevertheless he felt it had sufficient promise to be mothballed rather than scrapped. Sealed up the lab and everything with it. Equipment, books, box upon box of files—the works."

"How did the others take it?"

"You mean, Martin and Edwin? About as you'd expect. It hit Martin especially hard. Even though Edwin pioneered much of the technology that made the work possible, Martin was the one who first stumbled onto the process. We parted ways immediately. None of us wanted to talk about it—even if we'd been allowed to. I moved back to Massachusetts, found work in a local hospital. Martin eventually killed himself."

A brief silence settled over the room. Logan glanced up at the curtained windows. "Let me ask you just a few more specific questions about the equipment. We found several bulky suits hanging in one corner of the room. I'm assuming those were used by the operators of the machinery to shield them from negative effects."

"If we'd been successful, those suits would no longer have been necessary."

"The central device has two settings: beam and field."

"The therapy was meant to be administered in two distinct ways. The first way would be to have several patients assembled together, so that they could be treated as a group."

"I see. That would explain the roman numerals on the floor. So that would be the field setting?"

Sorrel nodded.

"And beam?"

"That allowed people to be treated individually, in remote locations. A radio wave would be sent out at a particular frequency to one of several small devices we constructed. When one of the devices received a signal, it would in turn emit an ultrasonic wave."

"These small devices you mention. Were they stored in a recessed drawer on the central machine?"

"Yes."

"How were they powered?"

"The usual way—by electricity. They had wall plugs, solenoids, vacuum tubes."

Logan thought a moment. "The displays on the faceplate of the Machine. They were graduated from one to ten."

"That's right."

"What was the standard medicated dose you administered?"

"Normally, two. Sometimes, as high as five—but those were only in the cases of the most floridly psychotic."

"This was in the field setting, I assume."

"Correct."

"What would happen if you redlined it?"

Sorrel frowned. "Excuse me?"

"Turned it all the way to ten."

"Ah. I understand." Sorrel passed a trembling hand over his lips. "We never 'redlined' it."

Logan hesitated before asking the final question. "In a few decades, the quarantine will be lifted. A small panel will be convened to discuss whether Project Sin should be revived—whether technology has advanced sufficiently so that your work could never be used against humanity. Do you think that will prove to be the case?"

The old man looked at him a moment. Then he shook his head. "I've wanted to think so. All this time, I've wanted that. But no—I don't think it will ever happen. Project S is a Pandora's box. I hate to say it, but they were right to close it down. And if you're right, young man: if someone has secretly opened it again . . . they'll be opening a window into hell."

A window into hell. Logan stood up. "Thank you, Dr. Sorrel—for your time, and your candor."

"Good luck." And Sorrel raised a withered hand in farewell. "Sounds like you're going to need it."

42

As evening fell, and heavy rain lashed the gables, parapets, and spires of the Lux mansion, a cell phone rang in the small set of rooms in the far section of the second floor.

It was picked up on the third ring. "Hello."

"Abrams," came the voice from northern Virginia.

"I know who it is."

"Logan's up in Fall River, Massachusetts."

"What's he doing there?"

"He went to a retirement community. He visited with the last of the three still aboveground."

The person on the second floor did not reply.

"We think he knows everything," the man named Abrams said.

"That old scientist is probably in his dotage. The likelihood is Logan just heard a lot of rambling."

"Our information suggests the old scientist's memory is just fine."

"Even if that's true, all Logan would learn is the backstory. He doesn't know about me. About us."

"He'll learn soon enough. It's only a matter of time. We're going to handle this."

"Like you 'handled' the architect?"

"Yes. Time is of the essence now. We've waited long enough. We can't afford any more delays."

"I told you, I'll deal with Logan."

"You had your chance," said Abrams. "It's out of your hands now."

"No. That's not the way. People will get suspicious—"

"With this hurricane bearing down on Newport? You must be joking. It's perfect. Logan's on the way back there now. Are people leaving the mansion?"

"The evacuation is voluntary. But, yes, many have left already."

"All the better. After the hurricane passes, they'll find Logan's battered body washed up on shore. They'll be saddened—but they won't be suspicious."

"It's dangerous to kill him."

"It's more dangerous to let him live. And he's

not the only one who knows too much. You'd be surprised how much collateral damage this storm may cause." There was the briefest of pauses. "You wait. We're going to take care of this, once and for all."

43

Two hours later, around eight thirty p.m., Kim Mykolos was sitting cross-legged on her bed, typing industriously on a laptop. A sudden slam caused her to look up abruptly.

She glanced in the direction of the bathroom she shared with Leslie Jackson. It was unoccupied, and Leslie's own room, beyond the bathroom, was also dark and empty—she'd left that afternoon to ride out the hurricane with relatives inland. Kim had no relatives within easy driving distance, and she'd turned down an offer from a friend to stay with his parents in Hartford. Despite the hurricane, the huge stone mansion seemed as safe a place as any . . . and besides, she was onto something interesting.

Another slam. This time, she realized it was a wooden shutter banging against a nearby casement, shaking the butterfly cases that sat on her bedside table. Earlier in the afternoon, maintenance had come by to make sure all windows were secured against the blast. One of the shutters must have come loose in the wind.

The phone on her pillow began to vibrate. She picked it up, glanced at the number of the incoming call. "Yes?"

"Kim. It's Jeremy."

"Where are you?"

"At a gas station, just north of Roger Williams University."

"I thought you'd be back here hours ago."

"That's what I thought, too. But the Sakonnet bridge is out, so I had to take the long way, via Warren and Bristol. And with this weather, traffic on 103 and 136 is crawling. I guess you're not leaving?"

"No. I'm here for the duration."

"In that case, you can do something for me."

"What?"

"You know those two small devices we found, stored in the Machine?"

"Know them? I've been slaving over one for what seems like days now."

"I want you to hide them away someplace. Someplace safe. And get the one from inside the radio in Strachey's rooms, please. Hide it as well."

"But I'm in the middle of . . ." She hesitated. "Got it."

"And then I'd like you to search my bedroom for another device, just like those others. It would most likely be hidden somewhere along my common wall with Wilcox, maybe behind a dresser or a bookcase. If you find one, put it with the others. I'd do it myself, only I don't know when I'll get there—and I don't want to leave this to chance."

"What is all of this about, exactly?"

"I told you why I went up to Fall River, who I was hoping to see. Well, Sorrel revealed a lot about Project Sin. It seems they were working on a way to treat schizophrenia using high-frequency sound waves."

Mykolos caught her breath. *No wonder . . .*

"They'd managed to reproduce schizophrenia-like symptoms in normal people, using a particular sound frequency, and hoped a different frequency would have the opposite effect in actual schizophrenics. But they never succeeded. In fact, modifying their experiment only made the effects worse. So the project was mothballed."

"And the small devices you want me to stash?"

"I think you were right. They're tone generators—built to emit the ultrasonic wave Project Sin was studying."

"That makes sense," Kim said. "Because I've analyzed the Machine further, and as best I can make out it's some kind of amplifier. A primitive, yet nevertheless very complex, amplifier." She paused a moment, thinking. "But why do you want me to hide those things away?"

"So they can't be used to hurt anybody else."

Kim froze as the meaning of Logan's words hit home. "Are you saying—"

"I'm saying that whoever found the forgotten room and resurrected the research is using those devices—first on Strachey, and then, I suspect, on me."

"So he, or they, intentionally drove Strachey crazy?"

"In order to halt work on the West Wing."

"Then why didn't . . . sorry, but I have to ask: why didn't it have the same effect on you?"

"I've been asking myself the same question. I think it has to do with our, ah, 'ghost catchers.'"

"Those necklace things we're wearing?"

"Yes. The hemishell of a nautilus is the central component. I'm no acoustical engineer, but I'll bet the logarithmic design of the shells' chambers breaks up, distorts the sound waves, reducing their effect. Reducing, but not nullifying—because I've been feeling rather unstable myself these last few days."

"And you suspect I'll find that device along the wall you share with Wilcox because he had no such . . . protection."

"Exactly. Instead of me being incapacitated, Wilcox ended up in the ICU." There was a pause. "Kim, I just didn't see it. I was convinced the Machine was a device for detecting, maybe communicating with spectral entities. Given my line of work, I guess that's the kind of assumption I'd easily slip into."

"Well, I'd say the Machine *is* a device for communication—just not the kind you initially thought."

"All those materials I found in Lux's files about 'ectenic force.' No doubt somebody *was* looking into paranormal phenomena—but it wasn't those three." Another pause. "Look, I'd better get back on the road. Traffic's looking a little lighter and the storm's growing worse—I don't want to risk a closure of Route 114. I'll get there as soon as I can."

"Okay."

"Thanks, Kim. And please—be careful. Don't take any chances." There was a click as Logan hung up.

As Kim placed the phone back on the pillow, she heard another noise. But this was no slam of a shutter—it sounded like a footstep, coming from the direction of Leslie Jackson's room.

"Leslie?" Kim called out. "What, you decided not to go after all?"

No reply.

Frowning, Kim rose from the bed and walked to the middle of the room, peering through the common bathroom and into the room beyond.

"Leslie?" she called again.

Was that movement, black upon black, amid the woven shadows of Leslie's room? If Leslie was there, why wasn't she answering? Why hadn't she turned on the light?

Had somebody been there all along, in the darkness, listening in on her phone call?

Suddenly, and for the first time, Kim felt, *understood,* the full weight of the danger she and Jeremy Logan were now in. If somebody had resurrected the work of Project Sin, and was willing to let Willard Strachey die to protect their secret . . . what would happen if her own role was discovered?

Be careful, Logan had said. *Don't take any chances.*

Was that more movement in the deep shadows? The cold gleam of metal?

Instinctively, Kim wheeled toward the door. As she did so, her feet slipped on the carpet; falling, her skull impacted the wainscoting of the nearby wall with an ugly sound of bone against wood, and her body dropped to the floor.

A moment passed. And then a tall, thin man emerged from the darkness of Leslie Jackson's room. His expressionless eyes surveyed the scene. Then he slipped a heavy blackjack back into a pocket of his tweed jacket and dragged Kim's body into a nearby closet. And then, plucking the pillow from the bed, he dabbed away the blood and tossed the pillow into the closet, as well.

"I'll be back for you shortly," he murmured, then slipped once again into the shadows.

44

Half an hour later, Logan pulled his Lotus Elan into the long, curving drive that led to Lux's parking area. The normally fastidiously tended greensward ahead was a riot of twigs, leaves, and—strangest of all—seaweed and spindrift, blown all the way from the coastline a quarter of a mile away. He had to negotiate around heavy branches that had fallen across the drive; he could make out at least half a dozen trees uprooted from the greenery that stood before the encircling brick wall. The main massing of Lux itself reared up against a black and furious sky, its battlements winking ominously in the flashes of livid lightning.

He managed to gain the relative safety of the near-empty parking lot in the shelter of the building's East Wing, turned off the engine, and then paused a moment to catch his breath. The entire journey back from Fall River had been tense—with the traffic, howling wind, and lashing rain—but the final ten minutes had been the worst. When he'd turned onto Ocean Avenue for the last leg of the drive, the full, unconstrained brunt of the hurricane hit: merciless buckets of rain, and a straight-line banshee wind that threatened to pick up his car and fling it into the surf. More than once, he'd thanked the automotive gods he owned a hardtop Elan; a canvas top would have been ripped away hours before. And he'd made it back just in time; the guard in the security house by the front gate informed him that the governor had just declared a state of emergency and instituted a curfew, effective immediately, and that the National Guard was being mobilized.

Logan waited another moment, then—peeling his fingers from the steering wheel and taking a deep breath—grasped the handle and opened the door. A screaming gust of wind forced the door right back at him, and he had to manhandle it open again with all his might. He gathered his strength, then rolled away toward the rear of the car as the wind flung the door closed. And then, bent forward until his head was almost level with his waist, he bulled his way toward the mansion's side entrance through air so thick with seawater he was almost drowning in it.

Just as he reached the door, he heard the buzzing sound of a motor cut through the wind. There was a light behind him, and he turned to see Ian Albright, the infrastructure supervisor, pulling up in a large golf cart, two men seated behind him. The cart stopped beside Logan and the three got out, all wearing identical sou'westers.

Albright stared at Logan as if he was from another planet. "Dr. Logan?" he asked. "You've just arrived? Don't tell me you've been motoring through this dirty great storm?"

"Something couldn't wait." Logan pointed at the cart. "What's your excuse?"

"A dozen slate tiles have blown off the kitchen roof, and the water's pouring in. We've got to get a tarp over it before . . ." The rest of his sentence was cut off by a shattering peal of thunder, followed by the crash of another tree falling over.

"Well, now that you're here, you'd better get inside," Albright said. "Dr. Olafson, Dr. Maynard, they cleared out hours ago, along with almost everyone else. There's just a skeleton crew now, a handful of security and maintenance and a couple of stubborn eggheads that refused to leave. But the storm's just been upgraded to a category three, and the worst is—"

A sudden shriek of wind staggered the four men, and the golf cart promptly turned over onto its side. "Sweet mother of *fuck*!" Albright cried in dismay, making for the cart as he simultaneously motioned Logan toward shelter.

Inside, the thick walls of the mansion dulled

the roar of the hurricane to a constant, low-pitched moan. Logan made his way through the strangely deserted halls to his rooms. Save for the never-ending boom of the weather, the entire place seemed cloaked in a watchful silence. He placed his duffel on the desk, sat down, and transferred the notes he'd taken during his meeting with Sorrel to his laptop, along with some observations and questions that had occurred to him during the exhausting drive back. And then he glanced at his watch. Almost half past nine. He shut the laptop and stood up from his chair. It was high time he checked on Kim.

As he turned to exit his rooms, the internal phone rang. He glanced back, saw the caller's four-digit number on the LED display. It was a number he didn't recognize.

"Hello?"

The voice on the other end of the line sounded breathless. "Dr. Logan? Dr. Logan, is that you?"

"Yes. Who's this?"

"Thank God you haven't left. It's Laura Benedict. We met in my office a few days ago. You might not remember me."

The young, rather shy quantum computing expert. "Of course I remember you. I'm surprised you're still here."

"Believe me, I wish I weren't. The bank of hotel rooms Lux booked in Pawtucket filled up hours ago. There's no place left to go." A pause. "But as long as I have to be here, there's something I need to talk to you about."

Logan took a seat behind his desk once again. "Go on."

"It's about Roger." Benedict's breathless voice grew softer, almost a whisper. "Roger Carbon."

"What about him?"

"I know why you're here. You're investigating the death of Willard Strachey. That was obvious when you interviewed me. And you think . . . you think that it was something other than suicide."

Logan went quite still. "What makes you say that?"

"It's hard to keep a secret in a place like Lux. Nobody knows exactly what's going on, but there's been speculation. . . ." Benedict went silent for a moment. "The thing is, Carbon's been acting a little . . . frightening the last couple of days."

"Frightening."

"Maybe a better word is 'suspicious.' I can make out some of his phone conversations—through the wall, I mean. The things he's been talking about . . . hinting at . . . are very alarming."

"Why didn't you come to me sooner?"

"I wanted to. But the fact is that I'm . . ." Another pause. "Well, I'm *afraid* of him. It was all I could do to gather the nerve to call you. But I haven't seen him around today. I think he may have left the island, and . . . and if what I think is true, then I shouldn't keep it to myself. I have to tell you—because I think you may be in danger."

"*I* may be in danger?" Logan repeated.

"I think so."

"Would you like to come by my office so we can talk about it?"

"No!" This came out in a frightened rush. "No, this storm . . . Please, let's meet in the basement. I have a lab here. We'll be safer."

Logan rubbed his chin. He really ought to check up on Kim.

I think you may be in danger. . . .

"Please, *please*," Benedict said in a voice like a supplicant's. "Before I lose my nerve."

"Very well. How will I find you?"

"Do you know the basement layout?"

"Not well. I've only been to the archives."

"That's sufficient. Take the elevator or the main stairway down, then head in the direction opposite from the archives. I'll be waiting for you by the barrier."

"I'll come immediately."

"Thank you, Dr. Logan." And she hung up.

45

Logan, his satchel slung over one shoulder, reached
the base of the central staircase without seeing a
single person. Turning left, he once again made the
journey down the dimly lit corridor of undressed
stone toward the gleaming metal door that led to
the basement laboratories. This time, however, he
could see the thin, birdlike face of Laura Benedict
on the far side of the perforated Plexiglas window
set into the heavy steel door. As he approached, she
punched a series of numbers onto a keypad set into
the wall—apparently, the door was locked from
both sides. With a low beep and an audible click,

the door sprang ajar with a sigh of positively pressurized atmosphere.

Looking briefly over Logan's shoulder to satisfy herself they were alone, she let him in, then pulled the door shut behind her. The air here was cool and smelt faintly of ammonia.

"Thank you for coming," she said.

Logan nodded. Once again, he was struck by the woman's evident youth. She led the way down the gleaming corridor with the sharp, almost abrupt movements he recalled from their first meeting. Before, he'd been struck by the aura of sadness she'd seemed to wear almost like a garment. Now, however, he sensed a different emotion: anxiety, even fear.

"We can talk in my lab," she said as they walked. "It's not far. There's nobody else in the secure area— I've already checked."

"I would have thought you had all the computers you needed in your office."

Benedict smiled wanly. "It's true. I could probably get by without this lab. But it gives me a quiet place where I can be alone when I'm working on a particularly thorny problem—or when I need a break from Roger."

As they walked, Logan glanced around curiously. Most of the doors were closed and bore simple airbrushed nameplates, but a few were open, revealing modern and sophisticated labs sporting equipment that he couldn't even begin to comprehend. Unlike the rest of Lux, the lighting here was bright, fluorescent, even a little harsh. It was as different from the polished wood and leather of the mansion above as a level-4 biohazard facility was from a London gentleman's club.

He followed Benedict around one corner, then another, and then—just as the basement was beginning to resemble a chrome-and-glass labyrinth—she stopped at an open door labeled BENEDICT. She ushered him into a sizable room that contained a steel desk surrounded by several Herman Miller chairs in matching gunmetal gray; a whiteboard, currently devoid of writing; two computers linked to a digital projector; and a rack of blade-server CPUs similar to the one in her upstairs office.

Benedict closed the door, then sat in one of the chairs and motioned Logan to do the same. Her face was pale with anxiety.

"Okay," Logan said, taking the proffered seat and putting his satchel on the floor beside him. "Please tell me exactly what your suspicions are concerning Roger Carbon, and why you think that I, in particular, might be in danger."

Benedict swallowed. "It's hard to know where to begin. Honestly, I'm not sure I can pinpoint just when it started. Roger has such a corrosive personality, you know; he's always getting into fights with somebody or other." She paused. "I guess it started three months ago. I noticed that, all of a sudden, he'd become a little secretive. That wasn't like him—normally, he doesn't care who hears what he says, what he does. But he started closing his office door. Just occasionally at first, and then more frequently. And every time he did so, he'd get on the phone—I could hear murmurs through the wall, you see. And then, just a couple days before Will Strachey's death, the two men had a dreadful argument in Roger's office."

"Strachey and Carbon? What was it about?"

"I'm not sure. Something about the West Wing. Roger had advocated for him to be in charge of that, you know."

"That's always struck me as odd," Logan interjected. "If Carbon had wanted the work done quickly, you'd think he would have argued for somebody with more experience."

"As it happened, I only caught the odd line or two of what was said. Will mentioned something about 'I'm moving ahead whether you like it or not.' And Roger replied, 'I'll see you in hell first.' I have to tell you, I've never seen Will Strachey like that before—livid, really livid."

"Go on," Logan said.

"Then, just a few days ago, Roger made another one of his clandestine phone calls. Only this time he didn't close his door all the way. I made out a little more of the conversation. It was something about a setback . . . a temporary setback. He seemed to be trying to persuade somebody not to take a certain course of action."

"Can you provide any more details about the call?"

"Sorry. I wasn't listening that carefully. It was only after overhearing those bits and pieces, and comparing them to the other things I'd noticed, that I began to grow . . . afraid."

"Why do you think that I might be in danger?" Logan asked.

"Isn't it obvious? You're looking into Will's death. You're also looking into the West Wing. If Roger is somehow involved with what's happened, even your presence here is a threat to him."

"I see."

Benedict hesitated. "Three days ago, I saw him coming out of your set of rooms."

"Really?"

"He seemed surprised to see me. Almost nervous—completely out of character. But then he said that he'd recalled something you should know, and, since you weren't at home, would look for you elsewhere." Benedict looked curiously at Logan. "Did he find you?"

"No, he didn't."

"Well, don't you see? It's clearly not safe for you here."

"It's not exactly safe for me out there, either."

"The hurricane? You can go stay in one of those block of rooms Lux reserved at the Pawtucket Hilton. I mean, anything could happen here now, with the place deserted like it is. If your life is at risk, don't you think the best thing would be to leave—leave immediately?"

Logan nodded, but absently, almost to himself. He hesitated. And then slowly he reached across the table and took Laura Benedict's hand in his. Her eyes widened in surprise, but she made no attempt to pull it away. He held it for perhaps ten seconds, and as he did so he became aware of several emotions: fear, of course; uncertainty; doubt . . . and something else.

He released her hand. "You haven't been at Lux very long, have you, Dr. Benedict?"

"Just over two years."

"Yes. And I recall you saying that Will Strachey was your mentor when you first came here."

"He was friendly, kind to a newcomer. It made all the difference in the world."

"Lux provided me with a brief dossier on you—on all the people I've interviewed, in fact. As I recall, before coming to Lux, you taught at the Providence Technical University."

"Yes, that's right. For about four years."

"Quantum mechanics, correct?"

Benedict nodded.

"Not quantum computing—the discipline you're pursuing now."

Benedict frowned, clearly confused as to where this was going. "They're closely related fields."

"Are they? I wasn't aware of that. In any case, I understand your doctorate was in mechanical engineering. Pardon my ignorance. Is that related, as well?"

Benedict nodded again.

Logan leaned back in his chair. "Providence was your childhood home, wasn't it?"

"Yes. Just east of College Hill."

"Ah. That would be near the large research lab . . . the name escapes me . . ."

"Ironhand."

"Ironhand. That's right. As I recall, they have a rather shady reputation for operating in the gray areas of science, sometimes doing weapons research for the highest bidder."

"Dr. Logan, why are you asking all these questions? Don't you think it's more important that you—"

"Why did you suggest that I go to the Pawtucket Hilton just now?"

"Why . . ." Her confusion deepened. "That's where Lux reserved all the rooms when the category of the hurricane was upgraded. It's the safest place for you to go."

"But over the phone, you told me that block of rooms had filled up hours ago."

"Did I?" Benedict hesitated. "Well, given your affiliation with Lux, I'm sure the hotel could make some accommodation—"

But Logan interrupted again. "Dr. Benedict, I'm going to ask what might seem like a strange question. I hope you don't mind. Is your maiden name Watkins?"

Laura Benedict went very still. "Excuse me?"

"Is your maiden name Watkins, by any chance?"

Another curious mixture of emotions—shock, incomprehension, perhaps annoyance—bloomed on her features. "Of course it isn't. Why would you ask such a thing?"

Logan spread his hands. "Just a hunch."

"Well, your hunch was wrong." And then Benedict stood up very slowly. "My maiden name is Ramsey."

46

For a long moment, the two simply looked at each other. The overhead lights flickered, dimmed, then brightened again.

"Of course," Logan said. "Sorrel told me that Dr. Ramsey pioneered a great deal of the technology that made Project Sin possible."

Laura Benedict did not answer. The anxiety had obviously not left her, but now her chin was thrust forward defensively.

"Why would you lure me down here with these dark rumors about Carbon—about wanting me to leave Lux for my own safety?"

"Because it's true . . . you *must* leave Lux,

immediately. If you don't, they'll kill you. I don't want that."

"Just like you didn't want Strachey to die."

Benedict's eyes reddened, and she turned away.

"Then you really did care for him. I'm sorry. What you told me about being beside yourself with grief—you weren't making that up."

She shook her head without looking at him.

"Who, exactly, is going to kill me?"

It took her a moment to answer. "I think you know."

"Ironhand," Logan replied. It was a statement rather than a question.

Benedict said nothing.

"How did you learn about Project Sin?" Logan asked gently.

Still Benedict did not answer. Then, with a sigh, she turned toward him. "From my grandfather."

"Dr. Ramsey?" he asked in surprise.

"A month before he died. Almost four years ago. My parents were already dead. He'd kept the secret his entire life. But it had eaten away at him, almost like the cancer that killed him." As she spoke, Benedict's voice grew stronger, more assured. "It was *his* research. He'd decided it was vital that his lone heir knew the truth. Dr. Martin's discovery was an accident. *My* grandfather was the prime mover behind the project. He'd told nobody. But he'd left behind certain . . . private papers."

Logan nodded for her to continue.

"The papers weren't comprehensive. But they explained the project, its potential, my grandfather's disbelief and chagrin that Lux had so abruptly halted it. I also learned the location of the lab where they had performed the work. It was a remarkable story, a maddening story. But it was all in the past, of course. It had nothing to do with me—I had my own life to live. And then . . . my husband died."

She sighed again—a deep, shuddering sigh. As she did so, Logan reached casually into his satchel and, hand hidden from view, quietly switched on his digital recorder.

"I was a scientist myself; it wasn't hard to secure a position at Lux. Nobody made the connection between me and my grandfather—and even if they had it would have meant nothing. I immersed myself in my new research into quantum computing. And I bided my time. For quite a while, I was of two minds about whether I should even explore Project Sin. After all, my work was quite fascinating on its own. But the longer I was at Lux, the longer I could hear my grandfather, calling to me from the grave. Calling on me to right the wrong. Nobody was in the West Wing anymore; it was off-limits. That's when I . . . I sought out the lab."

"And found all the paperwork, research journals, studies, laboratory notes."

"Yes. It was all very thorough."

"And I assume that made it easy for you to restart the work that had been mothballed."

For a moment, Benedict looked at him before answering. "The equations were complex. Certain aspects of the machinery were too obsolete to use and had to be replaced with modern equipment. That wasn't exactly cheap."

"In other words, you needed a backer. And that's where Ironhand came in."

"How do you know about them, anyway?"

"They approached the late Pamela Flood, descendant of Lux's original architect. She recalled the name as 'Iron Fist.' I know the area of Providence you come from quite well. It wasn't hard to put two and two together." He paused. "What did they want with the blueprints?"

"They wanted to know if there was another way into the secret room. They didn't want my work to be interrupted by any unexpected intrusions." She paused briefly. "At first, their role was small. They fund lots of start-ups, hoping to strike gold one time out of twenty. My relationship with them was no different. They well understood the need for secrecy."

"But over time, their role grew larger."

"Yes," Benedict said again. "When they began to understand the true possibilities of my work."

My work. Benedict was breathing more quickly now, her body language becoming restless. Logan wasn't sure how much longer she would be cooperative. "But you must have had other problems," he said. "Getting that work off the ground, I mean."

"It's not unusual. In fact, it's common."

"Let me guess. Some Lux Fellows who worked or lived near the West Wing eventually started to report strange things. Others were seen acting in a peculiar manner."

Benedict shrugged. "It was a relatively simple matter of adjusting the proximity beam."

"Yes. I understand the device has two modes, a field generator and a narrowly confined transmission signal. Those people must have been affected by your initial experiments with the field mode."

Benedict, who had been looking away, glanced back at him sharply. "As I said, it was a simple matter."

"But you had a more serious problem on your hands. Lux had decided to renovate the West Wing."

She looked at him, frowning.

Suddenly, Logan understood something. "You've told me that Carbon lobbied for Strachey to be the one put in charge of the renovation. And that's true—isn't it? What you left out was the fact that *you* convinced Carbon to suggest Strachey. What was it you told me—that Roger was a 'pussycat' in your hands? That doesn't jibe with your being afraid of him; I should have noticed that before. You assumed that Strachey would be slow at getting up to speed; that the renovation would take a lot longer than it did. That the forgotten lab—*your* lab, now—would remain hidden. But he moved more quickly than you'd expected."

"I was in the last stages of making the technology transportable," Benedict said, turning away again. "Of making the central amplification unit unnecessary; moving the hardware out of Lux and into Ironhand's secure labs."

"So you needed just a few more days . . . days that Strachey's death should have given you."

"He wasn't supposed to die!" she said, wheeling back. Tears sprung from her eyes.

"A double irony, since I was called to Lux to investigate his death and, in turn, found the room—preventing you from finishing."

Benedict said nothing.

"And then you tried to stop me, the same way you stopped him. Only it didn't work . . . not the way you intended, at least. I imagine you're wondering about that."

Benedict looked at him but remained silent.

"What about Pamela Flood? Was she supposed to die? That's the way your friends at Ironhand work. Doesn't that tell you something about them? And how did they learn about Pam, anyway—was my phone tapped?"

When Benedict's only response was to shake her head, Logan placed one hand on the desk and folded the other over it. "Tell me about the research, then," he said. "Have you succeeded where your forebears did not—creating a wholly safe treatment for schizophrenia, with no possibility of misuse?"

Now Benedict answered. "I did try. At first. But I soon learned that what was true in the 1930s is even more true today. You can guess the rest for yourself."

"I don't understand."

"Oh, please don't be coy, Dr. Logan. After all, you've already seen Sorrel."

Logan nodded slowly. So she knew about his visit to Fall River—a journey undertaken only that day. "In other words," he began again, "the problem has become more porous, rather than more solvable, as technology has advanced. So I assume you put aside its beneficial effects in favor of enhancing its harmful ones. In other words, weaponizing it."

"Simplistic, but correct."

"Interesting." Logan paused, thinking. "If all efforts to use the sound waves to *cure* schizophrenia were abandoned, and attention paid solely to the effects that the wave caused *naturally*—and enhancing them—no doubt some extremely disagreeable reactions would result."

"Hallucinations. Paracusia. Delusions. And that was just the start."

"The start of what?" Logan asked.

"My refinements."

"What refinements, exactly?"

Benedict gripped the back of the chair, leaned in toward him. "You know, it's almost a relief to talk about it with somebody who can understand—even, perhaps, appreciate. The Ironhand people are mostly interested in the end result. You see, I've been able to accomplish two things in particular: widen the perceived effects of the beam and enhance its functionality."

Logan waited, listening.

"My grandfather and the others, of course, weren't interested in intensifying the schizoid effects," Benedict went on. "Nor was I, initially . . . until I realized the so-called negative effects were the only ones the device could produce effectively. Initially, the sonic waves only affected certain 5-HT$_{2A}$ serotonin receptors in the frontal cortex."

Logan nodded. Sorrel had hinted as much.

"But I was able to create not just a single wave, but a harmonic series that would not only trigger additional effects on the brain but also enhance the effects of the initial carrier wave."

"The devil's interval," Logan murmured.

She looked at him. "I'm sorry?"

"The flatted fifth. G flat, for example, over C. It was a particular interval between two notes banned from church music in the Renaissance for its supposedly evil influence."

"Indeed? In any case, this synergistic wave—of two hypersonic pulses—caused a far wider spectrum of serotonin receptors to, in essence, overload. This effect could be maintained long after the wave itself had been cut off—I've witnessed serotonergic abnormalities lasting for eight, even twelve hours. Theoretically, with an initial pulse of sufficient strength, they could be imprinted indefinitely."

Indefinitely. Logan felt a sudden chill. "Witnessed these abnormalities in what?"

Benedict paused. "Lab animals."

"And in Strachey, too. And perhaps other

human subjects—willing or otherwise—at Iron-hand?" When there was no reply, Logan added: "What kind of abnormalities?"

"I've already mentioned a few." She drew in a breath. "Perception distortion, for example."

"As in synesthesia."

Benedict nodded. "All manner of false sensory signals. Enhanced sight, sound, taste, combined with hallucinatory factors. Eidetic imagery. Ego death. Altered sense of time. Catastrophic shifts in cognition. Complete dissociation from reality—"

"My God!" Logan interrupted this catalogue of horrors. "You're talking not only about complete psychosis here—you're also talking about the worst LSD trip of all time!"

"Scientists once thought LSD and schizophrenia were connected," Benedict said, shrugging. "And there were a few files in the room concerning early tests on ergotamine derivatives—that was a few years before LSD was actually synthesized from ergotamine, of course. But my hypersonic interval is so much cleaner."

"Cleaner." Logan shook his head, unable to keep the disgust from his voice. As she'd spoken, Benedict's voice had grown stronger, the shine of her eyes brighter; she took obvious pride in what she'd accomplished.

"Of *course,* cleaner," Benedict told him. "Isn't that what we want—clean, effective weapons? This is the cleanest weapon there is."

"Laura, how . . ." Logan stopped, momentarily baffled. "Can't you see how wrong this is?"

"Wrong? I'm helping my country."

"How, exactly?"

"By giving it a new way to defend itself. Look what's happening in the news *every day*. We're being attacked, not just on one, but on many fronts. And we may insist on fighting fair, but our enemies don't. Not anymore. That's why, without this technology, we're going to lose the war."

"But don't we have enough weapons as it is? And this—this *device* of yours is cruel. It's unthinkable. To drive somebody, perhaps an entire army, insane, or to send them on an endless bad trip . . . Laura, there are reasons chemical weapons were outlawed. And what if this weapon *is* deployed? Just how long do you think it will take for the technology to be leaked—and the same diabolical ordnance used against our own men and women?"

Logan fell silent. For a moment, the two merely looked at each other. Once again, the basement lights faltered for a moment before brightening again. At last, Benedict turned on her heel, opened the door to the lab, and began making her way back down the corridor. Logan jumped to his feet, turned off the recorder and slipped it into his satchel, and began to follow.

"Listen," he said as they made their way back through the passages. "I understand. You're in denial. It's only human. At the start, you were thinking—understandably—about a wrong done to your grandfather. And a weapon with as much potential power as this one . . . well, it could be worth a great deal. It meant money."

"Naturally it meant money," Benedict said, stopping to face him. "My grandfather was a brilliant man. He practically invented this technology single-handedly—only to be marginalized, to have his greatest creation swept under the rug. He was never recognized for his achievements. He *should* be recognized. Compensated. My *family* should have been compensated." She turned back, continued down the hall. "This is my rightful legacy," she said over her shoulder. "My inheritance."

"What is it you want to inherit, Laura?" Logan asked. "Ruin, madness, death? Listen: I'll bet you haven't spent much time really thinking about how this would end—about the damage this research would cause if placed in the wrong hands. It's true—your grandfather, and by extension yourself, have accomplished something remarkable. But if you'd take a moment to step back, to see the ethical reality of the situation, you'll know that this isn't the way."

Ahead, the metal of the secure barrier came into view. As Logan spoke, Benedict slowed, then stopped. "I was wrong," she said quietly, without looking back.

She paused, her thin body rocking slightly. And then she began walking again.

"Yes," Logan said as they came up to the barrier and she unlocked the door with a quick punch of her fingers over the keypad. "But, Laura, given what happened to your grandfather, I understand. What happened to him, to the others, was awful—shameful. And yet Lux was right to stop their work.

Do you see now why you can't go ahead with this? Why the research must end? Why you can't involve Ironhand in these secrets?"

Benedict stepped through the doorway.

"I meant," she said, punching in a sequence on the keypad beyond the barrier, "I was wrong about you."

Before Logan could react, the security door clamped shut, sealing him in.

"It was a mistake to try saving you," she said through the ventilation tubes. "They were right all along."

Logan grasped the door and shook it, but it was immovable. As he watched, Benedict picked up an internal wall phone and dialed. "Where are you?" she spoke into the phone. "First-floor library? I'm almost directly below you, at the barrier to the secure labs. Logan's inside." A pause. "Yes. Come right away. I'll meet you at the staircase, give you the entrance code. Do what you have to do, but I don't want to know anything about it."

She replaced the phone. Then she looked at Logan, gave him a regretful smile. "I'm sorry it had to end like this, Dr. Logan. You seemed like a good person. I wanted you to run. But I can see now that never would have worked." She lowered her voice. "Their way, unfortunately, is the only way."

Then she turned and began walking briskly down the corridor, in the direction of the central staircase.

47

For a moment, Logan simply watched through the Plexiglas window as Benedict walked away. He felt stunned with surprise. And then—with a sudden motion born more out of instinct than reason—he wheeled around and began running back down the cold, steel-clad corridor as quickly as he could.

After a moment he paused midcorridor. He'd never get out if he just ran blindly. More slowly now, he continued, jiggling the knobs of the doors as he passed, opening those that were unlocked and turning on the interior lights to create the illusion that someone might be inside. Time was his enemy; he had to buy as much of it as he could.

Just as he reached the T intersection at the end of the corridor, he heard a low beep as the security door was unlocked.

Logan ducked around the corner, breathing hard. Under the pitiless glare of the corridor lighting, he felt like a rat in a maze. He heard low voices in the distance and the crackle of a radio.

Taking a deep breath, he pressed himself against the wall, venturing a quick glance back around the corner. Some thirty yards down the hall, he saw three men. They were advancing slowly, looking into the open doors as they advanced. Each held a radio in one hand, and in the other something that Logan suspected to be a Taser. One of the men was wearing a tweed jacket. As he moved, his jacket swept back to reveal the glint of a handgun.

Logan pulled back. *Three men.*

As quietly as he could, he moved down this new corridor—opening doors and turning on lights whenever he could—and then ducked around another bend. He was approaching Benedict's lab now. Ahead on the right was a lab marked KARISHMA, its door ajar. He slipped inside and looked around quickly. It appeared to be a chemical laboratory of some kind, festooned with workstations, glassware in wooden racks, mass spectrometers, gas chromatographs, and other tools he couldn't begin to recognize. There were also whiteboards, a conference table, and the same Aeron chairs he'd seen in Laura Benedict's office.

Closing and locking the door, he looked around again, imprinting the layout of the room onto his memory. Then he turned out the lights and made his way carefully back to a far corner, where he crouched between a pair of metal bookshelves.

He couldn't just continue to run like a fox from the hounds. He had to think this through.

Three men. Ironhand security, perhaps, or at the least hired muscle. These were the people, he felt certain, who'd burned Pam Flood alive in her own house. No doubt they were also the men in the big SUV that had tried to run his car off the road and into the ocean—there was no longer any thought of that being a mere accident. These men were here to kill him.

So why were they carrying Tasers? Would there be fewer questions later if his body wasn't full of bullet holes? He shook off the thought.

In the dark, Logan quietly slipped his satchel from his shoulder and began rummaging through it, searching for anything useful. His hand closed over a small but powerful flashlight; he slipped this into a pocket of his jacket. His cell phone went into a pants pocket. He also pocketed the digital recorder with Benedict's unwitting confession. A Swiss army knife with half a dozen gadgets he'd never used went into still another pocket. Nothing else in the backpack—cameras, notebooks, EM sensors, trifield monitors—seemed of any use. He owned a handgun, but it was locked in a gun safe back in his house in Stony Creek—regrettably, it hadn't seemed a necessary accessory for a trip to a prominent think tank.

Out of habit, he slipped the near-empty satchel

back over his right shoulder. Then he froze as he saw—through the screened-glass window of the laboratory door—a shadow approaching. A moment later, one of the three men appeared. He wore a waxed waterproof jacket and a cap set low over his ears. As Logan watched, the man stopped just outside the chemistry lab, pulled out a radio, and spoke quietly into it. He listened for a moment, then put the radio away. A Taser was still at the ready. He tried the door to Logan's hiding place, and—finding it locked—continued down the corridor.

Logan let the air slowly escape from his lungs. The men must have split up as they reached the fork in the corridor.

He crouched in the darkness, thinking. There had to be an emergency exit somewhere. He thought back to his first trip down these hallways with Laura Benedict, just twenty minutes earlier, but he didn't recall seeing anything like another way out. . . .

His cell phone. He could call the police. Better yet, he could call Lux security—he had the number programmed into his phone and they would likely still be on site.

He plucked the phone from his pocket, began to dial—then saw the NO SERVICE message on the display. He was too deep into the basement, and the walls were too thick, to pick up a signal.

But Benedict had called him from down here. No doubt each lab had a telephone, hardwired to a landline. He could use that.

Rising from his hiding place, he pulled the flashlight from his pocket, cupped his hand over it to shield the beam, shone it around the lab. There: to the right of the door, on a small table, sat a phone with a dozen buttons embedded in its faceplate.

He waited a moment, making sure all was quiet in the corridor outside. Then, moving slowly, using the rectangle of light from the window in the door as a guide, he approached the phone, reached for it.

As he did so, his right elbow brushed against a large, empty glass beaker, set into a wooden stand. There was a protest of old wood; the beaker wobbled; and then—before he could react—the stand broke into two pieces and the beaker crashed to the ground with a sound like thunder.

Christ. For a moment, Logan froze. Then—as quickly as he could—he opened the door, locked it from the inside, closed it again, and darted across the hall into another lab. He'd already turned on the lights here, and he didn't dare turn them off. The room was damnably bare—just some bookshelves and a computer, but at least it was free of glassware—and he ducked under the central table.

Seconds later he heard the sound of running feet approaching from farther down the corridor. It was the man who had been here just moments earlier. From Logan's vantage point beneath the table, he saw the man's feet as they paused outside the door. They pivoted this way and that. Logan didn't dare breathe.

Then came the sound of a radio.

"Control to Variable One, give me a sitrep," a voice crackled.

"Variable One," the man in the corridor said. "I'm near the source of the noise."

"Anything?"

"Negative."

"Keep looking. He must be close. And shoot only as a last resort."

"Roger that." This was followed by a metallic clicking noise. For an agonizing moment, the man stood in the corridor, waiting, listening. And then—slowly, stealthily—he moved on down the hallway, back in the direction of the T intersection.

Logan waited: a minute, two minutes, five. He didn't dare wait any longer; at some point the man would return, probably with the other two.

Emerging from beneath the table, Logan crept silently to the door, then paused again, listening. He hazarded a glance into the corridor, which was empty. He slipped out, past Benedict's now-empty lab, until he reached another intersection. This, too, was deserted. But it made him nervous: if all these various corridors were interconnected, the chance of meeting up with one of his pursuers—either from ahead or from behind—increased dramatically.

He darted left and trotted quickly down the hall, opening doors and turning on lights as he went. Reaching another bend, he peered carefully around it—empty—then proceeded around the corner.

There it was: perhaps twenty yards ahead,

332 • LINCOLN CHILD

the corridor ended in another steel door. Above it glowed a red EXIT sign.

Moving as fast as he could, making no further attempt to conceal his footsteps, Logan ran toward the door. Just as he reached it, movement sounded from behind. Slipping the satchel off his shoulder, Logan threw it into the open doorway of a nearby computer lab as a diversion, causing a tremendous racket, but it was too late—as he glanced over his shoulder, he saw the man in the waterproof jacket at the bend in the corridor, yelling into his radio and sprinting in his direction.

Logan opened the door at the end of the hall with the EXIT sign above it—the door was labeled BRONSTEIN—then dashed inside, closed and locked it behind him, and looked around quickly. This was clearly some kind of physics laboratory, its tables covered with spectroscopes, digital strobes, microburners, and something that looked, most bizarrely, like an oversize timpani mallet stood on end, surrounded by a chicken-wire enclosure.

At the far end of the lab was another door. This, too, was marked with a red EXIT sign.

Behind Logan, the doorknob rattled as it was tried from the far side. This was followed by a heavy thud.

Skirting the lab tables and equipment shelves, Logan raced across the floor and opened the far door. There was a short corridor beyond, its walls bare save for a large ventilation grate set near the floor. At the end was still another steel door.

Beside it, mounted on the wall, was a security keypad.

He ran forward and tried the door anyway, hoping against hope. It was securely locked.

Logan took a step back, then another, almost dazed by this bad luck. He glanced over his shoulder, across the physics lab, to the window of the door he had locked. He could see the man in the waterproof jacket throwing himself against it, again and again. The Taser in his hand had been replaced by an automatic weapon. A silencer had been snugged into the end of its barrel.

Logan stood there, frozen, as the pounding continued. Now the man was being joined by the others, and he could hear the sound of overlapping voices. And still he could not move.

There was no way out. He was trapped.

48

Logan stood in the open doorway, surveying the lab. At the far end, through the security glass, he could see the three men attempting to force the door open. He had only seconds until they were through.

The overhead lights dimmed, brightened, dimmed again—the full fury of the storm must be on them now. As the lights once again returned to normal, he looked around the lab in desperation. There was the phone: fixed to the wall . . . on the far side of the lab, near the door he'd locked. Near the men, desperately trying to get in.

Could he get to it in time?

As he stood, frozen in place, one of the men pulled out his gun and aimed it at the door lock. The sound of the shot reached him as a sharp crump.

At the same time, Logan's gaze fell on the strange device he'd noticed earlier: the oversized timpani mallet. He peered at it more closely as another shot sounded. It consisted of a spherical metal ball atop a red plastic belt, the belt looking almost like the ribbon cable of a personal computer, fastened at the base to what appeared to be a comb-shaped electrode. The entire thing was encased in a wire cage.

It was familiar. He'd seen something like it before.

A third shot sounded. With the whine of a ricochet, part of the door lock spun back into the room, leaving a small, ragged hole.

Logan did his best to ignore this as he stared at the device. Where had he seen this?

And then he remembered. It had been at a Yale freshman fraternity rush, back before the practice was banned. An electrical engineering club had exhibited just such a device: its metal globe had shot out sparks in all directions, eliciting shrieks and cries and making people's hair stand on end.

A Van de Graaff generator. That's what it was called. And that wire enclosure: it was exactly like the Faraday cage Kim Mykolos had speculated about, in the faceplates of the suits hanging in the forgotten room. What was it she'd said? *An enclosure, made of a conducting mesh, that ensures the electrical voltage on both sides remains constant.*

A fourth shot. This one had the effect of knocking out the rest of the lock, sending it scudding across the floor.

Logan was thinking furiously, cursing the time he'd spent as a junior, snoozing through Dr. Wallace's physics course. The cage surrounding the Van de Graaff generator—it acted as a protective device. If the generator was turned on, and the cage removed, the generator would produce a rapid buildup of negative electrons. . . .

He rushed up to the lab table. Knocking away the surrounding cage, he saw the device was powered by two small white wires and a toggle switch inserted into the base. The wires led away to a standard electrical plug, which he picked up and slid into an outlet in the side of the lab table. Nothing happened. He pressed the toggle switch. It must have acted as a fail-safe mechanism, because immediately the generator came to life, humming and vibrating. He fell back, ducking down into the doorway and out of harm's way. As he did so, the door at the far end of the lab flew open with a violent slam.

As the three men stormed into the room, the Van de Graaff generator went crazy; freed of the restraining mesh, it began shooting out bolts of lightning in every direction, glancing off metal chairs and tables and racks of equipment, the blue and yellow tongues licking their way up the walls in uncontrolled, spastic gestures.

The men paused a moment, staring at the awesome display of electricity streaming out in a hundred jagged lines from the metal sphere. Then one of them—the man in the waterproof jacket—stepped gingerly forward. Quick as a striking snake, a jumping, dancing bolt of electricity shot out from the generator and almost encircled him. His body jerked for a moment under the current, and then he fell to the ground, temporarily stunned.

Logan backed away still farther, out of the lab and into the short hallway. It was as he'd hoped: with the generator running, the constant stream of negative electrons it produced would jump to any conducting material . . . for example, a human body.

"Thank you, Dr. Wallace," he murmured. *One down, two to go. . . .*

Suddenly, silently, the lights went out.

For a moment, Logan remained in stasis, uncertain of what had happened. Almost instantly, he realized: the storm had cut power to the mansion.

Feeling frantically around in the complete blackness, patting himself, he found first his flashlight, then his knife. It was just possible that, in the dark, he could make his way to the three, grab a gun, and then . . .

Red emergency lighting glowed into view. Then—fitfully at first, and with increasing strength—the main lights came back on.

Had the power been restored so soon? But no—the lights were still a little dim and uncertain. Lux's backup generator must have kicked in.

On the far end of the lab, he heard a groan as someone tried to rise to his feet.

Logan peered around the doorframe at the Van de Graaff generator. It was dead, powerless. Activating it again meant using the toggle switch. To attempt to approach it again, exposing himself to a field of fire, would be madness.

He wheeled around, looking down the short hallway. His eye paused at the oversized ventilation grate.

Maybe, just maybe . . .

He rushed over to the grate and knelt, flipping out the blade of his knife and running it along the closest edge, trying with all his strength to pry it away from the wall. The edge of the grate moved an inch, then another.

He heard voices around the corner now, growing closer. Logan moved the knife to another edge of the grate, working it loose with the blade. . . .

With a faint snick, the blade snapped off near its base.

Jesus, what else! Pocketing the broken knife and grasping at the partially loosened grating, he yanked at it with a grunt. With a *pop, pop, pop* of screws tearing out of the wall it came away, and he flung it across the hallway. From around the corner came the sound of running feet.

In the faint light of the hallway, he could see that a forced-air ventilation duct lay on the far side of a square hole the grate had covered. The stainless steel of the duct looked thin but well secured, and its passage was wide enough to accommodate his body. It ran straight ahead for about three feet, then sloped upward, toward the first floor.

On hands and knees he ducked into the improvised crawl space, the steel skin around him wobbling and swaying fearfully. If he could just make it back up to the main floor, he told himself, he'd be able to—

There was a sudden shriek of rending metal, a crack of failing rivets, and then the duct gave way and Logan began to fall into an unknowable blackness.

49

He plummeted downward through inky darkness. And then, quite suddenly, he hit something hard and unyielding. White light exploded in his head, and he lost consciousness.

He came to slowly, laboriously, like a swimmer struggling to reach the surface. It seemed to take forever. One after another, his senses returned. The first thing he became aware of was pain—his back, right knee, and head were throbbing, all at different, nauseating cadences. Next was sight. He could make out a smear of light—no, two smears of light—against the blackness that surrounded him.

Next: sound. He could hear whispers, different

voices, speaking from somewhere above him, near the lights.

He blinked, blinked again, tried to sit up. A stab of pain went through his knee, and he bit down on his lip to avoid crying out. His sight was clearing a little, and he could now tell that the smears of light were actually flashlight beams. They were lancing here and there, probing down from the ruins of the ventilation duct.

Logan realized that, however it seemed to him, he must have been unconscious only a few seconds. His pursuers were still in the corridor above, crouching in the mouth of the ventilation duct, searching for him. He'd fallen into some kind of subbasement.

He tried once again to rise, and only now became aware that he was lying in six inches of cold, brackish water. It must be groundwater, he realized, leaching in from the saturated soil around the mansion's foundation: a result of the torrential downpour. This time he was successful in forcing himself into a sitting position.

He waited, breathing heavily, for the pain to recede and full alertness to return. The flashlight beams were still moving around, but he had apparently fallen into a small cul-de-sac whose walls shielded him from the lights.

More whispered conversation. As he watched, one of the men—glasses winking in the flashlight beams—began crawling gingerly out onto the broken ductwork. It immediately bent under his weight and he turned, dropping into a prone position, spreading his weight across the base of the duct. The duct groaned in protest and—grasping at its broken corners—the man worked his way down the steel until he was dangling from its lower edge. Light from a flashlight reflected off his glasses. Another few seconds and he would drop to the floor of the subbasement.

Logan realized he had to move. As quietly as he could, using the stonework of the cul-de-sac for support, he rose to a standing position. His head throbbed, and the world rocked around him, but he clung fast to the wall.

He waited a moment for the grogginess and the worst of the pain to pass. He didn't dare turn on his flashlight—assuming it hadn't been broken in the fall—but a second man was still crouching in the entrance of the ventilation duct, illuminating his companion's descent with his flashlight, and the faint glow of the reflected beam allowed Logan to make out his surroundings. He was in what looked like a catacomb: walls of ancient stonework and masonry; low ceilings, interrupted at intervals by Romanesque arches; thick columns—the Solomonic spiral columns found throughout the mansion—punctuating the dim spaces. Cobwebs were everywhere, and Logan could hear the faint squeaking of vermin. The close air stank of mildew and efflorescence. The place looked as if nobody had penetrated its recesses for a hundred years.

A faint splash a dozen feet away alerted Logan to the fact that the first of his pursuers had dropped into the subbasement. As the man turned to help the other descend, Logan—feeling his way along the damp stone—moved away as quickly and silently as he could.

As he waded through the frigid water, the reflection of the flashlight beams behind him grew fainter, but he could nevertheless see that the sub-basement ran away into a warren of separate chambers. Ahead and to his right, a black hole yawned, reeking like the breath of a charnel house, but he nevertheless made for its dubious protection, favoring his right knee, one hand sliding along the stone wall for support.

A second splash—another pursuer had slipped down into the subbasement—and Logan limped away more quickly. Ducking beneath an arch and rounding a corner, he found himself in pitch-darkness. Now he would have to try his own flashlight. Feeling for it in the black, humid space, he drew it out and—shielding its beam while at the same time crossing his fingers—he switched it on.

Nothing.

With a curse, he gave it a savage shake. Now it emitted a faint beam, disclosing a branching tunnel ahead.

The whispers behind him grew louder. Committing his surroundings to memory, Logan snapped off the light and moved forward in darkness. One step, two ... then his foot snagged on something and he fell heavily into the water.

In a moment he was back on his feet, his knee protesting violently. There were cries behind him; stripes of flashlight beams licked across on the stonework; feet plashed in his direction. And now Logan began to flee, heedless of the noise he made. One hand held out before him, flicking his flashlight on every few seconds just long enough to see what lay ahead, he half ran, half staggered through a bewildering labyrinth of corridors, storerooms, and low-ceilinged vaults. His pursuers, apparently having separated but now alerted to his presence, exchanged shouts: there was more splashing; a few brief flickers of light; then the dull sigh of silenced bullets, followed by ricochets off stone. The men were firing blindly into the dark—nevertheless, the bullets whined by awfully close.

Suddenly, there was a sharp pain in his leg, just above the injured knee. Logan gave an instinctual grunt and spun around, staggering out of the path of additional shots. Then he stood in the darkness, gasping for breath, waiting. He heard voices again: first louder, then growing quiet, apparently retreating in another direction. And then, silence. For the time being, at least, it seemed they had lost him in the rabbit warren that made up the subbasement.

But not before winging him—or worse—with a bullet.

Logan shone his light downward, inspecting the wound. The bullet had grazed the meaty part of his outer thigh, tearing a hole through his trouser leg, through which blood was already seeping. With black water eddying around his ankles, he knew his pursuers would have no way of following a blood trail—but nevertheless he'd have to stanch the flow before he grew any weaker. Removing his jacket, he tore off one cotton shirtsleeve, then wrapped it around the injured leg, tying it off tightly. He slipped into the jacket again, then pressed onward, a little more slowly now given the double injury to his leg.

He stumbled into what had apparently been a wine cellar. On both sides, tiers of age-darkened wood rose, arrays of semicircles carved along their lengths. They were all empty. Thick cobwebs hung from them like strands of rope.

Beyond the wine cellar was a stone passage with empty storerooms on each side, apparently— based on the layout of the shelving—once used as pantries or larders. At the end of the passage, a low arch led into a room so large that Logan's faint beam could not reach the far wall. This was clearly the mansion's original kitchen: banks of stoves ran along one side, and in a side wall was a huge fireplace in which sat a cast-iron soup pot, hanging above a tripod by a rusted chain.

Logan paused for a moment, listening. But there was no longer any sound of splashing footsteps from behind.

He stepped forward painfully through the chill, ankle-deep water. A large oaken table stood in the middle of the room, covered with long-disused kitchenware: heavy chef's cleavers, mallets for tenderizing meat, a jumbled riot of wooden spoons. Logan picked up a filleting knife, slid it carefully into the waistband of his pants, then continued on.

At last he reached the far wall. He had been hoping to find a passage out, or even a stairway leading back up to the basement level, but there was nothing save a large, odd-looking metal cupboard that was flush with the wall. He did a slow revolution, shining his flashlight in all directions, but it was clear that the only passage out of the kitchen was the one he had entered through. His heart sank.

As he completed the revolution, his beam returned to the cupboard on the wall before him. As he played his light over it, he realized it didn't look quite like any cupboard he'd seen before. Grasping the lone handle and pulling it toward him, he recognized it for what it was: the door of a dumbwaiter.

He shone the beam inside. It illuminated a box-like wooden frame, perhaps three feet by four, that hung freely within a brick shaft like the flue of a vast chimney. Several empty plates sat on the floor of the dumbwaiter's cart, heavy with dust, and he removed these quietly and slipped them into the water at his feet.

A heavy rope hung in front of the dumbwaiter, between its wooden frame and the brickwork of the shaft. Grasping it with one hand, he pulled.

Nothing happened.

Putting the flashlight between his teeth, he took hold of the rope with both hands and pulled harder. This time, the wooden cart rose a little.

Logan glanced over his shoulder. He could hear the voices again: closer now than they had been for some time.

He looked back at the dumbwaiter. He could

just fit inside. But how, from inside it, could he get sufficient leverage to raise it up the shaft?

In the dumbwaiter's ceiling was a trapdoor. Logan glanced down at the improvised tourniquet, satisfied himself that the wound was not bleeding too badly. Ducking his way into the small compartment, his injured leg protesting in pain, he pushed this trapdoor open and looked upward, shining his light to get his bearings. He could see that the shaft rose perhaps twenty-five feet to a roof of brick, where it ended in a grooved pulley around which the rope had been secured.

Twenty-five feet. That, he estimated, would take him past the basement, as far as the first floor.

The voices were still closer now, and Logan closed the door of the dumbwaiter, sealing himself in. Then, reaching upward, he managed to slither up through the trapdoor in the ceiling. Sitting cross-legged atop the dumbwaiter, injured knee and bullet wound protesting, he closed the trapdoor before any blood could drip onto the floor of the cart.

The voices faded.

He pulled gingerly on the thick rope. It was coarse and slippery from decades of ancient cooking. He examined his palms in disgust. There was no way he could shinny up twenty-five feet of this greasy line—especially with his injured leg.

Maybe there was another way. Placing the flashlight at his feet and angling it upward, he grasped the rope with both hands again, as high up as he could reach. Then he pulled with all his might.

From far above came a faint groaning as the

pulley guide protested under the weight. And then—slowly, slowly—the dumbwaiter began to rise.

Pull; secure the rope into position as best he could; take a moment to prepare—and then pull again. He rose five feet, then ten as the dumbwaiter ascended the brick shaft, creaking and groaning quietly. Then he paused to rest. The muscles in his arms and back were twitching with the unaccustomed exertion, and his hands were already growing raw from the coarse rope.

He continued to pull until he could make out, another ten feet above him near the top of the shaft, a door where the food from the kitchen would have been removed from the cart and served to the household. When he finally pulled himself even with the door, Logan was able to loop the line over a hook on the ceiling of the dumbwaiter cart, cleating it in place. He relaxed his grip from the rope, almost gasping aloud in relief.

Quietly, he rose to a kneeling position and pushed on the door. There was a low rattle on the far side and he stopped immediately. Something was in the way. What it was, he couldn't be sure—but he could not afford to let it tip over. He would have to try sliding it forward, bit by bit.

With exquisite care, he applied pressure to the base of the shaft's upper door. The rattle from the far side continued, but he could sense from the resistance that it was being pushed out of the way. Several long moments of anxious effort and the little door was open wide enough for him to fit through it.

Beyond lay darkness. Ducking first his head, and then his shoulders, through the opening, he slipped out of the dumbwaiter shaft and rose gingerly to his feet. Feeling his way through the darkness, he pushed the dumbwaiter door closed, then replaced the object in front of it—his fingers told him it was a display table of some kind—back against the wall. And then, muffling his flashlight once again, he switched it on.

The space was familiar to him—he'd entered it once, years before, on the mistaken assumption that it had been a men's bathroom. It was actually a small gallery across the main hall from the dining room, presently used by waiters and waitresses for storing linens. Logan wiped grease and grime from his hands. He guessed, based on his unpleasant climb, that when the mansion had been owned by Edward Delaveaux, this room had likely been the butler's and maid's pantry for receiving and arranging dishes sent up from the kitchen.

Logan slowly approached the door of the small room, opened it a crack, and peered out. Beyond a short side passage, and across the rich carpet of the main corridor, was the entrance to the dining room—and, a few yards beyond it, the sloping staircase that led up to the second floor.

He had to check on Kim. If he was being pursued, then it was entirely possible that she was under threat as well. He stepped out into the hall and began moving toward the staircase.

Almost immediately, he shrank back. One of the three men—the one with the tweed jacket—

was standing several yards down the hallway. The man had his back to Logan, and he was speaking into a radio: clearly, the radios had better reception than cell phones within the thick walls of the Lux mansion.

Logan looked from the man to the staircase and back again. Even if he did get past, there was no telling if others were in wait for him upstairs. He would have to find another way to get to Kim.

He looked around in desperate uncertainty. Where to, now? *Where . . . ?*

And then, even as he asked himself the question, his eye fell upon another door. It lay at the other end of the side passage, and in the indirect light its small panes of glass were unrelieved rectangles of black.

It was an emergency exit, leading outside.

Logan didn't hesitate. Turning away from the main corridor, he made his way to the door; made sure it was not alarmed; opened it as quietly as he could manage—and then slipped out into the howling storm.

50

Even though he'd driven through the hurricane on his way back to Lux, the redoubled, elemental fury took him by surprise. The wind pressed him against the dressed stone of the mansion's facade, ballooning his jacket up and away from his shoulders, threatening to pluck the contents from his pockets. Within seconds he was soaked to the skin.

Forcing himself back to the exit, he peered carefully around the doorjamb and through the little panes set into the door. The short corridor beyond was empty; no armed figure was rushing toward him. He had made his escape from the building without arousing notice.

He leaned back against the building. But now what?

He glanced down the gray sweep of lawn toward the ocean. The waves were beating against the rocky coast with a fury he had never before seen; spume and spindrift tumbled angrily upward to mix with the lashing curtains of rain, blending together so completely that it was impossible to tell where sea left off and rain began. The rain, driving straight into his eyes, stung badly and he turned away, shielding his face with his hands.

He glanced to the left. He could barely make out the vast bulk of the East Wing, standing like a Gibraltar against the fury, a few dim lights glowing on its three floors. He could make his way to the edge of the wing, then sneak around it to the parking lot, and . . .

And what? Might not his car be under surveillance, as well? He'd seen no sign of it upon his arrival—if he had, he'd have been more wary about meeting Laura Benedict in her basement office— but that didn't mean it wasn't there. These men were pros, and they weren't just here to send a message . . . not anymore.

Even if he managed to make it to his car, and get away from his place—what then? What about Kim? As he'd raced through the labyrinthine underground labs of gleaming steel, as he'd waded through the dim chambers and grottos of the ancient subbasement, he'd cursed himself for not thinking first about her safety. Instead of telling her to round up the transmitting devices for safekeeping, he should have ordered her to go someplace, *any*place, where she could hide.

Then again, he thought, Kim was a smart woman. She might have seen the strangers, put two and two together, gone to ground somewhere. . . .

But this thought was immediately answered by another: *Pamela Flood had been a smart woman, too.* . . .

He drove this from his mind as best he could. There was something else to consider: the Machine itself. If he simply ran away, there would be nothing to stop Laura Benedict and the team of Iron-hand enforcers from dismantling and making off with the equipment, under cover of the storm. After all, Lux was all but deserted. True, she'd said she was still days away from completing the work she needed to finish miniaturizing the technology to make it suitable for transport . . . but after what had just transpired, that impediment wouldn't stop her. She'd take whatever she could, now, and then disappear.

As he stood there, in the black shadow of the vast facade, the words he'd spoken to Benedict in her laboratory came back to him. *This device of yours is . . . unthinkable. To drive somebody, perhaps an entire army, insane . . . There are reasons chemical weapons were outlawed. Just how long do you think it will take for the technology to be leaked—and the same diabolical ordnance used against our own men and women?*

The device had to be destroyed. She still needed it if she was to complete her work—she'd said as much. But what could he do? He was unarmed, facing a trained squad of killers. As he stood there in the shelter of the mansion's south wall, he patted at his pockets, even though he knew the gesture was futile. A flashlight. A kitchen knife. A digital recorder. A cell phone . . .

As his hand closed over this last item, the vaguest outlines of a plan began to come together. And as it did, his heart began to accelerate once again. He took a deep breath, then another, looking around to make sure the coast was clear. But there was only him and the howling storm.

Logan pushed himself away from the protective wall and forced himself out into the wrath of the elements. Turning his back to the East Wing, he began plodding forward. The hurricane was like an animal force, trying its best to spin him around, force him back, prevent him from staggering on. He took one step at a time, laboring against the appalling force of nature. As he did so, the shriek of the storm intensified, as if outraged by his attempts to defy it. His injured leg, and the blow to his head, throbbed and protested with the effort. Once, his feet slipped from under him and he fell face forward into the sodden grass. It was so thick with water that, for a crazy moment, he felt as if he were lying at the lip of a lake. It would have been easy, so very easy, just to close his eyes and drift into unconsciousness. Instead he forced himself to his feet

355 • THE FORGOTTEN ROOM

once again, but was almost immediately knocked down once more by the hurricane. The howling of the banshee wind rang painfully in his ears. Against all reason, the tempest was still escalating.

Logan realized he couldn't fight against the elements. The storm would sap all his strength before he even reached his destination . . . strength he would need for what lay ahead.

He veered out of the teeth of the storm and made his way back to the facade of the mansion. It seemed to tower endlessly over him, its crenelations and beetling gables invisible in the raging night. But here, under its eaves, the storm abated somewhat. Not much—but enough to allow him to continue forward.

One step, another, another. He soon lost track of time and, stupid with exhaustion, could not even begin to guess how far he'd come. The only way he was able to orient himself, to know that he was making any progress at all, was by sliding his right hand along the stonework of the mansion. . . .

And then, directly ahead, something loomed up out of the darkness, black against black. At first, he sensed rather than felt it. And then, as he began to trudge forward yet another step, he walked straight into it. Half blinded by the wind-driven rain, he pressed his hands forward, feeling his way, trying to determine what it was that impeded his progress.

It was another wall of dressed stone, taller than he could gauge and perpendicular to the one he'd been following, dark and unlit and uninhabited, stretching away to his left into unguessable distances.

The West Wing.

Turning now ninety degrees to the south and leaning against this new support, Logan moved forward until he found what he was looking for: a small window, low, barely at knee height. Dropping to the ground, heedless of the pain in his leg, he applied numb fingers to the sash, tried pulling it upward.

Locked.

Taking shallow breaths, coughing out the rainwater that kept filling his mouth and eyes and ears, he took off his jacket, placed it against the glass, and then beat at it—first with his fists, then with his left shoe. On the third blow, the window gave.

Using his jacket for protection, he gingerly plucked away the remaining shards of glass. Then he slipped through the window, careful this time to slide down to the floor feetfirst.

He shook the glass from his jacket. A brief circuit with the flashlight showed him he was in a small storage room, apparently used by the workmen who'd been engaged in the reconstruction. There were wooden sawhorses, stacked cans of paint, boxes full of caulking tubes, carefully folded tarps covered with Pollock-like drips and sprays in a multitude of colors.

His flashlight made out an open door on the far side of the room. He'd grab one of the tarps and stuff it into the window, then close the door behind him as he left the room; that would mute the sound of the storm, conceal the fact that he'd broken into the wing.

Just as he grabbed the topmost tarp, he hesitated. *No,* he told himself. First, there was something he had to do.

51

Putting his flashlight aside, Logan reached into the pocket of his sopping trousers, searching for his phone. He found it, shook off the beads of water that had accumulated on its face, then pressed the button to wake it from hibernation.

Several rows of faint orange light appeared beneath its number keys: a good sign.

He examined the tourniquet on his right thigh. It was as sodden as the rest of him, but it seemed to have stanched the flow of blood.

Now, raising the phone, he dialed Kim Mykolos's number. No answer. He tried once again with the same result.

Then he paused in the darkness, phone in hand, carefully thinking through his next move. Finally, he raised the phone once more and dialed another number from memory. It was the internal extension that had appeared on his phone when Laura Benedict dialed his Lux apartment, perhaps one hour before.

The phone rang five times before it was picked up. "Hello?" came the tense voice on the other end of the line.

"Hello, Laura," Logan replied. He moved closer to the broken window, made sure that the storm could be clearly heard behind him.

"Who is this?"

"Who do you think it is?" Logan breathed raggedly, careful to add a manic, desperate tone to his voice.

"Dr. Logan?" Benedict sounded shocked, dismayed, uncertain.

"Right the first time. Want to come out and play? The water's fine."

There was a pause. "What happened?" she finally asked.

"What happened? Your boys led me on a merry chase. It took a lot of doing, and a lot of running, but I managed to escape them."

"Where are you now?"

Logan let out a chuckle he hoped wasn't too high-pitched. "I'm outside of the East Wing, near the parking lot."

"Parking lot?" Alarm sounded in her voice.

"Oh, don't worry. I'm not going anywhere. Actually, that's not true—I am going somewhere."

Silence.

"Care to guess where I'm going, Dr. Benedict?"

The silence continued.

"No? Then I'll tell you. Why shouldn't I? You may get me, but by the time you do it'll be too late."

"Too late—" the voice began.

"I tried to make you see reason. But you refused. You even sent mercenaries to kill me. So I'm going to do it myself."

A brief pause. "Do what? Kill yourself?"

Logan chuckled mirthlessly. "Destroy the forgotten room."

"Dr. Logan . . . Jeremy—"

"You said yourself that your work there isn't complete. So I'm going to make sure your work *never* gets finished. I'm going to torch the whole goddamned room, and the rest of the wing with it if I have to. Just like your mercenaries torched Pamela Flood. And then I'm going to find the old notes and journals and lab reports—they'll be around here somewhere, maybe in your lab, maybe in your private rooms—and I'll torch those, too."

"Jeremy, listen—"

"No. *You* listen!" Logan shouted against the roar of the storm. "That thing can't be allowed to exist. Do you hear me? I'm going to make sure that weapon never sees the light of day—*if it's the last thing I do.*"

Then he hung up.

Slipping the phone back into his pocket, he picked up the tarp again and stuffed it into the broken window. Then, plucking up the flashlight from where he'd placed it, he moved to the doorway, stepped through it, and closed the door behind him. Instantly, the sound of the storm grew muffled.

Almost the entire Lux faculty and staff had deserted the mansion ahead of the hurricane. This wing, he knew, would be utterly deserted.

Laura Benedict thought he was standing outside the East Wing. That meant time—if nothing else—was, for once, on his side.

But first he had to find his way back to more familiar ground. And, time or no time, he'd have to hurry: Benedict would already be on the phone again, rallying her men and telling them where to go. At least, he thought, that would take any heat off Kim. It was a calculated risk.

He shook the water off his shoes, squeezed the damp from his trousers. Then, pointing the flashlight ahead of him, Logan moved down the corridor, heading north in the direction of the West Wing's entrance. He realized that, based on the height of the window through which he entered, he must be one floor below the main level. The hallway, which consisted of bare plaster walls, jogged left, then left again. Logan pushed away the pain in his leg and his head and tried as best he could to estimate his location by dead reckoning. Was he near the portal leading to the main building? Or was he lost somewhere in the maze of narrow corridors and rooms that filled the rest of the wing?

Ahead, the hallway ended at a circular metal staircase, its triangular rungs heavy with dust and the imprints of booted feet. Logan shone his light up the staircase, then climbed the treads carefully, one step at a time, dragging his injured leg behind him now. He stepped out into a side corridor that he didn't recognize, full of timber and lath and the stacked detritus of demolition. Here he paused a moment to squeeze the blood and water from the improvised dressing, then reapply it to the gunshot graze across his thigh. And then he moved forward again.

Following the narrow corridor, flashlight beam licking over the walls and ceiling, he emerged shortly into a wider space. This he immediately recognized: to his left was the staircase leading up to the second floor, and the jumble of intersecting rooms that lay beyond. In the distance, he could see the dark bulk of the nearest standing stone: a silent, grim sentinel in this ghostly, echoing place.

He switched off the flashlight for a moment and stood motionless in the darkness, listening. All was silent, save the moan of the storm as it beat against the building's exterior. It was too soon for Benedict's goons to be upon him—but it would not take them long. He had to hurry.

Making his way up the staircase—glancing behind to make sure he was leaving no trail of blood or rainwater—he slipped past the ruined offices, piles of plaster rubble, and half-destroyed walls, following the path by memory, until he reached the vague outline of Strachey's shadow-haunted lateral corridor A. Turning down it, shining the flashlight ahead of him, he advanced until he reached the improvised HAZARDOUS AREA sign and the tarp barrier that lay beyond.

He paused another moment to reconnoiter and listen. Then he moved past the sign, ducked through the hole he'd made in the tarp barrier—had it really been less than two weeks before?—and entered the forgotten room.

He knew the room had been wired for electricity, but he did not turn on the light switch. Instead, he used the flashlight to get his bearings one more time: the Machine, its various controls, the heavy armorlike suits that hung from the rear wall. He noticed that the strange, elevator-like device remained corkscrewed into position on the third floor, its base flush with the ceiling.

Good.

In the close, listening silence of the West Wing, he now began to make out the faint sound of voices.

Quickly, he turned toward the rack of metal suits. He found himself recalling the long days he'd spent here; now he was angry at himself for never trying on one of the suits, familiarizing himself with their operation.

He moved the beam of his flashlight over the row of bulky garments, quickly selecting one that seemed like his size. Then—placing his light on a nearby shelf—he unhooked the suit from its tether and lifted it down.

He was surprised by how heavy it was. It seemed to be constructed of a single, unibody design, and for a sickening minute he could not figure out how it was meant to be put on. Then he noticed a series of hooks and grommets—flush with the suit and almost invisible if one didn't know where to look—that extended in a long line from beneath the right armpit to the hip. As quickly as he could, his cold and wet fingers fumbling stupidly, he undid the fastenings. The seam was padded and reinforced on the inside by felt and leather. He pulled the knife he'd obtained from the old kitchen out of his waistband and let it drop to the floor. Pulling the suit wide, he took off his shoes, and then, raising his hurt leg gingerly, began to slip into it.

The fit was very tight, and the built-in metal slippers that served as shoes hurt his feet, but there was no time to search for a more comfortable replacement. He slipped his arms into the metal sleeves, pushed his fingers into the flexible, accordion-like metal fins of the gloves. Thank God: they, at least, fit.

Leaving the helmet dangling from the neckpiece, he pushed the protective felt back into place, then began fastening, as quickly as he could, the hook-and-grommet arrangement that sealed the suit. With his fingers in the heavy gloves, this proved even harder than undoing the fasteners had been.

The voices grew louder. They were still indistinct, but one of them, he now realized, was that of a woman. She did most of the speaking, as if giving directions.

Of course. Benedict knew the way into the room far better than he did. She would want to get her men into position, ready for the ambush, as far in advance of his arrival as possible.

Buckling the last grommet, Logan stepped forward. Walking was awkward and it took him several steps to get his balance. Grabbing the flashlight and playing it over the Machine, he found the primary switches set into the side of its central housing. He bent stiffly over them, curling the fingers of one glove around the power switch; he snapped it on, waited several seconds, then engaged the load switch.

Softly, almost below the threshold of hearing, as if more sensation than sound, the Machine began to hum.

Now Logan could hear footsteps overhead. It was as he'd hoped: Benedict would have her men approach via the weight-actuated spiral elevator, the method she no doubt had always used to enter the secret room herself. The voices were louder now, and he could make out her words.

"Close the retaining doors," came her muffled voice. "Then give the winch on the other side, there, a clockwise turn. One turn will be enough."

"You're not coming?" returned a masculine voice—one Logan recognized from his pursuit in the mansion's basement.

"I'll wait up here."

More shuffling of feet, a hollow boom, then an odd creaking noise.

Logan retreated to the front panel of the Machine, where the operating controls were located.

He ducked down, so that he would be less visible. The elevator, he knew, would spiral to a spot directly in front of the Machine—and its doors would open to face him.

He grasped the helmet, pulled it over his head, and gave it a twist to seat it into position.

Immediately, the room, already dark, grew blacker still. The faint hum of the Machine, the noises from above, were attenuated almost beyond the threshold of audibility. There was a small breathing orifice below the visor, lined on the inside with felt. Through the wire mesh of the faceplate, he could just make out the words on the control panel before him. The rest of the room was a blur.

Except for one thing: near the ceiling, the decorative circle that marked the base of the elevator was now descending, rotating smoothly and silently down into the room. And from within the curved surfaces of its matching outer doors came the yellow glow of multiple flashlights.

52

Logan looked over the controls, thinking quickly, recalling what Kim had said. *Beam and field. Local and global. A local mode, very specific and sharply directed. . . . And a broader, more general mode.*

That's the one he'd have to use: the field controller. It would be directed in a broad arc toward the front of the room, where the markings had been set into the floor. Where the now-descending elevator would land.

I believe I've studied these controls long enough to test my theory, Kim had told him. But had he been watching closely enough to reproduce what she'd done?

The elevator had now descended halfway to its resting place. He could hear the muffled voices within, see—through his faceplate—haloes of flashlight beams beyond the housing. They weren't trying to hide their movements. For all they knew, he was still somewhere out in the storm, making his way to the West Wing.

Crouching behind the Machine, Logan made sure that the master switch was set to field mode, then ran his eyes over the row of controls, blinking against the darkness and the obstructing faceplate in order to make out their legends. There—he recognized the first one Kim had used after turning on the device: a toggle switch marked MOTIVATOR.

He reached for it, switched it into position.

The elevator reached the floor of the room, bumping against it quietly. More chatter from inside. On the floor above—where Laura Benedict was waiting—all was silent.

Logan scanned the controls, located the next one: ENGAGE.

As the curved doors to the elevator swung open, he activated the control.

Flashlight beams flooded the room now, and he ducked farther behind the protective bulk of the Machine. Peering over its upper housing, he could see three forms, all of whom he recognized: the man in glasses who had first followed him into the subbasement; the other in the waxed raincoat; and, in particular, the hawk-faced, cruel-looking man in the tweed jacket. All held flashlights in their left hand; all held weapons in their right.

He glanced over at the set of controls. Just above those he had activated was a rotary dial, the numbers 0 to 10 inscribed into its faceplate. Next to it was a VU meter, its analog needle resting at the leftmost setting.

Recalling what Kim had done, Logan reached up and turned the knob to the 1 position.

The hum of the Machine increased ever so slightly. As if in reply, he heard the men now talking among themselves: low, uncertain.

He realized that he had only a few moments to make this work. If the men discovered him now, they'd simply shoot him.

He turned the knob to the 2 setting. The needle of the VU meter came sluggishly to life, bobbling back and forth along the indicator marks at its leftmost edge.

The men went silent. One spoke briefly, in an alarmed tone, only to be shushed by another—no doubt the ringleader, the figure in the tweed jacket.

Logan knew that, when he and Kim had briefly tested the Machine, it had been in beam mode, set to emit an ultrasonic pulse at a specific, discrete target. Even so, he'd felt its effect. Now, with the Machine set in field mode—directed at the entire space ahead of him—he could only imagine what his pursuers were beginning to experience.

It was time.

He took a deep breath. "I'm in control of the Machine," he called out through the sound hole in the faceplate. "I'm directing it at you right now."

There was an expostulation of surprise, followed by a metallic racking of weapons. "For fuck's sake," one of them murmured. "Be careful what you shoot in this place."

"You know what it's capable of," Logan said. "I'll use it on you if I have to."

More muttering. He heard stealthy footsteps coming toward him.

In response, he turned the switch to the 3 setting. The Machine began to sing—a basso profundo sound from deep within its workings—and one of the men gasped.

"Stay back," Logan said. "I won't warn you again."

A shot exploded from among the flashlight beams in front of him, and a bullet ricocheted past his ear. In response, he dialed the machine up to 4, then 5.

There was a cry from the group of men—a howl of pain.

Now, Logan dared to peer over the faceplate of the Machine. One of the men—the one in the waxed jacket—was bending forward, hands to his ears, mouth open in a rictus of pain. Next to him, the one in glasses was fumbling with his weapon, as if trying to unjam it. And beside him, the hawk-faced man in the tweed jacket was aiming—directly at Logan.

He dropped back behind the Machine as another bullet whined past just above his head. Craning his neck awkwardly in the bulky suit, he reached up with a gloved hand . . . then spun the knob over to the 7 position.

The howl of pain returned; only worse now—a shriek of agony. As Logan leaned against the Machine, it seemed to vibrate like a living thing, shaking and bucking, filling the room with its presence.

He ventured another look forward. The man with the waxed coat was still in the same position, bent over, apparently incapacitated. But the man in the glasses had cleared his weapon and was raising it toward him, steadying it. Blood was dripping from his nose and ears but he was ignoring it, wiping at his eyes with the back of one hand. And the man in the tweeds not only had his weapon leveled, but was *advancing*. . . .

Logan ducked back, breathing fast. He knew he had only a second or two if he was going to act; otherwise, he'd be dead.

He glanced back up at the controls. The rotary dial was set in the 7 position, the VU meter jerking and bounding along its semicircular course like a mad thing. He thought back to his conversation with Sorrel: *We never redlined it. . . .*

With a brief, muttered curse, Logan reached up and cranked the dial all the way to 10.

Immediately, several things happened. The deep-throated song of the Machine became a sudden roar as it threatened to tear itself from its moorings. The VU meter abruptly pinned itself all the way to the right. The sounds of pain he'd heard from the direction of the spiral elevator became first shrieks, then yelps, then strange, guttural, animalistic sounds. There was a tremendous bang, fol-

372 • LINCOLN CHILD

lowed by the crash of something heavy collapsing to the floor.

Once again, Logan dared to rise up, take a glance over the top edge of the Machine.

The man who'd been bent forward, hands to his ears, was now on his knees, blood pouring from his nose and mouth. The man with the glasses was spinning around, keening dreadfully, as if in time to the song of the Machine. Droplets of blood flew out from all the orifices of his head as he twirled—nostrils, ears, mouth—forming a horrible corona of matter, coruscating in crimson circles as if spun by centrifugal force, flying out in all directions. The man in the tweed jacket had knocked over a lab table and was now walking in strange, jerky motions, like an automaton. As Logan watched, he crashed into one wall as if blind, turned with a laborious gesture, began walking in another direction.

All three had forgotten their guns, which lay on the floor of the lab.

Very carefully, keeping his eyes on the three men, Logan crept slowly around the front of the Machine. He gathered up the guns, then retreated back to the bank of controls. Only then did he slowly dial the setting back, first to 5, then to 2, and finally to 0.

The hum of the Machine, the terrible animal trembling, slowly subsided. But the strange, guttural noises of the man in the waxed jacket did not go away.

After several moments, Logan stood up. Care-

373 • THE FORGOTTEN ROOM

fully, he unscrewed the faceplate, then undid the fastenings of the suit and climbed awkwardly out of it. And then—one gun in his hand, the other two snugged into his waistband—he reached over to snap on the lights, then stepped forward.

He looked at the three incapacitated figures for a moment. Then, turning away, he ducked beneath the tarp and walked a few yards down the rubble-strewn corridor until he found what he was looking for: a recessed wall panel containing an extinguisher and a fire ax. Shoving the third firearm into his waistband as well, he reached out for the ax; hefted it once, twice. Then he ducked back under the tarp.

Two of the men remained where they had been when he left them. The one with the glasses had stopped his ghastly toplike spinning and collapsed to the floor. The leader—the one in tweeds—was still shuffling robotically, bumping into things, turning away again, staggering off in another direction. All three had blood running from their noses and ears—and now, most horribly, leaking from their eyes as well.

Logan regarded them for just a moment. And then he turned toward the Machine. Bending down, he snapped off the switches that disengaged the electric current. He rose again, fingers tightening on the ax. There was a moment of stasis. And then— with a grunt of effort—he swung the ax down onto the Machine. There was a shriek of something like pain as the blade buried itself in the metal. He freed the blade, raised it, and swung the ax down again, taking out the front panels and the control mechanisms. Another several swings destroyed the strange, futuristic devices that sprouted from the lateral cowlings, the field generator and the rotatable pickup coil. He hacked at the device again and again, as if all the uncertainty and fear and pain of the past two weeks was now compressed into this single convulsive act, burying the quickly dulling blade into the metal flanks of the terrible device as large and small pieces—metal, glass, Bakelite— went flying in all directions. Finally, his breath coming in short, sharp gasps, he lowered the ax and looked toward his attackers.

The man in the waxed jacket was now stretched out on the floor, immobile save for occasional involuntary spasms, a pool of blood spreading away from his head. The man with the glasses was crouching in a corner, his own face a mask of blood. He was batting his hands in front of his face, as if to ward off some unseen attackers, and he was making strange gurgling noises—as if trying to scream from a throat whose voice box had closed in on itself. And the ringleader—the hawk-faced man—was now seated awkwardly on the floor, as if he'd dropped there, slowly and methodically tearing the hair from his head in ragged patches. As Logan watched, the man stared at one of the clumps, bloody scalp still affixed to the roots— turned it over curiously—and then stuffed it into his mouth.

Now, moving gingerly forward, Logan stepped beneath the spot where the elevator had come to rest. Its contents unloaded, it had already spiraled silently back into the ceiling, waiting in the abandoned third-floor closet for such time as it would be needed again.

From above, he heard—or thought he heard—the sound of quiet weeping.

Logan stared up at the decorative circle that marked the elevator's base. Then he cleared his throat. "Dr. Benedict?" he called out. "You can come down now."

EPILOGUE

The tall casement windows of the director's office were flooded with sunlight. Beyond the leaded glass, the impossibly green lawn sloped slowly down toward the rocky coast and the Atlantic—remarkably calm today, as if penitent for the angry histrionics it had so recently displayed. People in Windbreakers and light jackets walked in groups of ones and twos along the manicured paths—now rather disheveled—and a painter had set up her easel down near the shoreline. Here and there, groundskeepers and maintenance workers were picking up twigs and other debris and, in general, repairing the damage done by Hurricane Barbara.

Despite the brilliant sunshine and the tranquility of the scene, there was something in the very sharpness of the azure sky, the way the people bent instinctively forward into the occasional puffs of wind, that spoke of winter.

Jeremy Logan walked across the office carpet, favoring his right leg slightly, and took a seat in one of the chairs across from Olafson's desk.

The director, who'd been on the phone, hung up and nodded. "How's the leg?"

"Improving, thank you."

For a moment, the two sat in silence. So much had been said over the last few days—so much done—that now it seemed speech was almost superfluous.

"You're all packed?" Olafson said.

"Everything's in the Lotus."

"Then I guess there's nothing left but to say thank you." Olafson hesitated. "That sounded a little facile. I didn't mean it to be. Jeremy, it's not too much to say that you've saved Lux from itself—and in so doing, I think you may have saved the world from a very serious situation, as well."

"Saved the world," Logan repeated, tasting the words as he spoke. "I like the sound of that. Then perhaps you wouldn't object if I doubled my fee?"

Olafson smiled. "That would be most objectionable."

Another silence settled over the room while Olafson's face took on a serious cast. "It seems almost unbelievable, you know. When I first returned after the hurricane, saw you staggering out of the

West Wing, Laura Benedict huddled under your arm—it was like something out of a nightmare."

"How is she doing?" Logan asked.

"She's responding to stimuli. The doctors liken it to an extreme nervous shock. They predict a full recovery, although it may take six to eight months. Her short-term memory, however, is irretrievably gone."

"So she did get a significant dose of ultra-sound," Logan said. "That's a shame."

"It was unavoidable. In any case, our debriefing is long over, and there's no need to revisit it. You did what you had to do."

"I suppose. Still, perhaps the memory loss will prove a blessing in the end." Logan had been glancing out the windows, not looking at anything in particular. Now he looked back at the director. "What about the other three, from Ironhand?"

Olafson's face became clouded, and he glanced down at a sheet of paper on his desk. "Not good. One is 'floridly psychotic—presenting with extreme homicidal paranoia, delusions, ungovernable mania.' Another is in a state that the evaluators in the psych ward at Newport Hospital, frankly, have never seen before. There is no analogue for it in the *DSM-5*. One of the doctors characterized it"—he quoted again from the sheet—"'as if the action potential of the serotonin receptors are always in transmission mode.' Basically, the man's brain is being flooded by sensory signals—grotesquely enhanced, distorted, and unavoidable—that are simply too overwhelming and violent to be processed. They have no idea how to treat him except to keep him, for the time being, in a medically induced coma."

"Long-term prognosis?"

"They wouldn't say. But reading between the lines, it would appear the condition, barring some miracle, could be irreversible."

Logan took this in for a moment. "And the third?"

" 'Severe catatonic disorder, marked by stupor and rigidity.' Again, the doctors are at a loss for an explanation, because CT scans show none of the damage to the limbic system, basal ganglia, or frontal cortex that would normally explain catatonic schizophrenia."

Logan let out a deep sigh. Slowly, he returned his gaze to the window.

"Fortunes of war, Jeremy," Olafson said in a low voice. "These were bad, bad men. They were responsible—directly or indirectly—for Will Strachey's death."

"And Pam Flood's," Logan added grimly.

"Yes. If you hadn't acted, thousands—tens of thousands, perhaps—might soon be living under threat of similar fates."

"I know." After a moment, Logan turned his gaze back toward the director. "And what of that? Has the threat been neutralized?"

"In the aftermath of the storm, I had a few well-picked men, under the direction of Albright, remove everything from the room. They also dismantled the central machine—although you'd already done a pretty good job on it—and had it destroyed in the ovens of a foundry in Wakefield."

"What about Benedict's work?"

"Again with Albright's help, our security staff performed an interdiction. We cleaned out her office, her basement lab, her private quarters. Burned everything. With the help of the local authorities, we also emptied her family home in Providence, which she'd inherited—that was where we found most of the notes and files, actually."

"Local authorities?" Logan repeated.

"There aren't many large cities up and down the New England coast that don't owe Lux at least one favor." Olafson paused. "We've also taken the precaution of destroying all other paperwork in our own archives relating to Project Sin. And I'm not speaking merely of those files in my safe—I'm talking about the early work that led up to the project's formation in the late 1920s. Anything and everything, no matter how indirect or remotely linked." He glanced at Logan. "I hope you agree."

"Enthusiastically. But what about Ironhand?"

Olafson's expression clouded again. "We're in discreet conversation with the Feds. We've destroyed all evidence we can get our hands on, done all we can to put a protective bubble around anything Benedict might have accomplished." He paused. "What do you think?"

"I think that if she had enough material to continue her work off campus, say in the Ironhand labs, she wouldn't have acted with such desperation—

382 • LINCOLN CHILD

neutralized Strachey, tried to kill me, done her utmost to buy the time necessary to reduce the footprint of the weapon, get it off premises." He shook his head slowly. "No—if you've destroyed all the equipment and burned all the paperwork, Ironhand won't have enough to restart her work."

"Not on their own, perhaps," Olafson replied. "But that won't stop them from trying. I'd be lying if I said they'll go away easily."

This observation hung in the air for a moment. At last, Logan rose to his feet. Olafson did the same.

"Can I walk you to your car?" the director asked.

"Thanks, but I've got one final errand to take care of before I leave."

"In that case, I'll say good-bye." Olafson shook his hand warmly. "We owe you more than we can repay. If I can ever do anything personally, as director of Lux, just let me know."

Logan thought for a moment. "There is one thing."

"Name it."

"The next time I come here to undertake some open-ended research project, make sure Roger Carbon is on extended sabbatical, far away from Lux."

Olafson smiled. "As good as done."

Leaving the director's office, Logan made his way slowly down the elegantly appointed corridors and sweeping staircases. In the three days since the storm, the think tank had returned to normal—scientists speaking in hushed tones as they passed by, wide-eyed clients waiting for an audience in the Edwardian splendor of the main library. Passing the dining hall—the clanking of silverware and porcelain beyond its closed doors indicating that lunch would soon be served—he turned down a side corridor, went through a set of double doors, and stepped out onto the rear lawn.

The bright sunshine, and the unmistakable undercurrent of chill in the air, hit him immediately. He made his way past the small knots of strolling scientists and technicians, the painter at her easel, until he reached the long scatter of rocks that marked high tide, flung carelessly along the coast as if by a giant's whim. Kim Mykolos sat on one of the larger rocks, hands in the pockets of a gray trenchcoat, staring out to sea. An ugly yellow bruise, just now beginning to fade, stood out on one temple.

"Hello," Logan said, taking a seat beside her.

"Hello yourself."

"I hear this sea air is great for convalescing."

"It's not the sea air I have to thank, Dr. Logan. It's you."

"Please—Jeremy."

"Jeremy, then."

"Why should you thank me?"

"You came to my rescue. Called nine one one. Practically drove me to the hospital yourself."

"If anything, I should be apologizing for getting you involved in the first place."

"Most excitement I've had in years." Then, quite abruptly, the jocular tone faded. "Honestly, Jeremy. After what happened to Will Strachey . . . well, I needed to see this through, see things right. And that's what you gave me. I wish I could do something in return."

"You can. Did you bring them?"

Kim nodded. Then she pulled her hands out of the pockets of her trenchcoat. Cradled in each hand were two items, wrapped in tissue paper.

Logan took the two from her left hand. They were the small transmitting devices they'd discovered hidden in the flanks of the Machine, in Strachey's radio, and behind a bookcase in Logan's office.

"You remembered. Thanks."

She looked at him. "Is everything good? I mean, has Lux swept all this crap away?"

"As well as they could, yes."

"Then there's just one thing left to do."

As if with a single mind, the two rose. Tearing away the tissue paper and wadding it into his pocket, Logan hefted the devices, and then tossed them—one, then the other—into the sea. Kim followed his lead.

They remained silent a moment, watching, as the sea swallowed them greedily, the small plashes quickly covered over by creamy breakers, one after another after another, until even the memory of their sinking was gone.

" 'O spirit of love,' " Logan said almost under his breath,

How quick and fresh art thou,
That, notwithstanding thy capacity
Receiveth as the sea, naught enters there,
Of what validity and pitch soe'er,
But falls into abatement and low price
Even in a minute.

They stood together in silence for a long moment, staring out over the blue ocean.

"So it's over, then," Kim murmured.

"Walk me to my car," Logan replied.

Within five minutes they were standing in the parking lot in the shadow of the East Wing. As the wind stirred the lapels of Kim's shirt, Logan saw the lines of the ghost catcher pendant beneath. "I'll take that off your hands, if you like," he said.

She shook her head. "I've kind of gotten used to it."

There was a pause. "What's next for you?" Logan asked.

"It's like I told you when we first met. I'm going to finish up Strachey's work, secure his legacy. And then I'm going to continue my own work on strategic software design. Perry Maynard, the vice director, tells me that's a discipline totally in line with Lux's future plans."

"Well, when you found the next Oracle, be sure to sell me some stock options," Logan said.

They embraced. "Thanks again, Kim," he said. "For everything."

She smiled just a little sadly. "Mind how you go."

———

As Logan fired up the Lotus Elan and made his way out of the parking lot, he saw a dark, late-model sedan pull away from a parking space and follow him down the long graveled drive. As he drove, slowly and thoughtfully, through the crooked downtown streets of Newport, the sedan continued to follow him at a discrete distance.

"I don't know, Kit," he said quietly to the spirit of his dead wife, who in his fond imagination was sitting in the passenger seat. "Do you think they'll follow us all the way to New Haven?"

Kit was considerate enough not to respond.

"I hope these Ironhand operatives aren't too dedicated in their surveillance," Logan went on. "I've got a class in the medieval trade guilds of Siena to prepare for, and this kind of attention could cramp my style."

And with that he pointed the car toward the Claiborne Pell Bridge, Connecticut—and home.